SECRET OF MEMPHIS

SABRA WALDFOGEL

CONTENTS

AN APPRAISAL

NEW YORK TO MEMPHIS MIGHT BE A DIRECT ROUTE FOR the airlines, but in real life, most people don't go that way. Even so, it was the path I took after my marriage fell apart. I left my job at Sotheby's in Manhattan and returned to the city I'd left fifteen years before, swearing I'd never go back.

Once there, I opened an antique shop, which wasn't exactly a portable business, and to anchor myself further, I bought a house. Why not? The asking price was a tenth of the sum my ex and I had received for our apartment in Manhattan. I fell in love with the Memphis house at first sight, a 1920s bungalow in Evergreen, a neighborhood that reminded me of Brooklyn.

I wasn't going anywhere, even though my first three months as an antique dealer involved an appraisal that I didn't get paid for and a big fight with my father, which meant that we still had a lot of fence-mending to do. Other than that, I was happy—for the moment, anyway— in Memphis.

My brother, Josh, who had my back in the family fight, was often in touch with me. Josh was an estate attorney who got his law degree at Vanderbilt, and he was enmeshed in Memphis's good old boy network as well as the tightly knit community at Temple Israel. Josh and I were betwixt and between in Memphis. Our family name was Raskin—my father was the third generation of Jewish haberdashers in town—but my mother was descended from the Beardsleys, who settled Shelby County in the 1820s and who made their fortune, before and after the Civil War, as cotton planters.

When Josh called, I was opening the shop. My shop, Minerva's Place, was on Main Street in Midtown Memphis, in the building that once housed my grandfather's clothing store, the cornerstone of the family business until my father moved to the suburbs. As our website said, the antique shop mingled the old South and the new. Customers could find a nineteenth-century silver coffee set sitting on a mid-twentieth-century teak coffee table. Or a diamond necklace worn by a belle from the 1870s next to a 45 from the early days of the Stax Recording Studio.

Two dealers helped me run the place. One was Jude Phelps, who'd been my classmate at Germantown High School, once a bouncy debutante, now a Southern goth with a sharp eye for the bottom line. The other was Gideon Fairchild, who'd spent years in Nashville as a session musician until he realized he'd never be out front. Now he was a dealer in vintage guitars who'd educated himself about antiques in general. He could sell anything to anyone, and I was indebted to him every day because of it.

In our backyard, where an ancient live oak grew, lived a great horned owl. Our avatar nested there and preyed on the mice and rats drawn by the restaurant dumpsters down the street. Minerva's owl was supposedly a smaller species, but I'd come to love her deep hooting call and the sight of her wide wingspan.

Now, on the phone, Josh said, "I hope I haven't caught you at a bad time, Nat."

"No, we aren't open yet. This is fine."

"How's it going?"

Business was the love language of the Raskin family. "The shop? I'm always pleasantly surprised by how well we do, between Mama's referrals and the tourist walk-ins. I can't complain."

"That's great. I'm sorry I haven't come by to see it. Work is crazy, and the kids have soccer. Two different leagues. We're always at a soccer game."

"Don't apologize. I wish I could come to the games. I'm always at the shop."

"You're working, too. Like Dad is."

I laughed. "Retail is in our blood, I guess. Like snappy dressing."

"Not a bad legacy. Hey, are you still interested in doing appraisals?"

"Only if someone is paying," I said.

"I hear you. That's actually why I called. I have a client who needs an estate appraised."

I could use the money, but I was cagey now. "Are they making a will?"

"No. Mrs. Powell had a will, and it's very well constructed. She just died, and she left the house and all its contents to her heirs. A son and a daughter in their forties. They don't have a clue what's in there or what it's worth."

"Powell? The old family Powells?"

"Yep. They were probably neighbors to the Beardsleys when Shelby County was brand-new in 1820. The planters next door."

"Serious money?"

"Not by New York standards, no. But certainly by Memphis standards."

"Are they difficult?" Without realizing it, I was asking the questions that had been reflexive when I worked at Sotheby's.

He hesitated, and I knew he was going to sugarcoat it, because he wanted me to say yes. "They want to value the estate quickly so they can sell."

"No attachment to the house? Or the stuff?"

"I don't get that feeling. I think they just want the money."

"Where's the house?"

"In Cordova."

It was impossible to spend a million dollars on a house in Memphis proper. For that, you had to go to Cordova, where old money and new money mingled. I wondered what Mrs. Powell had left to the son and daughter who were so indifferent to her things. "You didn't force me down their throats?"

"No. All I said was that my sister is a licensed appraiser

with fifteen years of experience valuing antiques at Sotheby's."

I felt the familiar stirring of hope that there would be something interesting. A quickening at the thought there might be something exceptional. "I'm interested."

"I can't tell you how happy I am. I'll call them and set it up. Hey, Nat, would you be free to join us at Temple this Friday night?"

Temple Israel, founded by merchants who needed to be in the shop on Saturday, had always held its Sabbath services on Friday night, and I couldn't beg off because of my own shop. I knew what my mother would say. "Aren't you curious about catching up with people you haven't seen in ages?" And if it was easy to talk to my father these days—which it wasn't—he would remind me, "You could talk up the shop." As he had been doing at Temple for years.

I had to go, whether I wanted to or not. Now I had to find something to wear besides my New York LBD.

I asked Gideon, who shared shop duty with me on Fridays, if he minded closing by himself. "I have to leave a little early."

"No, of course not." He looked at me with the beginning of a grin. "You got a date?"

I said, "I wouldn't leave early for that. I have to drive out to Temple Israel in Germantown."

"For the service? That ain't so bad."

"How would you know?"

"I've been to a temple in Nashville."

"What, you got religion there?"

He grinned. "No, I just went to a wedding."

Throughout my childhood, I'd attended Friday night services at Temple Israel. I'd been bat mitzvahed there, the occasion for a big party that was the envy of all my friends. I'd been active in the youth group throughout high school. And I hadn't been back—save for my grandfather's funeral—since I left for college at eighteen.

But it didn't matter. Of course they remembered me, both my parents' friends and my old high school classmates, the ones who'd gone to school at Vanderbilt or Emory, or less fortunately, at the University of Tennessee in Knoxville, and who'd come back to establish themselves in careers and marry each other. They pressed my hands. My parents' generation said, "You haven't changed a bit!" My own generation told me they'd heard about the shop—no doubt from my mother—and that they'd love to stop by. I found myself reciting "Thursday through Sunday, ten to five," a merchant's mantra. *This isn't so bad,* I thought. I wouldn't come here every week, but I could manage one homecoming.

"Nat."

I looked up in surprise because I never thought I'd hear that voice again. It belonged to Adam Levy, who'd been my boyfriend when we ran Temple Israel's youth group together, back in high school. Adam Levy, whose heart I'd broken with so little consideration fifteen years ago. "Adam! What a surprise to see you here. Are you visiting?"

"No, I'm back in Memphis for a while."

"Really? When did you come back?"

"A few months ago. I was working for Warner Music, and they downsized. They laid me off." He shrugged and kept his tone light. "Then my wife downsized and laid me off, too. I'm divorced. So I'm back in Memphis."

I recognized that tone, the breezy note to hide bitterness and pain. "I'm sorry to hear that."

"What about you? I thought you'd never come back."

Ouch. He remembered that. "Well, you say a lot of things at eighteen that you regret saying once you grow up."

"What happened?" Curiosity gleamed in those still-beautiful brown eyes, but so did sympathy.

"I got divorced, too."

He nodded, and I rushed in to fill the silence. "What are you doing these days?"

"I'm at a law firm. IP law."

"So you went to law school." That had always been a source of conflict between Adam and his father.

"I succumbed and got my law degree at Vanderbilt. What about you? What are you up to in Memphis?"

I began to remember things I wished I didn't. The touch of Adam's fingers on my cheek. The brush of his lips on mine. The look on his face when he watched me undress for the first time. Those memories crowded out the recollection of our last hurtful words to each other. I hadn't felt a throb of desire for months. Now I did, and I felt a blush come to my cheeks.

I'd never expected to see Adam Levy again. I never thought I'd retrieve any of these memories from the deep archival storage where I'd left them fifteen years ago.

I'd been wrong.

I pulled myself back to the present. "I didn't stray too far from my old job," I said. "I opened an antique shop."

"I heard about it," he said. "My mother's always kept

me up to date on the old youth group crowd. I visited your website. It looks terrific."

Suddenly in retail mode, I said, "It's a lot of fun. You know, you should stop by. We're open from ten to five, Thursday through Sunday. We're online, too. Minerva's Place."

He laughed. "You sound just like your father."

I didn't mind. "Retail is the Raskin legacy. We're in the old Raskin clothing building on South Main."

"Natalie Minerva," he said, reminding me that he was one of the few people in my life who had ever called me by my middle name.

"A better name than Raskin's Place, that's for sure."

He smiled. "It's good to see you again, Nat."

"You too," I said, telling a half-truth as the past over-shadowed the present.

I turned to see Josh, who was looking at me with a quizzical expression. I shook my head. All my courtesy and bravado drained away. "I need some air," I told him, and I abandoned the crowd, buzzing with goodwill and gossip, for the sidewalk outside. At dusk, the air was cool and still. I breathed it in and wondered if owls nested in the trees in the open spaces near the building.

Adam Levy. Not the only reason I'd left, but a lot of it. I had a history of running when I got hurt. Or hurt someone else. And it had caught up with me in Memphis, as it had in New York.

When Jude walked into the shop the next morning, I said to her, "You'll never guess who I ran into at Temple Israel last night."

"I won't, because you're dying to tell me," she said, stashing her shoulder bag behind the counter.

"A ghost from the past."

"How big and bad a ghost?"

"High school, if that helps."

"I remember high school. Help me out."

"High school sweetheart."

She laughed. "Adam Levy? I haven't seen him for decades. Married, fat, and balding with three kids?"

"No. Grown up, gorgeous, and divorced."

"Any sparks?"

Gideon surprised us by coming in the back way, which was right next to the counter. "Sparks? Don't tell me we have an electrical problem in here." But he was kidding.

"Nat ran into her high school sweetie at Temple last night," Jude said.

"Thanks a lot for keeping a secret," I said.

"We have no secrets here," Jude said, winking at Gideon, who still hadn't told me where he lived in Memphis or where he'd grown up in Tennessee.

"Speak for yourself," I said.

"Flame still alive?" Gideon asked me.

"None of your business, either of you."

Saturday was our busiest day, when employed locals joined the tourists, and we didn't sit down all morning. I was delighted at the constant effort to open cases, answer questions, and educate brand-new collectors. We sold a pair of silver candlesticks and a set of caviar spoons. I overheard Jude telling the customer they were just the thing to serve wasabi. We sold a mid-century nightstand and a mid-century lamp to sit atop it. We sold a Carl Perkins 45 from the early days of Sun Studios, and someone asked Gideon to take one of his Fender Jazzmasters down so he could finger it and yearn for it, even though he didn't buy it. We sold a Bohemian garnet necklace and a Navajo turquoise ring and a pair of funky plastic earrings from the 1960s. We sold my least favorite painting in the shop, a loving portrait of someone's redbone hunting dog. I'd always gotten a thrill from watching auctions at Sotheby's, where a lesser thing was in the thousands of dollars and the great things sold in the hundreds of thousands or millions. I was just as happy to fire up our card reader for objects priced at less than a hundred dollars.

We finally had a lull around three and managed to eat something in the momentary quiet. As I was finishing my sandwich, the electronic bell jangled. I crumpled the plastic wrap, tossed it into the wastebasket, and said to Gideon, "Showtime!"

Adam walked into the shop and came up to the counter. He smiled as he said, "Are you surprised again?"

I was, but I said, "I'm delighted you found us." I said, "Jude, this is Adam Levy. Remember, from high school?"

"I remember you," she said with just the right note of surprise, as though I hadn't prepared her.

Perplexed, he said, "I'm sorry, but I don't remember you."

"Judy Phelps. I was a blonde in high school."

"It's been a while," he said.

"I know I look different. And I go by Jude now."

He recovered his politeness. "Then we'll start over. Nice to see you again." He turned to Gideon. "I know you didn't go to Germantown High."

"As a matter of fact, I didn't," Gideon said.

I introduced him. "Gideon specializes in vintage musical instruments." I gestured toward the guitars hanging on the wall in their sculptural display. "Those are his."

"You're a musician?"

"I was a session guitarist in Nashville for a long time. Worked for Warner Music."

"I used to live in Nashville myself. I worked for Warner, too. Lawyer."

"Keeping us bad boys out of trouble."

"IP. Intellectual property. Keeping your copyrights out of trouble."

"I know what IP is," Gideon said. I knew that tone. It was his "I ain't a stupid hillbilly" tone.

"What brought you to Memphis?" Adam remained polite.

"Got tired of Nashville and wanted a change. What about you?" Not so polite.

"Warner downsized."

"So they picked you to take the fall."

What the hell, Gideon? I thought.

"It was a business decision," Adam said, his voice still polite.

Before Gideon could say anything ruder, I said, "Adam, I'm glad you stopped by. Is there anything in particular you're looking for?"

He returned to me, still sounding perfectly pleasant. "Not that I know of," he said.

"Well, take a look around. If you see anything in a case, we're happy to open it for you. And if you have any questions, just ask."

He smiled at me and nodded to Jude. "Thanks."

When Adam was out of earshot, I whispered to Gideon, "What the hell was that? What have you got against lawyers?"

Gideon didn't reply.

"While he's in here, he's a customer."

"Yes, ma'am."

"You aren't the least bit sorry, are you?"

Gideon gave me his aw-shucks grin. "No, I ain't."

Adam had a question about one of Jude's lamp tables. I could hear her doing her best to convince him he needed it. She asked after the style of his place. "It's 1980s generic," he said, and she said, "Oh! A blank canvas! You can put anything in a place like that."

I heard him say, "As long as it isn't repro English country. That was my ex's taste."

She said, "This is a fun mid-century piece. Heywood Wakefield. About as far from English country as you can get."

"I can see that."

When she returned to the counter, Gideon asked, "He didn't go for it?"

"He's still looking."

Gideon stifled a snort. "He didn't come here for anything in the shop," he said, looking at me.

I said, "What's gotten into you today?"

We let Adam wander around, and he finally came to the counter to set down a paperweight with a skyscape of Memphis inside. An advertising piece from the Holiday Inn, which got its start here in the early 1950s. I gave him my best retail smile. "You found something."

"It will look good on my desk at work."

I said to Gideon, "Should we give him the friends and family discount?" I wanted Gideon to have a chance to redeem himself with Adam.

Gideon inclined his head, very slightly. "That's up to you."

Adam, who was still being polite, said, "For a $10 purchase? I'll pay the freight."

"Suit yourself," Gideon said.

As Gideon made change, Adam said to me, "You have a lot of nice stuff."

"We do our best."

Gideon wrapped the piece and put it into a bag. I knew he still wasn't sorry. I handed Adam the bag and gave him another retail smile. "Thanks for stopping!"

ON SUNDAY AFTERNOON, Gideon answered the phone and handed it to me. "I think it's your friend with the paper-weight," he said.

Adam asked, "Did I catch you at a bad time?"

"I'm in the middle of something." I wasn't. "Let me call you back." I wanted to talk to him on my cell, in the back-yard. In private.

He gave me his cell number, and in five minutes I

escaped to the yard. It was so hot that the shade of our live oak offered little relief. I'd forgotten the weight of the humidity that misted off the river and hung over the Delta. With spring's arrival, I'd lived and worked in air conditioning, and my body hadn't readjusted to the weather I thought was normal when I was growing up. "Sorry about before." I lifted my hair from my neck.

"Are you busy on Sundays?"

I laughed. "Recreational retail. We're busy all weekend."

"I should talk. I worked more weekends than I want to think about."

"Lawyers do," I said. "Is there something I can do for you?" When he hesitated, I teased him a little. "Sell you more desk accessories?"

"I'm set, thanks. Did I do something wrong to set off your business partner? He seems to have quite an attitude."

I said, "He was a session musician in Nashville for years. He must not like lawyers."

"IP lawyers? I'm innocent."

I wondered, not for the first time, what lurked in Gideon's past. "Entertainment, IP," I said. "Birds of a feather."

Now Adam's tone turned flirtatious as well as apologetic. "I certainly didn't stop by your shop to pick a fight with Mr. Fairchild."

"That's good to know. I'll tell him."

"No, that's all right." He laughed and the sound was intimate in my ear. "I came by to ask if you'd like to meet for a drink sometime. Preferably soon."

I wiped the sweat from my forehead with the back of my hand. "Ever since I've been back, whenever I do anything—it doesn't matter what—someone asks me, 'Is this a rebound thing?'"

"Probably. But who cares? It's our business, no one else's."

But I hesitated. "All things considered?"

He knew what I meant. "Already taken into account. The answer is yes. Rebound."

"You did turn into a lawyer," I said, teasing him.

"I've changed that much," he said, teasing back.

"Then let's do it. When are you free?"

"Anytime," he said.

Back in the shop, the cool air was like an embrace. I pulled a tissue from the box behind the counter and wiped my face. "It's too hot for spring," I said.

Gideon said, "I can tell you said yes to something."

"As though it's any of your business."

Jude said, "Don't tell me you gave him your cell."

"What is this, high school? Cut that out, both of you."

"How long since your divorce?" he asked. "Not six months?"

"I'm not counting, and you shouldn't, either."

But that night, at home, I poured myself a glass of wine and cranked up Otis Redding, too loud, to keep me company. I sat in the embrace of my big mission chair. "I've Got Dreams to Remember," Otis sang, his song about betrayal in love, and as I listened, I let the past return to me. I was newly divorced, but my breakup with Adam returned as though the past, to paraphrase the Faulkner we'd read in high school, wasn't past at all.

What was I doing? The voice in the back of my mind didn't remind me, *It's too soon.* It spoke loud and clear. *This is a bad idea, and you know it.*

I CALLED THE POWELL FAMILY, Josh's referral for an appraisal, and set up an appointment. On Thursday, the shop door opened and the alarm system beeped. I looked up; it had become a reflex, readying myself for a customer. But it was only Gideon, who looked the worse for wear this morning. He didn't smell of alcohol, but his eyes were bloodshot. I wondered if he'd been playing in a pickup band. I wondered if he'd been drinking. "Late night?" I asked.

"Don't ask."

"I feel for you."

He looked at me. I saw the shadow of a grin. "Even though it's none of your business."

"Fiddlesticks," I said, channeling my grandmother Beardsley. "Why is it a state secret that you had a gig on Beale Street?"

He rubbed his forehead. "All right, I did."

"I wanted to ask you for a favor. A business favor."

"It depends. What do you need?"

"I need you to cover for me tomorrow."

"You're going to Temple again?"

I snorted. "No. I have a lead on an appraisal job, and it's the only time the family can meet."

"Are they paying you?"

"I'm just at the proposal stage. But if they won't, I'll say no."

"I owe you." That was an apology for the last appraisal, which had cost us in time and grief and hadn't netted either of us a dime. "It's no problem."

"Thanks."

He perked up. "Will you need any help? Research? Inventory?"

"Depends on what I find. I've got my antenna up."

"What's the client like?" He was the antique dealer again.

I said, "My brother won't admit to it, but I bet the heirs are being difficult. Could be grief or could be cussedness, as my mama's relatives might say. Old money, or what passes for old money in Memphis. They might have something good. But you never know."

He managed to smile. "That's the hook, isn't it? Gets us in the door every time, no matter how cussed they are?"

I was sure he drank too much. I knew he no longer used cocaine, the musician's drug of choice. But he was hooked on the thrill of the chase for an object of desire, and I was as badly addicted to that as he was. "It surely does."

He grimaced and admitted, "Do we have any aspirin around here?"

I rummaged in my purse and handed him the bottle I'd brought for myself. "Ibuprofen. Will that do?"

"I reckon it will."

ON THURSDAY, when I was due to meet the Powell heirs at their house in Cordova, I hesitated before my closet. I needed to look like I deserved a consulting fee of $150 an hour. And I needed to be ready to crawl under a piece of furniture and get dirty.

I could imagine Gideon laughing at me.

Knock it off, I said, to him and to myself. I pulled out a black suit from Bloomingdale's and a pretty blouse I could throw in the wash. It had been good enough for Sotheby's, and it should be good enough for rich snobs in Cordova, Tennessee.

I drove northward to Cordova in bright sunshine, on a summer day that promised to come close to a hundred degrees, with the mist from the river thick in the air. Cordova wasn't far from Germantown, but I'd rarely visited when I lived here. Germantown was middle and upper middle, and full of Reform Jews at home at Temple Israel. Cordova was serious money, brand-new as well as old, and if I went there, I needed to call on my Beardsley side to pass as an Episcopalian. I am, sort of. We went to Christmas Mass every year at St. Mary's. My father would kiss my mother and tell her, "Barbara Jean, you know how much I love you, but I can't set foot in a church for Christmas Mass. Take the kids, and we'll all go to your parents' house to eat dinner and open the presents tomorrow."

When Josh was little, he called the two of us "half Jewish and half Christmas."

Cordova was the land of mansions and McMansions. The houses were too big and they sat on huge lots, fronted by swaths of landscaped greenery. I drove past a vast front lawn where a Black man drove a riding mower, his red cap as bright as a cardinal against the unrelieved green. In Memphis, that green never went away. I would miss the leafless trees of a New York fall. When December came, I would miss snow, too.

The house had a discreet numbered sign, and it led me up a long, curving path, meant to imitate the approach to a plantation house. The house itself, built twenty years ago like the rest of this part of Cordova, was a vast structure, white with tall pillars in front, a Memphis developer's fantasy of Tara plantation. I'd never liked these houses because I knew the real thing. As a child, I spent weeks in rural Shelby County at the old Beardsley plantation house. The original, put up in the 1820s, had been replaced by a graceful four-up-and-four-down a decade before the Civil War. Its pillars were modest, in the style that my adult eye would know as federal. That was a planter's house. The house before me was like something on a movie set.

I rang the doorbell, wondering if the housekeeper would answer the door, but the woman who met me was small, fine-boned, sharp-featured, her hair still artfully blonde. She looked nervous. "I'm Joyce Enright," she said. "Evelyn Powell's daughter. My brother, Owen, is here too. Come in and meet him."

In the foyer, before the grand staircase—Tara again—I met Owen Powell, who shared his sister's fair complexion and sharp features. His looks, once boyish, were fading, and his hair, once gold, had dulled and receded. His handshake was hearty, but he was ill at ease.

I was used to that. Estate appraisals were contingent

on a death, and I could feel that someone who lived here had died. The house gleamed inside, as though Mrs. Powell hadn't used it much at the end of her life. I suspected the hand of a housekeeper as well as a nurse's aide, two long-suffering Black women who needed the money. They were now gone, as the hospital bed and medical equipment were gone.

I said, "Is there someplace comfortable we can sit? I can tell you more about myself and what I do as an appraiser."

"Can I get you something?" Joyce asked. "Coffee?"

There was no smell of coffee in the house. Only lemon wax and the faint scent of lavender. "No, I'm all right."

We sat in the living room, a big space with a fifteen-foot ceiling and a cathedral window that someone had to get on a ladder to clean. The room was exquisitely tidy. Mrs. Powell hadn't been a hoarder. But the room had a huge china cabinet, which was full, and many small tables, on which decorative items were carefully arranged. I spotted what looked like a Tiffany lamp, a big Newcomb vase, and a silver tea set, post–Civil War American silver. Under our feet lay a lovely Isfahan rug, circa 1900. Somebody had money during the cotton boom of the late nineteenth century.

I said the obvious thing. "I'm sorry for your loss."

They both looked uncomfortable. I didn't see grief. I wondered if they'd been estranged from their mother, or if she'd been estranged from them.

I asked if they lived in Memphis. Joyce lived in nearby Bartlett. Her husband was a senior manager for Holiday Inn, the corporation native to Memphis, a point of pride for Memphians. She said, "I stay home with our three kids. They keep me busy." Owen was a broker for Edward Jones. When he told me he lived in Germantown, I said, "I grew up there." We talked about neighborhoods and tested our connections with neighbors. He asked me how I'd liked living there. "It was a great place to grow up," I said.

"Where did you go to school?"

"Germantown High. It was a good school when I was there. They sent kids to the Ivies. I got into Columbia University. Are your kids there?"

He shook his head. "They go to Westminster," he said. He exchanged a look with his sister. "It's not cheap, but it's worth it."

Westminster was a Christian academy that had popped up as white people fled Memphis and its heavily Black public schools. He was right, places like Westminster cost a bomb. I allowed myself a moment of spite. *Your racism costs you a bomb.* But I quashed it. These were Josh's clients, and if I behaved myself, they would be mine. I'd worked with rich people before, people I wouldn't want for friends.

I told them about my experience with Sotheby's, and they nodded politely. It was hard to read them. Sometimes grief took the form of blankness.

Owen said, "We want to sell everything and we want to get it cleared out fast. We want to sell the house, too."

I explained what was involved in an estate appraisal and why it might take a while. "It's a spacious house. There's a lot to value."

Owen shifted uncomfortably on the sofa. Joyce twisted

her hands. Her skin was very fair; her veins showed through it, blue and delicate. She said, "Just go through it, as fast as you can."

I said, "Let's make sure we find everything and value it properly. You don't want to leave money on the table."

That got to them.

"May I look around? Get enough of an idea to give you a realistic proposal for the appraisal?"

"Sure," Owen said.

"Let me know if there's anything you want for yourselves. I'll value it, for your insurance, but we'll keep it out of any sale."

Joyce shook her head, but Owen said, "Actually, there is something. It belonged to my dad."

I nodded.

"It was from a baseball game he went to in 1959. The St. Louis Cardinals. He caught the ball, and the whole team signed it. It was Bob Gibson's rookie year. I remember him telling me about the game."

"Bob Gibson?"

Owen broke into a smile. "Great pitcher. Great player. My dad loved that baseball."

Owen had loved his father, and they had loved that baseball together. I wondered again what had gone wrong between Owen and his mother.

"We'll keep our eyes peeled."

"It was always in the study."

I started in the living room. The lamp was Tiffany Studios. The vase was a Newcomb, decorated by their best artist, Sadie Irvine. The silver was Gorham, from New York. The dining room table was in the Duncan

Phyfe style. The wood was too glossy, too new, to belong to the eighteenth century. I'd have to crawl underneath it to find out the label that made it a good twentieth-century copy. I thought of Gideon, who had once given me a hard time about not dealing with dust and dirt at Sotheby's.

And then I saw the chairs.

I told myself not to jump to conclusions. Chippendale chairs, like Duncan Phyfe tables, had been imitated since the day Thomas Chippendale first made them in the 1750s. English chairs in the Chippendale style, even if they were old, were so common that they didn't have much value. And a set from Ethan Allen, circa 1950, would have a nice look and would have so little value they'd be impossible to sell.

"Do you know anything about these chairs?" I asked them.

Owen said, "Just that we sat in them for Thanksgiving dinner."

"The last time we came here for Thanksgiving dinner," Joyce said, with surprising bitterness. "When was that? Three years ago?"

An estrangement, then.

"Please, Joyce," Owen said.

"I just wish—"

"I know this isn't easy. Don't make it harder." He put a gentle hand on her arm. Had he been the protective big brother when they were small?

Joyce pulled herself together and put her good Southern persona back on. "They've been in the family as long as I can remember. That's all we know."

"May I take a good look at them?"

"Go ahead," Owen said.

"I think they're old," I said. I had an inkling, but I'd learned not to raise a client's expectations. "I think they were made around 1800, give or take a decade."

"Is that good?" Owen asked.

"A chair made in 1800 is worth more than a chair made in 1950."

"How much more?" Joyce asked. Even without the burden of Westminster's tuition, she was eager for money, too.

"I can't say for sure until I get a good look. I don't know who made them. Or exactly when they were made. That makes a difference."

I was now itching to run my hands over the carving on the legs and to upend them to look at the secondary wood of the seat. I reached for the nearest chair.

"Take a good look," Owen said.

I bent down and passed my hands over the carved back. Mahogany. Very fine carving. I stroked the seat. Red brocade, not original, probably reupholstered at the same time the Tiffany lamp came to Memphis from New York. I knelt and examined the carving on the cabriole legs. Stroked it. Felt the satiny wood under my fingers. I upended the chair. I touched the supports and felt for the unfinished and unstained secondary wood. Poplar, which was right. It wasn't marked. They never were. The carving was as distinctive as any maker's mark.

Thank God, they hadn't been made by Ethan Allen in 1950. But they hadn't been made by Thomas Chippendale in the mid-1700s, either.

They'd been made in Philadelphia, probably just before the Revolutionary War. I'd seen chairs just like these before. Those chairs came from the workshop of Thomas Tufft, one of the finest cabinetmakers in colonial Philadelphia. Were these chairs their siblings? I wondered if the family had saved the papers that would give the chairs the provenance that Sotheby's insisted on.

I set the chair aright. "How many chairs like this are there?" I asked. "I count ten in this room."

Joyce said, "I think I saw a another one like this in the study."

Owen led the way, Joyce close behind, and we went to look. The room was empty, save for a desk and a chair. Aside from the computer, the desktop was bare.

Owen said, "The baseball was always in here."

"Maybe it's in the drawer," Joyce said.

He moved the chair to open the drawer. It was empty, too. "It's not here."

"Maybe Mother sold it," Joyce said.

"She kept everything of Dad's after he died. She held on to his clothes for years. Why would she sell the baseball?"

I said, "I doubt your mother sold it. I bet it's here somewhere. I'm sure it will turn up."

Owen shook his head and shut the drawer. He looked down at the chair. "It looks the same as the others," he said.

"May I take a look?" The wood, the shape, the carving, and even the secondary wood underneath were a match. "You're right." I carefully set the chair upright. "It's odd, though. No one ever ordered a set of eleven. Always twelve. Is there another one somewhere in the house?"

Owen said, "Now I'm curious. Joyce, do you have time? Let's look through the house, see if it's here." When she hesitated, he said, "Maybe we'll find the baseball, too."

They led me through the house. Upstairs, we scanned the six bedrooms. Everything was painfully neat; the housekeeper had earned her money here. I was on alert for another Chippendale chair, but all I saw was a fair amount of nice Victorian furniture. Desk chairs. A ladies' wing chair. A rocking chair. But nothing that matched the dining room chairs.

The dressers were full of scarves and cashmere sweaters, but we didn't find the baseball there, either.

We climbed into the attic, which was insulated enough to be bearable in weather hot and cold. It was full of banker's boxes, and I felt another itch to lift their lids and rifle through the papers. But it was empty of furniture. There was no Chippendale dining chair.

It would take a lot of work to find a baseball in these boxes.

Up north, we would have gone into the basement, too, but houses in Memphis were built without them. A foot down and there was soggy Delta dirt. Not even this house, built at great expense, had a basement.

Back in the living room, Owen looked at me. "I wonder what happened to the chair."

I said, "When people split up the sets, they always did it in even numbers. A pair. Four. Six. This one could have been broken somehow, or it could have gone missing. A lot of things in the South went missing during the Civil War."

Joyce sniffed. "You mean the War of Northern Aggression."

I couldn't bring myself to say *Excuse me,* but I couldn't let it go, either. I smiled and made my voice light. "Whatever you want to call that dustup we had down here between 1861 and 1865."

My heart was pounding. It was enough of a gift to have found the eleven chairs. But now I was as curious as Joyce and Owen.

Where was the twelfth chair?

2

ELEVEN CHAIRS FROM PHILADELPHIA

On Saturday morning, Jude shared the shift in the shop with me, and as soon as she'd put down her purse, she asked, "How did it go yesterday? Did they have anything good?"

I felt a thrill in thinking about the chairs, a secret I wanted to hold close. "They do. Lots of nice turn-of-the-century stuff."

She knew what I meant. Both of us still thought of the twentieth century as *this* century. "Any jewelry?"

"I didn't get to see it. Probably."

"Are they okay to work with?"

I couldn't help it. "Rich people out in Cordova? What do you think?"

She snorted. "Like my ex's family," she said. "Sweethearts."

Not for the first time, I wondered how bad her divorce had been.

"They're going to have a pile of money from that estate," I said. "And my fee is coming out of it."

Gideon wasn't on duty, but he stopped by shortly after we opened. "You're grinning like a Chessy cat. What did you find?"

"A great big Arts and Crafts Newcomb vase," I said. "Signed by their best decorator, Sadie Irvine."

"You don't care about Sadie Irvine. They've got something better than that."

"It might be," I said. "I don't know yet."

Jude asked, "Did you see anything you want for yourself?"

I want those chairs to be Thomas Tufft's work, I thought.

I was well aware of the power of wishful thinking in the antique business. I'd met dealers who squinted and looked sideways and lied to themselves to prove they had something great instead of something ordinary. My ex knew a collector and part-time dealer who'd bought an etching he hoped, against all evidence, to be a de Kooning. We had a saying at Sotheby's. "In God we trust. Everyone else has to bring provenance." Our word for documentation. In a court of law, proof.

I CALLED the woman who'd taken my job at Sotheby's when I resigned. I'd left on friendly terms, and it was a pleasant call. She asked me how I liked living in Memphis.

I was surprised by my own answer. "I like it. Not all of it. I haven't found a decent Thai restaurant yet. But otherwise it's good. I opened an antique shop downtown, and it's going well. I have two business partners, local dealers who know what they're doing, so I can't hurt myself too badly."

She said, "You sound better than you did in New York."

I surprised myself again. "I feel better. Look, I won't keep you too long. Do you remember the Thomas Tufft chairs that came up for auction a few years ago?"

"How could I forget? I never saw such a feeding frenzy. Why? Did you find some down in Memphis?"

"I found some Philadelphia chairs. My memory tells me they're the spitting image of the Tuffts. But I don't trust my memory. Can I get any of the photos? Even an old catalog would help."

"Let me look around. I don't think anyone would mind if I sent you photos for a comp. It's still in the family, so to speak."

"Thanks." It warmed me to hear that Sotheby's still thought of me as a member of the family.

She asked, "How would a Tufft chair turn up in Memphis?"

"Old Tennessee family. They probably came here in the 1820s from Virginia, and Virginia planters bought Philadelphia furniture before the Revolutionary War. That's how." I caught my breath. "If it's a Tufft."

"How many are there?"

"Eleven."

"Where's the twelfth?"

"That's what we're all wondering."

A FEW DAYS LATER, I was at home, putting together the proposal for the Powell estate appraisal and hoping the mail would include the photographs from Sotheby's. The phone rang. It was Jude, and I wasn't sorry to be distracted. "What's up?" I asked her.

"I'm in the neighborhood, and I wanted to drop off my rent check. Since it's due today."

"It can wait until Thursday." I felt protective of Jude, who looked so fragile, as though she'd been sick.

"No, you need the money too. Besides, I'm dying to see how you've arranged your house."

I laughed. "Oh, that's it? You're snooping?"

"Busted!" she said.

"Come on over."

On the steps, under the portico, she said, "Evergreen is such a cute neighborhood." Once inside, she said, "And such a cute house." Looking around, she began to laugh. "Mission furniture!" she said. "Is that a Stickley chair?"

"What's so funny?"

"I thought you'd live in a house that looked like your great-grandmother's plantation."

"I bought the furniture from the former owner," I said. "It's right for the house. And comfortable." I pointed to the big Stickley chair. "My perch." I drank my morning coffee there, and my evening glass of wine.

"Now I'm dying to know what you collect, since it isn't Staffordshire and Sevres."

The stuff I'd had in storage in New York had arrived, and I'd filled the china cabinet. "I'll show you."

Before I had a chance to open it, she peered inside. She

punched me gently on the upper arm. "You little dickens," she said. "Is that a Hamada?"

"Busted," I said. "Mid-century studio pottery. Hamada, Bernard Leach, Warren Mackenzie. An antidote to all that nineteenth-century sugar."

She smiled. She was tucking that information away, as all dealers did, hoping to make a match between a collector's yen and an object when the object came into her hands.

I said, "Do you want to stay for a bit? I have wine, I have sparkling water, and I have cheese and crackers, too." I hoped she'd say yes. She needed fattening up.

"No, I've got to move on." She pulled the check from her purse and handed it to me. She put a finger next to her nose, a kid's gesture. "Hamada!" she said, laughing, as she left.

I PUT TOGETHER the proposal for the Powell heirs and waited to hear back. A few days later, I sat in my Stickley chair, sipping a glass of white wine and paging through the *Maine Antique Digest*. I scanned an article on prices realized at a recent auction in Boston. They'd sold a pretty piecrust table made in Boston in the 1760s and a primitive portrait of a wide-eyed little girl holding a tabby cat that had a bilious expression.

My phone rang. It was Josh. "Hey, Nat."

"What's up?"

"Owen Powell called me earlier today."

I sighed. "So this isn't a social call."

"I'm afraid not. He called me about your estimate." He sounded apologetic.

I suspected that Owen had hit the ceiling—probably about the fee—and Josh didn't want to upset me. "He wasn't happy, I take it."

"He thought it was a little high."

"Did he use a word like *outrageous*?"

"Nat, he told me what you proposed. It doesn't seem unreasonable to me, even for Memphis. But he said he was pretty surprised by it."

I said, "What do you think? Is he just a skinflint, or is he hurting for money?"

There was a long pause on the other end.

"Josh? You know something. You saw his credit report, didn't you? You talked to his banker?"

"You know that's all confidential. You understand what that means."

Did I. "Of course I do. You didn't tell me a thing," I said. "But now I know what I need to know."

"Even that's confidential," he said.

"In a situation like this one—where the heirs are looking forward to the money—it's common to take the fee out of the estate after it's valued. Would he feel any better about that?"

"Would it put a dent in the estate?"

"The house alone is worth over a million. The contents are just gravy. You know it wouldn't begin to put a dent."

"I can make that clear to Owen," he said. "That might change his mind."

I said, "I do need some money up front. I'll have some expenses. I'm hiring two of my dealers to help with the inventory and research." I'd been thinking that over, but now I'd made the decision for sure. "Their time would cost me $15 an hour. The total will run less than $5,000. I'd like to get that much so I can pay them."

"If Owen balks at that, how low can you go?"

"Half that. But I need some earnest money."

He said, "What did Freud say? That if they pay for it, they value it?"

"I'm glad you didn't suggest that I discount the job. We do that all day long at the shop. This is different."

"I get it. Lawyers don't discount, either. I'll talk to Owen to see if I can smooth things over. I feel responsible because I referred them to you. Let me work it out."

Now I knew how the Powell heirs were going to be difficult. Owen Powell was in a hurry because he was hurting for money. Even after the check came, $5,000 or half that, now I had reason to worry, too.

THE POWELLS AGREED to the lowest possible upfront money, and I invoiced them for it. Now I'd be paying Jude and Gideon out of my own estate. But that wasn't their concern.

We met in Cordova on a Monday morning, standing outside in the already muggy heat. As we waited for Joyce to let us in, Gideon looked around and said, "Nice shack."

Joyce looked askance at Jude's appearance, her boho clothes and the purple streaks in her hair, but she recognized the Phelps name, and they chatted politely about Jude's relations and connections in Cordova. Gideon just yes-ma'amed her and charmed her. I thought, not for the first time, that it was a good thing that Gideon had decided on a life as an antique dealer and not as a con artist.

Joyce offered to make us coffee. While she was in the kitchen, I whispered to Gideon, "I should take you with me wherever I go. Soften them up."

"She ain't such a hard case."

"Easy for you to say."

Joyce returned with cups on a tray and smiled at Gideon as she set everything on the sideboard. She said to me, "I have your check," and she handed it to me.

It bothered me that she was paying me the way she'd pay her gardener or her cleaning service. "You can mail it to me next time, if you want," I said.

She glanced at Jude and Gideon. "I have to run," she said. "But you all have a good day."

After she left, Jude looked at me. "So she thinks you're the help," she said.

"I'm not going to let that bother me, as long as the check clears."

Gideon said, "You aren't sure?"

I tried to laugh it off. "Are we ever?" I tucked the check into my handbag. "You two work on a formal estate appraisal before?"

"Oh, we have," Gideon said. "Under Miss Beverley's velvet-clad fist."

Jude snickered.

"Who's Miss Beverley?" I asked.

"Grande dame of high-end antique appraisals in Memphis," Gideon said. "Blue blood, old money, knew everyone who was anyone. Clients loved her. Had the market to herself for decades."

"Until?"

"Until she started to miss things. She did an appraisal for an old Shelby County family and didn't bother to go through the family papers. Told the family to throw them out. Someone was smart enough to take a look first and found a packet of letters from Varina Davis. That's Jeff Davis's wife. Those went for a bundle at auction, didn't they, Jude?"

"Near $75,000, if I remember right," Jude said. "The client was furious. Talked trash about her all over town. She shut up shop after that."

"So that's how I got this job. I'm the only appraiser in town who still has her marbles."

"And you have us," Gideon said. "For you, Miss Minerva, I promise we'll do our homework."

"We all will."

Jude rose. "I can see a lot of pretties in this room."

"I'll give you the tour."

"Is there jewelry?"

"It would be upstairs."

Gideon said, "You look in the garage? The shed?"

"Not yet."

"We should. Is there an attic?"

"There is. Full of banker's boxes. Papers, I'd guess."

He grinned. "Miss Varina's letters?"

"Who knows? I'll ask before I look. Families can be sensitive about papers. By the way, keep your eyes peeled for a baseball. Signed. St. Louis Cardinals, 1959, Bob Gibson's rookie year."

Gideon said, "I'd love to have that."

"I'm afraid you can't. It's the only thing the son wants from the estate. We couldn't find it the last time I looked. But it's got to be here somewhere."

Jude asked, "Can we set up on the dining room table?"

"Don't worry about the table. It's a twentieth-century repro."

Jude walked into the dining room and stopped to get a good look at the nearest chair. She touched the top rail and let her hand trail down the curve of the backsplat. She bent to take in the medallion and squatted down. She followed the curve of the legs and patted the ball-and-claw foot as though it were alive. She rose. "This isn't a repro," she said.

"No, it isn't."

"So that's what you've been grinning about," Jude said.

Gideon said, "Chair? I thought it was your lawyer friend from Nashville."

"Oh, hush," Jude said. She rested her hand on the chair's back. "Are these as good as I think they are?"

"I hope so. And if I can find the provenance, they'll be even something more."

"What else have they got?" Gideon asked.

"I'll give you the tour."

Jude was happy about the closets full of St. John suits and the drawers stuffed with Hermes scarves and Bottega Veneta handbags. She opened the jewelry case for a scan. "Costume," she said. "Really nice, but costume. I wonder if she kept the good stuff in a safety deposit box."

"I can find out."

"Do you know what's in those boxes in the attic?"

"I haven't looked at them yet, but it's probably papers."

We waited in the living room while Gideon checked the garage and the yard. He came back sweating. And smiling. "There's a late model Lexus in the garage," he said. "And the shed! I've lived in apartments that weren't as nice. Garden furniture, new, but worth putting in an estate sale. Hey, why are the two of you grinning? You find anything else I should know about?"

WHEN THE PHOTOGRAPHS from Sotheby's arrived, I pored over them, trying to match them to my memory of the chairs in the Powell house. It didn't help. I needed to see the image and the reality side by side. I wanted Jude and Gideon to see it, too. I asked them to come back to the house in Cordova with me.

Joyce, who'd come early to let us in, met us at the door. She looked tired, and her hair was mussed and dull. I asked her, "Was traffic bad?"

"No, it's just that I feel like I'm in the car all day, between errands and the kids." She looked at the table, covered with vases and figurines to value. "How are you coming along?"

"We're doing fine. Everything from the china cabinet is appraised. This is stuff from upstairs."

She eyed our laptops. "Will the table be all right with all that stuff on it?"

"Don't worry about the table. It's nice, but it isn't old. It's worth what you'd pay new at Ethan Allen."

She flashed a tired smile. "I thought you couldn't tell me what anything is worth."

"Believe me, when it sells in the estate sale, you won't be disappointed. We haven't missed anything."

Now I saw Gideon smother a smile.

She sighed. "I guess it's all right. I really want to get this appraisal done. Owen and I want to sell the house."

"I know."

She asked, "Is there anything I can do to help?" She was hovering because she was anxious.

"No, just let us work. You take off and try not to worry."

After she left, Gideon said, "She doesn't know whether she's coming or going, does she?"

"I guess she's disoriented from driving so much. You should meet the brother. He doesn't like me or trust me, and he doesn't care if I know it."

"The best kind of client," he joked.

"When you feel like taking a break, there's something I want you and Jude to take a look at."

"You have that Chessy cat look again. I'm ready now. I'll get Jude."

Jude came downstairs and said, "I've never seen so many Hermes scarves in one place. What have you got?"

I took out the envelope and laid the photos on the table. They weren't the eye candy for the catalog. They were the research photos, with close-ups of the carving and a good shot of the secondary wood of the underside of the seat.

I pulled out a chair and looked from the real thing to the image and back to the real thing. Jude and Gideon followed my gaze as I assessed the curve of the back rail. The shape and the design of the splat. The medallion on the seat front. The set of the legs. The ball-and-claw feet.

I thought of the question my first boss at Sotheby's had asked me when I looked at an object, the basis of connoisseurship. "What do you see?"

I saw. I saw what was there, not what I hoped to find there. And I knew. I said, "The chairs in this room are the same as the chairs in the photographs."

Gideon looked from chair to photo and back. He grinned. "They're a dead ringer," he said.

Jude asked, "What are the chairs in the photos?"

"They sold at Sotheby's a few years ago. Eighteenth-century, made in Philadelphia."

"How good are they?"

I leaned against the table because I felt giddy. "Pre–Revolutionary War, 1770s, made in Philadelphia. From the shop of Thomas Tufft, the best cabinetmaker in the colonies."

Gideon said, "How much did they go for?"

"There were five of them, and they realized $25,000 apiece."

"Not bad," Gideon said, pretending to be deadpan, but Jude let out a whoop.

I said, "Let's keep it quiet for the time being. I don't want to make an appraisal until I've done enough research."

In God we trust. All others bring provenance.

If I could find it.

AFTER A WEEK of going through the Powell house, I met with Owen and Joyce to apprise them of my progress. They weren't pleased. "Can you work any faster?" Owen asked, frowning.

"We're moving along. But we don't want to miss anything."

Owen said, "There are days when I wish we'd put it all in the dumpster and walked away."

I'd heard that kind of frustration from clients before. I also heard the underlying bitterness. "Your mother had a lot of lovely things. Believe me, they have value. Let us go through everything for you."

Joyce said, "I've been wondering about those chairs. The dining room set. Did you find out anything more about those?"

"I have, as a matter of fact. I'm sure they're Philadelphia chairs, and I'm fairly certain they were made by Thomas Tufft, one of the best cabinetmakers in Philadelphia."

"What are they worth?"

I said, "With pieces like these, a great deal of the worth is in the provenance. The documented history. An auction house will want to see invoices or wills that document their ownership in the family. Is there any chance your mother had papers like those?"

Joyce said, "There are all those bankers' boxes in the attic. We didn't know what to do with them. Who knows what's up there."

"Look through our family papers?" Owen asked. "You want to let her look through our private papers?"

I thought, *They think I have the ethics of an interior*

designer. "As an appraiser, I'm bound by confidentiality," I said. "Whatever I find, I wouldn't reveal without your approval."

"But you don't know what you'll find," Owen said.

"I might find the baseball," I said, hoping to soften him up a little.

"Still hasn't turned up?"

"We'll keep looking."

Owen shook his head. Joyce patted his arm. "Owney," she said, likely his childhood nickname. "We want to sell everything, but we want to get as much as we can for it. Let her look in those boxes. Maybe she'll find something to make the chairs more valuable. And maybe she won't. It's worth a try."

I was surprised. Neither of them knew or cared about the family's history. What were they worried I'd find?

"Top dollar," Owen said, as though he was talking himself into it.

"Top dollar," Joyce echoed, looking at me.

AFTER ADAM CALLED to make a date for a drink, I went into my bedroom, stared into my closet, and worried about my appearance as I hadn't for years. My father's words in his shop, his retail mantra for anxious female customers, came back to me. *How do you want to look? How do you want to feel?*

I wanted to look as though I wasn't trying too hard. Attractive but not seductive. Like I'd look in my own shop. Put together but not corporate. Polished but casual.

How did I want to feel? The throb of desire I'd felt when I ran into Adam at Temple Israel returned. Alone, in my own house, I pressed my hands to my hot face. I was the high school girl who'd fallen in love with a beautiful boy and learned every inch of his skin after two years of serious sex. And I was the recently divorced woman, lonely and full of self-doubt, who hadn't dared to think about intimacy for months.

I was having a hard time being both at once.

Adam had suggested a place in Midtown that hadn't existed when we were growing up, a wine bar with imported beers, expensive wines by the glass, and appetizers in the Southern nouvelle mode. It had exposed brick walls, and big plate windows that let the summer light through, and it smelled of white wine and crabcakes. It held no memories for either of us.

We'd supply those ourselves.

Adam waved to me from a table. He'd already ordered a beer. As I sat, his face lit in a smile. "You look great, Nat."

It had been a while since a man looked at me with pleasure, and I'd forgotten how satisfying it was. "Thanks. You look pretty good yourself."

He'd come directly from work, but he'd taken off his jacket and loosened his tie. He looked a little wilted, but we all did if we walked more than a few steps outside. His hair, like mine, curled like crazy in the wet heat of summer in Memphis. I remembered the feel of those curls springing beneath my fingers. Now that was a ghost, fifteen years past.

"Older," he said, raising his glass.

I leaned forward to get a better look. I knew I wasn't

risking any cleavage. "Wiser," I replied.

"We both hope," he said. "What would you like to drink?"

I glanced at the menu. "White wine by the glass," I said. I'd learned not to be a snob about wine in Memphis, but when my drink came, I sipped it and thought, *Nouvelle Memphis. Not bad.*

Adam and I had always known each other. We'd never had to get acquainted before. I continued to struggle with the difference between our all-too-familiar past and our ignorance of each other in the present.

I said, "We used to know each other so well. And now I feel like we don't know each other at all."

He smiled. He now had the slightest crows' feet when he smiled. "We still know each other. We just have some catching up to do."

"Really? Is it that easy?"

Along with the charm, his smile was now sadder. "It is, and it isn't."

I sipped my wine. "So, catching up. You went to law school. After you swore you wouldn't."

He nodded. "I realized it was never about going to law school. I stopped being mad at my father."

If that was true—and why wouldn't it be?—he had changed. "And then you ended up at Warner Music."

He nodded. "They hire a lot of lawyers. The work sounded interesting. When I interviewed, they told me that I'd meet the celebs and the stars. I said, 'That sounds like fun.' They assured me it was."

"We had some of that at Sotheby's, too. It was fun."

"I'm surprised you left Sotheby's. You were there—

how long? Since college?"

"How did you know?" I hadn't told him that.

"My mother kept me up to date on you. Temple gossip. That's how I heard that you'd gone to work at Sotheby's and that you'd gotten married."

My mother, who heard all the Temple gossip, had not kept me similarly informed. I answered the question I'd been asked. "Fifteen years."

"And now you're running an antique shop."

"It's different from Sotheby's, that's for sure, but I really enjoy it. I get a kick out of dealing with the customers. And I love selling stuff. Retail really is in the Raskin DNA."

He laughed at that. "I saw the picture of your grandfather in the shop."

I kept my grandfather's picture in a prominent spot, with a little tag beneath it as though it was on exhibition. "Our resident spirit."

"I heard that he died. It was a few years ago. I'm sorry."

"He did. That's the only time I came back to Memphis. I miss him."

"He looks like he's happy to be back in the shop. He looks like he's proud of you."

He hadn't known my grandfather well, but his condolences were genuine. I appreciated it. "He would be."

"Was it hard to come back to Memphis?"

I wondered how he'd answer that question himself. "After I got divorced, I needed a big change. And it turned out to be coming home." I met his eyes. "A rebound thing."

He asked, "Bad divorce?"

I said, "My friends in New York told me, 'When you

start dating, don't lead with the divorce.'"

"You didn't. I asked you."

Our eyes met, and I was afraid he'd see everything I'd felt since I got divorced. *What went wrong? Was it my fault? Will anyone ever love me again? Do I dare find out?* "Is there such a thing as a good divorce?"

"I haven't seen one yet." His beautiful dark eyes were full of sympathy. Oh, he knew. He knew about waking up in the middle of the night, when there was nothing to distract from the grief and the guilt.

The sympathy got to me as no flirtation could. "Careful," I said.

"I know," he said. "Rebound, both of us."

"No kidding," I said.

He shook his head.

"What?"

"I'm just thinking of what an idiot I was after we broke up." He leaned forward. "There were phone lines between Nashville and New York. Plane flights, too. I was such an idiot."

I was startled into laughter. "Now you say so."

"And you were, too, even though you won't admit it." He laughed too.

I hadn't forgotten how to talk like a teenager. Sass. "Speak for yourself!"

He looked at me with a warmth that went back to the earliest days of our friendship, the only people on the youth group board who got things done. "Do you think we could start from a different place? Wherever we are now? And see where we go?"

I said, "Do you remember," before I realized what he

might be remembering.

He smiled. "What?"

"That Faulkner quote our high school history teacher kept on the wall in her classroom?"

"About the past?"

"How it isn't dead. Or over. Still with us, haunting us."

"Yes, I remember," he said, but his smile told me he remembered more than that, and my face grew hot again.

"We can try," I said. "But I want to take it slow."

"Then we will."

Thank you. I thought about taking his hand and decided against it. "Let me call you."

He smiled. "Promise?"

"Promise."

———

THE NEXT DAY, after I opened the shop, both Jude and Gideon followed me in. They both carried boxes. Gideon looked tired again, and his eyes were bloodshot.

"You need ibuprofen?" I asked him.

He set the box on the counter. "No, I'm all right."

"Where were you last night?" Jude teased.

He ignored her. "I need the key to my case."

Jude gave it to him. He said to me, "See? A perfectly good reason to be here. New merch."

"You know you can be here all you want," I said. "We do better when you're here." I heard the multiple meaning, and I colored a little.

Jude said, "And we love you, too. Don't we, Nat?"

"What's in your box?"

As she set it on the counter, she asked, "How was the ha'nt?"

"Ha'nting."

Gideon said, "I didn't think white people said ha'nt. Who was it?"

I sighed. "I think you know."

As Gideon turned the key in the case lock, he asked, "Is he Mr. Right?"

I blushed. "I'll make a deal with you. When I find Mr. Right, you"—I took in Jude, too—"both of you will be the first to know."

Jude started to laugh.

"Oh, hush," I said, still blushing. "I have better news than that. It's about the appraisal."

"They have provenance?" Jude asked, her voice eager.

"They have papers in the attic. They gave me permission to look at them."

"Permission?" Gideon asked. "What are they hiding in there?"

Jude snorted. "Old family that goes back before the Civil War? Take a wild guess."

I said, "In the Powell house, that's the War of Northern Aggression."

Now Gideon snorted. "Are those old papers all dusty, Miss Minerva?"

"I don't know. I'll find out." I looked at Jude. "What did you bring in?"

She pulled it out, unwrapped it, and set it on the counter before me. "I thought you'd like this."

It was a lovely little stoneware vase, hand-thrown, with a crackled, speckled gray glaze. I cradled it in my hands, liking the feel of it. I turned it around, looking for the mark.

She caught my eye as I said, "Warren Mackenzie. The early mark, the one conjoined with his wife Alix's initials. I bet she designed it." Jude smiled as I held up the vase and crooned to it. "What are you doing so far from home, little fella? All the way down the Mississippi in Memphis?"

Jude said, "I know someone who went to Minneapolis to visit friends. He found it at an estate sale up there. As soon as I saw it I thought of you."

"I'd like to go to an estate sale like that." I set the piece down. "What are you asking?"

"I'd take $100 for it."

I said, "You will not. Market on a piece like this is $250, $275."

"He picked it up for nothing, and I got it cheap."

"No, no. Like my grandpa used to say, 'Buy low and sell high. And don't discount the new stuff.' Market is $275, and I insist on paying you that much."

She shook her head, and I remembered the realtor who sold me my house, joking about asking the sellers for a higher price to accommodate my New York sensibilities. This was different. I pulled out my checkbook and wrote her a check.

As she tucked it away, she said, "What else do you want?"

"You know what I want. A Hamada, in the original box. You find me one of those, I'll be more than happy to pay you full market for it." I laughed. "Now *that* would make me happier than finding Mr. Right."

3

THE POWELL PROVENANCE

Back at the house in Cordova, I opened the door to the attic and turned on the stairway light. The attic, like the rest of this house, was in pristine condition and perfect order. As I led Jude and Gideon up the stairs, I thought I'd never seen an attic less eerie than this one.

We stood at the head of the stairs and stared at the boxes. Piles and piles of banker's boxes. My heart sank.

Jude said, "Have you peeked inside at all?"

"No."

She took the lid off the nearest box, topmost on a stack of three. "It's organized. Neat. Utility bills, all the way back to the eighties."

Gideon opened another box. "Bank statements and canceled checks," he said. "Decades' worth."

"There must be fifty boxes up here," I said. "And we've got to go through everything."

Jude said, "Let's do the first pass on the spot. It's not bad up here. Enough room to stand up and spread out, and it's not stifling, either."

We looked. Everything was carefully organized and neatly labeled. Evelyn Powell had the instincts of an archivist, but these were the dullest kind of household papers. Invoices for servicing the a/c. Receipts for appliances going back decades. Tax returns, thirty years' worth.

Jude said, "Oh, look! Every vet bill they ever paid. The last bill for the last dog. And this." She lifted up a clay disk to show us.

"What the hell?" Gideon asked.

"A memorial paw print. The dog's name was Biscuit."

I sat back on my heels and sighed. "Unless there's a market for antique bills from Bell South, I don't think we'll find anything up here."

Gideon shot me a glance. "Unless something's been misfiled."

I groaned.

Jude said, "It's strange that there's nothing personal, except for that thing from the vet. No letters, kid stuff, clothes, anything like that."

"There's nothing personal downstairs, either. No photographs of her kids or her grandkids."

"She doesn't strike me like the kind of person to throw stuff away. Where's the rest of it?"

I shook my head and met Gideon's eyes. "I guess we need to go through every folder and every piece of paper," I said. "Just to make sure we've seen everything."

"Nat, what are we looking for?" Jude grinned at Gideon. "Besides Miss Varina's letters?"

"Ha-ha. We're looking for anything that might relate to the chairs. Wills, which might mention them as bequests. And if we're really lucky, correspondence. Or even the original bill of sale."

We lugged the boxes downstairs and stacked them on the living room floor. For the rest of that day, we opened every box, opened every folder, and touched every piece of paper.

"Gid, you know what this reminds me of?" Jude asked.

"Looking for a needle in a haystack?"

"Remember that guy who always came to estate sales and went through every book in the library, looking for money stashed inside?"

I snorted. "Did he find any?"

"It must have been worth his while. He kept doing it."

I stood up and put my hand to my lower back. My eyes ached, too.

At the end of the day, we shut the last boxes and stacked them neatly on the carpet. I said, "I'm too tired to take them back upstairs. Joyce is going to have to lump it for a day or two."

Gideon said, "The good news is we didn't overlook Miss Varina's letters. The bad news is that we got a lot of papercuts for nothing."

AT SOTHEBY'S, the pieces that sold best had a lineage, like a human being's, defined by their appearance in wills or family inventories, documenting their passage from generation to generation.

After two intensive weeks of touching everything that Evelyn Powell had owned, read, used, and worn, we'd made her acquaintance. She had always lived in the past. The objects she kept in her immaculate living room and her pretty china cabinet weren't things she'd bought for herself. She'd inherited them from her parents, her grandparents, and ancestors further beyond. Even the practical items in the kitchen belonged to a previous generation. Her everyday dinnerware was her wedding china from the 1950s, and her everyday flatware was silverplate that her parents had likely received as a wedding gift. The television in the bedroom and the computer in the study were glaring anachronisms in this house.

She liked order. She revered the past. She saved things.

I recognized her. My Beardsley grandmother was like that, too.

Had Evelyn Powell saved the wills, too?

Shortly after we combed through the boxes in the attic, Jude and Gideon took off around four in the afternoon, and Joyce showed up shortly after, looking frazzled. "Traffic is awful at this hour," she said. She opened the cupboard and took out a glass. She ran the water until it was cold and drank at the sink. "If I didn't have to pick up the kids, I'd have a real drink." She sat heavily in one of the Chippendale chairs. They were hers. I could hardly tell her to park her bottom in them carefully. "Is this about the papers in the attic?"

"We went through everything. Page by page."

She pushed the hair back from her forehead. "Did you find what you were looking for?"

"It was bills, receipts, old checks, and financial records. Your mother saved decades' worth. You'll want to keep the more recent tax records, but everything else can go into the shredder."

"Nothing about the chairs."

"Not up there, no."

She sighed. "Are they worth anything?"

"I still think so. If we can find some documentation."

"Like what?"

I explained about the provenance, and why wills mattered to it.

"No wills up there?"

"No. But your mother seems to have been a saver by nature. Did she have a safety deposit box?"

"She did. We haven't opened it yet. We've been over-whelmed with the house." To my surprise, she sighed. "I never expected to deal with any of this," she said. "The way things had been between us, I didn't think Mother would leave us a thing."

I didn't ask. I waited.

"We had a falling out when I got married. She didn't approve of my husband. Thought he was beneath me. Now that's something you don't hear people say much. But she was like that. Stuck in the past. I don't think she lived in the here and now. It wasn't like dementia. She was sharp as could be. But she acted like she wished she lived a hundred years ago."

I thought of the living room, with its museum-like quality. I nodded.

"When Owen joined a Baptist church, it made her furi-ous. She raised us Episcopal. Not much religion there, if you ask me. But she told him she didn't want him in the house. No Holy Rollers in her family."

"I have relatives who are hard-shell," I said.

"You?"

"Deep roots in Shelby County on my mother's side. Part of the family goes to St. Mary's Episcopal and part of it turned Baptist. Some of those folks found their way to being rock-ribbed Baptists."

"You get it."

"My mother used to bring me to the family picnics when I was a kid. Blood is thicker than water. There are just a lot of things you don't talk about."

"Owen's not like that. Oh, I can tell you don't like that his kids are at Westminster, getting a Christian education. It's all right, but it's a bit much, to my mind. My kids go to the public school in Bartlett, and we make sure they go to church and belong to the youth group. That's enough religion for us." She looked at me. "I can tell you don't have any religion at all."

I laughed. "On the contrary. I have too many options to choose from."

She smiled, and for the first time, I actually liked her. She said, "If we find the wills, are the chairs really worth a lot?"

"It's hard not to get your hopes up. But they might be."

SHE DIDN'T WANT me looking at the papers unless Owen said yes. He didn't like the idea of my inspecting legal documents like wills, but he was buoyed by the hope that the chairs were valuable. "How valuable?"

"I hate to raise your expectations until I can say for sure."

"Are you holding out on us?" He was edgy and he sounded accusatory.

"Of course not. Why would I?"

"Where's the damn baseball?"

Joyce tried to soothe him. "It's a huge house. It could be anywhere."

"I know how big the house is!" he snapped.

"Let's open that safety deposit box," Joyce said. "See what's in there."

I was beginning to feel troubled by Owen, hot and cold about this estate, unhappy that I was probing into the family history, but eager for the money. I called Josh.

"How's the appraisal going?"

"Great. Mrs. Powell had a lot of nice things. They'll have a bang-up estate sale."

"Clients acting all right?"

"Squirrelly."

"Worse than usual?"

"Owen Powell is on edge, more than before. I wish you'd let me know if he's in trouble."

"Well, we both know he has three kids at Westminster and a mortgage on a house in Germantown," he said. "Pretty normal overreach, I think. Haven't you seen that before?"

He wasn't going to give anything up. Well, I had my own reasons for confidentiality. "Yeah, and I've seen the gleam of greed, too. 'Wow, it's valuable? It's that valuable? Can it be more valuable?' Once they hear that, I think they'll be willing to wait to send it to auction for top dollar. Joyce gets it. Owen keeps wavering. He can't decide if he wants some money now or more money later."

"Keep reminding him about more money later."

"I will. If there might be a mess ahead, I just don't want to get in the middle of it without warning."

He said, "You've dealt with estates before. When is it ever clean and neat?"

Joyce and Owen emptied the safety deposit box, and Joyce brought us the contents, which she laid carefully on the Duncan Phyfe repro table, our workstation. "This box is full of jewelry cases."

"Have you peeked inside?" Jude asked.

I said, "Jude is a gemologist and an estate jewelry expert. Do you mind if she takes a look?"

Joyce said, "No. I'm really curious too."

Gideon, who was always curious, even if it was something he didn't deal in, hovered behind us.

Jude took out the topmost case. The dark blue velvet was as lustrous as it had been when it was new. She opened it and lifted out the necklace. Her face broke into a smile as she turned the diamonds to catch the light. "That's lovely," she said. "Edwardian, old mine diamonds, beautiful design. I'd guess French, but I'd need a loupe to be sure."

"Is it worth anything?"

She looked at me and smiled at Joyce. "My lips are sealed until I do enough research," she said.

Joyce laughed. "Oh, I'm learning. I know what that means. It's worth something, but you don't want to disappoint me by giving me a big number." She turned to me. "We found something for you, too."

The folders themselves were pristine, too, preserved by the safety deposit box. I glimpsed the labels in the now-familiar precise hand. *Stock certificates. Marriage licenses. Insurance policies. Wills.*

My breath caught in my throat. "Have you taken a look?" I asked.

"Owen did. He said the old ones were really hard to read," Joyce said. "They're handwritten."

"Contrary to popular belief, not everyone in the nineteenth century had good handwriting."

Joyce said, "The newer ones are typed up, but he said it was all legalese."

Owen Powell was a stockbroker. Surely he'd read a legal contract.

I said, "I'll look at all of them. I'll do my best to transcribe the handwritten ones for you. And if you have any questions, we can consult Josh."

She joked, "Do we get a break on his hourly rate because you're his sister?"

She must be feeling good about the jewelry. "Unfortunately not," I said, smiling at her. "But I don't think anything will be out of order."

She said, "By the way, keep your eyes open for a ring. Diamonds and sapphires. Mother always wore it, but we haven't found it yet, and I wondered if she put it away in the safety deposit box."

Jude said, "Will do."

She looked wistful. "She treasured it. She said it had always been in the family and it should stay in the family. I thought she'd give it to me."

I thought, *Another missing heirloom.*

After Joyce left, Jude lifted the box full of jewelry cases. "I'm going to take these upstairs so I can spread out and look at them properly," she said. "Let me know if you find anything interesting."

I rested my hand on the folder labeled *Wills*.

"You going to open that?" Gideon said. "Or just commune with it?"

I sat. "You never know what you're going to find."

"That's why you've got to open it."

I opened the folder. I'd handled documents this old, but never with my bare hands. At Sotheby's, we kept cotton archivists' gloves for items like this. It felt wrong to touch the paper.

"What are you looking for?" Gideon asked.

"Anything that helps with attribution. Who made it, and when and where. Bills of sale are good. Correspondence between the maker and the buyer is even better."

"Why the wills? What's in there?"

"Proof of ownership. If the piece matters enough to the family, they'll mention it in a will. If it's been sold, receipts are just as good. I've seen pieces that were sold and resold at Sacks—that's Israel Sack, the high-end furniture dealer in New York who went out of business in 2002—and his receipts are just as good as a bequest in a will for establishing who owned the piece."

My hand trembled as I reached for the topmost page. I squinted at the faded, untidy script. "Joyce was right.

Whoever wrote this had lousy handwriting." I wouldn't be able to scan the lines, as I would with anything printed. I'd have to decipher them, letter by letter and word by word, as I'd read Hebrew in Sunday School at Temple Israel. "I can make out the name. Ezekiel Powell. And the date, April 10, 1848."

"Any idea who he was?"

I said, "No. I wonder if they've done a genealogy. Not the kind of tree you can do online. An old-fashioned labor of love, put together by some Daughter of the Confederacy who wants to trace the family back to Charlemagne."

"We'll keep our eyes peeled. While we're scouting for the baseball. And the ring."

I turned the page and smiled.

"What?" Gideon asked.

"It's an inventory," I said. "You usually see it in much earlier wills, when every stick of furniture and every spoon was of value. It's not typical in wills written this late, but Ezekiel Powell decided to itemize everything he owned."

"Just the furniture?"

This I could scan. "Beds. Dressers. Sideboards. A dining table. Numerous side tables. Chairs. And silver. Candlesticks, a coffee set, and hollowware, a dozen table settings."

"Not shabby."

I laughed. "Not just an inventory. He assigned a value to every item. He went through his estate and appraised it." I kept reading. "Here we go. He mentions them separately. A dozen chairs in the Chippendale style. And there's a note: 'For my eldest son Lucullus, with the provision that he treat them with care.'" I looked up. "Why wouldn't he?"

"Maybe his dad knew he was rough on the furniture. What else have you got?"

I turned the page. "It's a list of names." I looked up, troubled. "His slaves." I took a quick census. "He had thirty slaves to bequeath to Lucullus."

I set Ezekiel's will aside to read the next document.

"This one is Lucullus Powell's will," I said. "His handwriting is a lot better than his father's. A better education, I bet, or else he asked his lawyer to draw it up for him. It's lovely copperplate." I showed Gideon. "Look at the date. 1861. April 14 of 1861. Looks like he made his will in a hurry, just before he enlisted in the Confederate army."

"Who got the goods?"

"Let's see. He left the estate to his wife, in trust for their son, Robert, until he turned twenty-one. He doesn't itemize the household goods, but he specifies that his widow gets the plantation house in Shelby County and all its contents. Look at this. He mentions the chairs. 'A dozen dining room chairs in the Chippendale style, to which I have been a good steward.'" I looked up at Gideon. "They had an attitude about those chairs."

I turned the page to find another list of names, longer than the one in his father's will. "He itemized all his slaves." Another swift count. "When he went off to war, there were fifty enslaved persons living on his plantation." I put the will aside, shaking my head.

"Nat?"

"My mother's family owned slaves before the Civil War," I said.

"They leave a list like that?"

"If they did, I've never seen it." Abashed, I reached for the next will and scanned it. "This one is Robert Powell's. Lucullus's son. Dated 1897. Wow, pages and pages. It's about the family business."

"Which was?"

"Powell and Sons, Cotton Brokers." I skipped over the language that described the transfer of assets from father Robert to son Jonathan. On the last page, one sentence caught my eye. "He mentions the chairs. He left them to his son. I'm quoting here. 'The set of Chippendale chairs, to keep them in the family.'"

"So far, so good," Gideon said.

"It's weird. They aren't treating the chairs like an American heirloom, a cherished item that gets passed down in the family. They're treating it like an English heirloom. That's a legal designation for something that can't be separated from the estate. No one ever owns it. They just have custody of it. It usually refers to things like coats of arms or jewelry that was a royal gift." I shook my head. "I shouldn't be surprised that a Southern family would have delusions of grandeur like that."

"What's up next?"

"We're in the twentieth century. It's typewritten! I can actually read it! It's not Jonathan. It's an Owen. I wonder if it's Robert's grandson." I turned the pages and broke into a smile. "He itemized his stuff, like Ezekiel did. He had a professional appraisal done. A catalog, just like the one we're doing."

"Let me see."

"Wait a minute. It's for insurance, so it probably isn't everything, just the most valuable stuff." I smiled as I read it. "The silver's in there, and so are the vases and figurines. So is the Newcomb vase! And the Persian carpet." I let my finger trail down the paper. I didn't mind touching twentieth-century paper. "Here they are. Eleven mahogany chairs in the Chippendale style. Everything valued."

"That I want to see." I showed him.

He said, "So that's what Sadie Irvine was worth in 1954."

"The prices don't help us. But the list does."

"First mention of eleven chairs instead of a dozen. Who got the goods next?"

"The Robert Powell who married Evelyn."

"Is her will in there?"

"It is." It had been word processed and printed from a laser printer in my brother's office.

"I wonder if there are any surprises in there. Anything we missed."

"My brother didn't think so. It's straightforward. She left everything to both her children." I put the will aside.

And saw the paper at the bottom of the pile. This was old, yellowed paper, the kind I shouldn't be touching with my bare hands. A letter, dated June 25, 1773, from Philadelphia. The handwriting was elegant and sure. I felt a prickle along my spine. I bent over the page and reminded myself, *See what's there. Not what you hope for.*

The letter was addressed to Mr. Jonathan Powell of Westmoreland County, Virginia, and it had come from the shop of cabinetmaker Thomas Tufft.

Below the salutation was a sketch. A design. I stared at the familiar back rail. The familiar splat. The familiar medallion. The familiar curved legs with their ball-and-claw feet. The sketch was elegant and sure, too.

"Look," I said to Gideon.

He looked at the page, then at me.

"Dead ringer," I said.

I picked up the page with trembling fingers. Underneath it was another piece of paper. It was the bill of sale, dated August 8, 1773. As promised, a set of a dozen mahogany chairs in the style of Thomas Chippendale, to be delivered to Virginia, at a cost of $100.

Gideon said, "I bet that was a pile of money back then."

I was hot and cold at the same time. I said, "It was a fortune back in the 1770s." I set down the paper, realizing that I shouldn't be touching it.

"And have they held their value?"

"You never know, at auction." I was shaking. "Drag Jude downstairs. Tell her there's something good to look at."

Jude bounded down the stairs after Gideon. "You found something?" she said.

I'd arranged the papers on the table in an artful fan, as though I were setting them up for viewing at Sotheby's. "Yes. Look at it. But don't breathe on it."

"What is it?"

I was shaking worse than before. "Provenance," I said.

WHEN I MET with Joyce and Owen, we sat at the repro table, and we sat in the chairs. Joyce looked eager, but Owen was tired and edgy. He had dark rings under his eyes and a pouchy look to his thin face, like a man who sat up late at night drinking instead of sleeping. He tapped his fingers on the tabletop and looked at his watch.

"Is this still a good time?" I asked him.

"As good as any. I have to be back in the office in Germantown in an hour."

I told them, "I've gone through the folders in the safety deposit box, and I have some very good news for you about the chairs." I could tell that Owen wanted to ask, "How much?" I said, "We now know when they were made, where they were made, and who made them. They're from Philadelphia, like I thought, and they date from 1773. They came from the workshop of Thomas Tufft. He was one of the best cabinetmakers and chair-makers in the colonies in his day, and his work is extremely desirable today."

"How do you know?" Owen asked. He wasn't curious. He sounded belligerent.

I pulled out the folder and carefully extracted the letter and the bill of sale. I laid them on the table. "Take a look," I said.

Joyce bent over the letter. "He drew a picture?" she said, delighted.

"He sketched the design."

She twisted around to stare at the splat. "And he didn't change a thing!"

"It's an excellent design," I said, smiling. "And there's more good news, too, from the wills. There's proof of uninterrupted ownership in the family, starting with the Powell who first commissioned the chairs."

Joyce was reading the letter. "Jonathan Powell. In Virginia, back in 1773."

"Does the name ring a bell?" I asked.

"No," Owen said. "Can we move this along?"

"Between the letter and the wills, the chairs have the kind of documentation that a major auction house is looking for," I said. "They'll be able to give the chairs a higher valuation because of it."

"How much?" Owen asked.

"Sotheby's sold a lot of five Tufft chairs a few years ago, while I was still there. Same design, same time period, same kind of provenance." I now had a number I could stand behind. What I'd value them for, if I were still at Sotheby's. I couldn't keep it from them any longer. "They went for $25,000."

Joyce said, "Each?"

"Yes, each."

Owen pulled out his phone. Calculating, he said, "That's—" He stared at the screen. "That's $275,000." He looked up at me. "Would they be worth more if we had all twelve?"

"They'd be worth $25,000 more. With chairs like these, it doesn't matter about having an even set. Having eleven is good enough."

Joyce had a dazed look. "$25,000 *each*," she said.

"I hate to burst a bubble, but no one knows what will happen at an auction. It's a crapshoot, like playing the stock market." Did I see Owen wince? "You price according to the comps, you assume the market hasn't changed, you get the right bidders in the room, and you hope for the best. But it's still a crapshoot."

Owen said, "How fast can we get them into an auction?"

"When you deal with a major auction house, it takes a while. They need to do their research, and they schedule auctions in advance to group and advertise the best pieces. At best, three to four months, and likely closer to six."

Owen tapped his fingers on the table. "I'd really like to sell them sooner," he said.

"We're almost done with the appraisal," I said. "You can start to think about scheduling an estate sale. They'll need some time to set up, and they'll want to advertise, too. But it's not like dealing with a New York auction house. They can move in a matter of weeks, not months."

"And then we can get the house on the market, too," Joyce said. "Talk about comps. We know what the house is worth."

Owen curled his fingers into a fist and pressed it into the table. "Okay, say we want to put the chairs into an auction. What happens next?"

"I can contact Sotheby's, where I have an in, and I'll do the same with Christie's. I have friends there, too."

"You had friends at the competition?"

"I have friends in every major auction house in the country, and some in Europe," I said. "It's a small, close-knit world. We'll see what they say, and we'll take it from there."

Owen uncurled his fist. "How much longer until you're done with the stuff in the house?"

"A week. Two at the most."

"You find the baseball yet?" He was still unhappy.

I wished I knew what was making Owen Powell so hostile. Josh wasn't going to tell me. I moved into full Sotheby's mode, making nice with an angry rich person. Smiling, I said, "We're still looking."

"I'm still wondering where that damn twelfth chair is. Aren't you, Joyce?"

"Does it matter, Owney?" She laughed, delighted.

It was as though the rest of the estate—the house, the decorative art, the jewelry—hadn't sunk in. The chairs were only a small part of the whole. I'd seen this before, too—the daze that accompanies the news that Grandma's old, ugly piece of furniture is worth enough to put the kids through college. It's more exciting than learning that the house you know is worth a million dollars will sell for a million dollars. It's the thrill of found money.

Joyce glowed with the news. "I bet the *Commercial Appeal* would love a story about this."

At that, I wasn't so pleased. "How good is the security on this house?" I asked.

Owen snapped, "Damn good."

"It would be better to keep it quiet," I said.

WHEN I GOT HOME that evening, my neighbors Val and Emmy were sitting on their front porch. I waved at them as I drove up, and they waved back. Val lifted her sweating glass and called out, "Want to join us?"

I hopped from my car and hightailed it up their walk. "What are you drinking?"

"Juleps," Val said. "Leo's staying with Grandma, and we're taking advantage of it to drink like grown-ups."

I laughed. "You're drinking a mint julep?"

"The mint's from the backyard. And Emmy's a madwoman with a muddler."

Val had grown up in the Black neighborhood of Whitehaven—she'd been a basketball star at Whitehaven High—but Emmy had come from a moneyed Southern family. I'd never pried to find out how they'd come to join their lives together. Evergreen, like the New York I'd left, welcomed them. They were our block captains. Val's height came in handy.

Emmy disappeared into the house to make me a drink, and when she returned, Val said, "You look happy today. Love or business?"

"Oh, business. I'm appraising an estate, and we found something really good. Old. Beautiful. Rare. Valuable." I thought of sending the photos and the copy of the bill of sale to Sotheby's, and I felt good all over again. "It's what you live for, if you're in the antique business."

Val lifted her glass. "Congratulations," she said.

I took a sip of the bourbon, but suddenly I didn't want to be tipsy. The natural buzz was better. I sat and chatted, to be polite, but after I walked in my front door, I pulled out my cell phone. I knew who I wanted to share my news with. I called Adam.

"Nat!" he said, and his tone, like his smile the last time we met in person, told me that I gave him pleasure. "How are you?"

"I feel like celebrating."

He laughed. "What happened?"

"I found something good in the estate I'm appraising. Really good. I'm a little light-headed." Eleven chairs at $25,000 apiece! Who needed bourbon?

"Let me celebrate with you."

Yes.

"Let me take you out to dinner."

I thought of sitting across the table from him, champagne glasses in hand, and I knew I wasn't ready for it. "I have a better idea," I said.

"What do you have in mind?"

"Meet me in Greenlight Park by the river," I said.

"Outside? Are you serious? It's hot as Hades out."

"Go home to change first," I said. "And it's always cooler by the river, because there's a breeze off the water."

He laughed. "You're serious."

"I'm a real Memphian again," I said, teasing him as I usually teased Gideon. "Are you?"

"If you insist," he said, teasing back.

"I do," I said.

I'd never spent any time by the river when I was a teenager, but not long ago, on the day when I wasn't sure whether I wanted to go back to New York or throw myself in the river, I'd stood on its bank and looked over the water. That day, the river had kept me in Memphis. Now the riverside was my favorite spot in the city, and I went there all the time.

I had my doubts that Adam would like it, since he was a suburbanite through and through, whose idea of wildlife was a backyard squirrel. But I hoped he might see the river like I did.

He met me in the parking lot, and I had to grin at the sight of him in shorts again. "It's just like Jacobs Camp," I said, where we had both been campers for years.

He laughed. "Just don't ask me to sing."

I hummed the first few bars of "Hiney ma tov u-manayim," the youth group anthem of togetherness. Returning to his younger self, Adam groaned. "Cut it out, Nat." But he was smiling.

This far from the water, it was hot and oppressively humid, the air thick and wet and hard to breathe, the Memphis I was still readjusting to. Adam's hair had curled in the heat, as had mine. He smelled of his own scent, an earthy cinnamon smell, combined with the tang of sweat. It was familiar, and it was not.

"Come on," I said.

"Where are we going?"

"We're going down to the water." I pointed. "Then we'll find a place to sit. Because you're right, it's too hot to move much."

We walked together at a leisurely pace. "There's a bench," he said.

"I want to get closer to the water."

As I led him there, he said, "How close? Do you want to fall in?"

"Trust me."

He snorted.

"Here." I led him to the spot I liked best. I sat first, and he joined me on the log that fit us like a loveseat, pushing us closer together. I didn't look at Adam, but over the river, murky even in daylight, sparkling where the summer sun hit it. This was slow-moving water, and I breathed in its smell, muddy and alluvial.

He said, "The muddy Mississippi."

I turned to him and smiled. "This is my favorite place in Memphis. This is the reason there's a Memphis at all. The mighty, muddy Mississippi."

He waved away a cloud of gnats and turned to me. "You really like this. You really live in Memphis now."

"I do. Sometimes I'm still too much the Yankee and it gets in my way. But I'm a Southerner who came home."

Adam shook his head.

I asked, "You aren't at home the same way, I can tell. Do you miss Nashville?"

"I do. Warner told me they'd be glad to rehire me if things pick up. I'd be glad to go back."

I couldn't imagine returning to New York, so much more attractive than Nashville. "Even though your ex still lives there?"

His laugh had an edge. "If I move and join a different synagogue, I'll never see her."

No good divorce, I thought.

Still edgy, he asked, "Are you in touch with your ex?"

I didn't want to say much. I had a light version for a cocktail party or a chat after the service at Temple Israel. "No. We finalized the divorce and split up our assets and we were done. That part was amicable. I guess he felt guilty about the rest."

"Which wasn't amicable."

"No." I waited before I told him the rest. "He left me for someone else. Younger. Taller."

He ignored my light tone. He offered sympathy. "That's rough, Nat. I'm so sorry to hear it."

His sympathy touched me, and I wasn't sure I wanted to be touched that way. Not yet. I shook my head.

He knew he'd hit a sore spot. He looked over the water rather than at me. "Tell me about this thing you found. The one you're excited about."

"I can't be specific, because I promised the client I'd keep it confidential. Appraisers have to do that, like lawyers do."

He hadn't worn a cap and he had to shade his eyes against the sun to look at me. "Tell me what you can."

"It's something every antique dealer dreams about, finding something so old, so rare, so beautiful, and so valuable. It's the kind of thing that we used to go crazy about at Sotheby's."

"Will you send it there?"

"I'll call them, but I'll call Christie's, too. It's that good a thing."

"You're really lit up about this."

"This is literally the find of a lifetime. I'm thrilled about it."

He smiled. "You'll have to let me buy you champagne."

"Sometime. Right now, this is nice."

As the sun began to sink a little in the sky, the breeze off the water was cooling and delicious. It stirred my hair and blew it across my face.

He reached out and smoothed the errant lock. "You're right, this is nice."

The touch of his fingers in my hair was like the first caress he'd ever given me when we were both sixteen. At the memory, I looked away. I gazed over the water, and his gaze followed mine.

"Do you see the willow flies?" he asked.

I nodded.

He smiled. "Do you remember?"

"What?"

"The youth group retreat in the spring of our junior year. We sat on the shore of a muddy, buggy lake, and we watched the willow flies."

It came back in a rush. Our first kiss on that lakeshore, months of longing concentrated in the brush of lips on lips.

He laid his hand on my cheek, just as he had fifteen years ago, his eyes alight with memory and desire.

I covered his hand with my own. "I remember too much, and it scares me."

"Rebound?" he asked softly, touching my cheek gently before he took his hand away.

I nodded. "Adam, where are we going?"

"I don't know yet. But we have a lot more catching up to do."

I saw the lines at the corners of his eyes that showed when he smiled. He was older and sadder, as I was. "Let's do that first," I said. We sat together, at ease for the moment, watching the willow flies dance over the water.

NEXT WEEK, when Gideon walked into the shop, he carried the *Commercial Appeal* under his arm. He tossed it on the counter. "You see the article?"

"Of course I did. It ruined my breakfast."

"Big local news. Great picture of one of the chairs. The chair looks better than Owen Powell, who was shooting his mouth off for the reporter."

"Yes, I know."

"All worked up about the odd set of eleven."

"Yes, Gideon, I know. I tried to talk them out of it. They think it's good publicity." At Gideon's disbelieving face, I said, "Their security's good, for a private home. I'm hoping that the chairs will be too recognizable to fence. And think about it. If you're a smart thief, what would you take? Something small you can put in your pocket. You don't want eleven chairs, even if they're worth $25,000 apiece at auction."

"Man, if you were hungry enough, you'd rent a truck and sneak there in the dead of night to disable that security system. You know people get worked up about guitars, and they don't fit in a pocket, either."

I leaned against the counter, feeling tired now that the anger passed. "I wish they'd listened to me. They don't need PR here in Memphis. They need the kind of PR I can get for them in New York."

After the article appeared, anyone with a Chippendale chair—any kind of Chippendale chair—strolled into the shop and wanted to know what it was worth. All of us, Jude and Gideon and I, had to tell people that there was English Chippendale, there was Philadelphia Chippendale, and there was Chippendale sold in Macy's department store. The latter, which most people owned, wasn't worth a dime. It wasn't even saleable.

A man who'd brought in his chair said to me, "It looks just like the chair in the newspaper article."

"That style of Chippendale chair has been copied since the day it was made. And in every decade since. It's still being made today."

"How do you know this chair isn't old?"

I came out from behind the counter. "Let me take a good look at it." I touched the wood. "First of all, the wood. It's the color of mahogany, but it isn't mahogany. Or even walnut. It's a wood used in commercial furniture today. Beech, I'd bet. And then the details. There's no carving on the front of the seat. You remember the medallion on the chair in the article?"

"I didn't see it."

I pointed to the seat front. "No carving. No medallion. And the legs."

"What about them?"

"These are straight. Not ornamented with carving. And no ball-and-claw feet. Those are details that required hand-turning and hand-carving at the time. These chairs are machine-made." I felt testy and I sounded like it. Gideon was watching me as though I was a pot just about to boil. "May I turn the chair over?"

"What are you looking for?"

"A maker's mark or a label." He watched as I upended the chair. Even mad, even handling a lesser thing, I was careful. "There it is. I can tell it's recent, even though I don't know this maker." I cut him off. "The font. It just looks contemporary." I righted the chair.

He was miffed. "I think you're wrong."

I took a deep breath. He was pig-ignorant about furniture, but he was an innocent bystander in the matter between me and the Powell heirs. I said, "What you have is a useful, attractive, contemporary chair that's derived from a classic eighteenth-century design. Please take it home and enjoy it."

"I bet I can sell it."

"I'm sure you can. There's a market for everything."

He picked up the chair and muttered darkly at me as he left.

Gideon said, "I never thought I'd see the day. You losing your temper with a customer."

"God help me if another idiot walks in with a Chippendale-style chair from God knows where. I won't just lose my temper. I'll hurt someone."

I HADN'T SEEN MUCH of our third dealer, Thomas Waverley, since he first filled his cases. Jude, who ran into him on her rounds as a picker, told me he'd been busy buying. As a case dealer, Thomas didn't have duty hours, and he was too contained and deliberate to drop by to socialize. I'd wondered about him. I'd asked Jude if she knew what he collected.

Jude said, "There's no way you can find something that will soften him up like I did for you."

"Why? What does he collect?"

Jude looked pained.

"What is it?" I asked. "Is it something kinky? Don't tell me he collects Klan stuff!"

She still looked pained. "He collects racist memorabilia. It's really bad and really scary."

"Like what?"

"I saw some. It gave me nightmares."

"Why? Why would he torment himself like that?"

She said, "He told me he thinks of it as educational. Lest we forget."

"Forget? I don't have to look at Nazi objects to remember the Holocaust!"

"Nat, it's not for him. It's for white people."

I thought of the wills with their lists of beds, silver spoons, and slaves. I shook my head.

But when Thomas came in today, he looked unruffled, his lips curved into their resting expression, a faint smile. He didn't bother with small talk. He rested his beautifully groomed hands on the counter. "I saw something you might be interested in," he said.

"Don't tell me it was a chair."

"It was indeed a chair."

I groaned. "Not another Chippendale chair!"

He leaned over the counter, and I could smell his aftershave, a light and pleasant citrus scent. "Not just any Chippendale chair. One that's the spit of the eleven you already found in Cordova."

4

THE WOODSON CHAIR

The woman who owned the chair lived in Orange Mound. Thomas insisted on giving me careful directions, as though Orange Mound, a historically Black neighborhood five minutes' drive from Evergreen, was a foreign country. He wasn't far wrong. Before I'd talked to a blues musician who lived there, as I was researching a vintage guitar, I'd never set foot in that part of Memphis.

Thomas stood on the sidewalk outside Letitia Woodson's house, looking anomalous in his three-piece suit and bow tie. There was no front yard, just a carpark. The house was half the size of my bungalow and built by someone who had no use for frills or ornaments. Or no money. Like all the houses on the block, it looked old and worn. The woodwork was weathered and cracked, and the paint was peeling.

Thomas said, "Did you have any trouble finding it?"

"No, your directions were perfect. How do you know Ms. Woodson?"

"She belongs to my church."

"Do you know how she came by the chair?" As soon as the words were out of my mouth, I realized what I sounded like. *Did she steal it?* I deserved Thomas's rebuke.

"How does anyone come by anything? She tells me it's been in the family for a long time."

The woman who answered the door was younger than I'd expected, in her late twenties, angular and tired-looking. A little girl clung to her leg. She greeted Thomas with a smile, and he hugged her. He knelt down and said to the little girl, "Will you give me some sugar?" The little girl laughed and walked into his embrace.

More than an acquaintance from church. I was suddenly tired of close-mouthed antique dealers whose private lives were in a vault.

Letitia Woodson looked askance at me as Thomas made the introductions. We shook hands. Her hand was chapped and rough. She asked us in and offered us coffee. "Please, don't go to any trouble," I said. The house was so small that anyone in the kitchen could easily see into the rest, which was divided into a tiny dining room, crowded with a dinette set, and a living room, dominated by a beat-up sectional sofa and a large-screen TV. The chair had pride of place in the living room. Even in this tiny space, I'd wait to be invited to look at it.

When I made house visits for Sotheby's, I always found something to compliment. But those people were well-to-do collectors who had lovely things to look at. This house had nothing. I was at ease with kids. I got along fine with my niece and nephew. But I didn't feel right talking to the little girl, either. I asked, "What do you know about the chair?"

Letitia said, "Just that it's been in the family forever. And there's a story that someone in the family made it. That's why we've hung on to it. We've always thought it was special."

Even at a distance, I could see the resemblance to the Powell family chairs. Chippendale style, dark wood, carved legs.

Letitia said, "You're an antique dealer, like Thomas?"

"Yes, I am now. I own a shop downtown, Minerva's Place. I used to live in New York, and I worked for Sotheby's Auctions."

She shook her head.

I'd need to explain myself without patronizing her. It was harder than it should have been. I thought, *Treat her like a customer—uninformed but interested*. "It's a big auction house with branches in Manhattan and London. They sell high-end stuff. After Jackie O died, they sold her estate."

Letitia nodded again.

I said, "I worked there for almost fifteen years. I specialized in American furniture from the 1700s and 1800s. I've seen a lot of chairs that look like yours."

She nodded again. I couldn't tell whether she was uncomfortable with me because of New York or Sotheby's, or just because I was white.

Thomas wasn't helping me.

"May I take a good look at it?" I asked.

"Yes."

Thomas was right. In terms of design, it was a dead ringer for the Philadelphia chairs, and it was beautifully made and beautifully carved. I knelt before it, looking carefully at the wood. I touched it as I'd touched the

Powell chairs. The wood was smooth but not as satiny. I turned it over with care to look at the construction. It mirrored the Powell chair. I touched the seat support. The wood felt rougher than the wood on the Powell chair.

I looked up. I said, "The design is the same, but the wood isn't. It isn't mahogany like the other chairs. And the secondary wood"—I spoke to Letitia—"the wood underneath that doesn't show. It's different."

Thomas said, "What do you think?"

"I think it's made of black walnut and stained to look like mahogany."

Thomas leaned forward. "What makes you think that?"

He was asking on Letitia's behalf, and I spoke to them both. "See the grain? It's nice, it's wavy, but it's not as fine as mahogany. And feel it."

He trailed his fingers over the wood of the leg.

"It doesn't have that satiny feel."

"What about the secondary?" Thomas asked.

I said, "It's poplar, but not the yellow poplar the Philadelphia cabinetmakers tended to use, when they weren't using cedar or pine. It's tulip poplar." Now I looked at Letitia Woodson. "Tennessee's state tree."

Thomas asked, "What are you saying?"

"I don't think this chair was made in Philadelphia. I think it was made in Tennessee."

Letitia's face fell. "So it isn't like the others."

"Well, here's the strange thing. It looks just like the others. Whoever made this chair was looking right at those other chairs. He—it's probably a he—used those chairs as a model for this one."

I don't know what moved me to do this, but I began to

feel all around the underside of the seat support. I don't know what I was looking for. But I felt something before I saw it. A spot where someone had dug into the wood. Not a gouge, but an intentional carving. It was an odd spot to carve, hidden from view. I turned the chair to peer at it, but I couldn't see what my fingers had found. "Do you have a flashlight?" I asked Letitia Woodson.

"We do." She turned to rummage in a kitchen drawer.

I pointed the flashlight at the spot I'd felt. I still couldn't see it. I had to angle the chair nearly on its side.

And I found it.

I said, "Ms. Woodson, did you know that this chair is marked?"

"No."

I showed her. "It has a maker's name carved into the seat support. Underneath. It's hard to see," I said, angling the flashlight for her. "It's easier to feel it."

She bent down. "I see it," she said, and her face curved into a smile.

"Show me," Thomas said. He bent to look. "It looks like the name Tobey," he said. He looked again. "Nat, did you see there's a date? 1838."

I asked Letitia, "Does the name Tobey ring a bell with you?"

"No, I've never heard it," Letitia said.

All three of us looked at each other, and the unspoken question echoed in the room.

Who was Tobey?

AFTER WE LEFT, Thomas and I stood on the sidewalk outside the house. Furniture expert to African American expert, I asked him, "Who was Tobey?"

"I have a hunch."

"What is it?"

"It was a common name for enslaved people in the eighteenth century. A nickname for Tobias."

"I love a hunch as much as anyone," I said. "But after fifteen years at Sotheby's, I don't trust a hunch. I want provenance, and that needs documentation. I want to look for a workshop run by someone named Tobey in Nashville or Memphis first."

"A white cabinetmaker?"

"Let me talk to someone at MESDA." I meant the Museum of Early Southern Decorative Arts. "Let me see where that goes. If I can rule it out, then I'll think about following your hunch."

I DIDN'T KNOW anyone at MESDA, the decorative arts museum in Winston-Salem, but the curator was gracious to me. "Let me take a look in our archives," she said.

Her research didn't turn up a cabinetmaker named Tobey anywhere in Tennessee. She said, "All that means is that we don't have any records for him. Not that he didn't exist. You're talking about Shelby County? Probably someone local who did cabinet- and chairmaking for his neighbors. He might turn up in the census."

"Thank you, but I already looked. No luck."

"Shelby County records? Tax records?"

"I hadn't thought of those, but I'll look there too."

She said, "Now you've got me curious. If you find him, let me know. We'd like to add the information to our archive."

"I'll do that."

Thomas's comment nagged at me. *A common name for an enslaved man.* I thought of the wills with their lists of human chattel, which I hadn't scrutinized in my eagerness to find the chairs. I thought of Ezekiel Powell, who had owned thirty human beings.

I'd scanned the wills, but I'd only transcribed the portions relating to the chairs. I opened Ezekiel Powell's will and paged through it. I wanted to see the slave inventory written in his own handwriting. Here it was, the last page of the will, a list of enslaved persons.

Damn the handwriting. I deciphered the first entry:

He'd made an appraisal of his slaves as he had for his non-human property. The enslaved, unlike the silver or furniture, had names. First names only. He distinguished them further by their gender and their age, noting their skills or conditions. And their value.

Gus, male, 24, $500, prime field hand.

And the second:

Mary, female, 54, $100, crippled.

I kept looking. I found Susie, female, 34, $300, a laundress. And a few entries below hers:

Tobey, male, 48, $1000, a cabinetmaker.

I sat back in my chair. The name was right. The occupation was right. The dates fit. Something else didn't.

How had an enslaved man in the Tennessee hinterland learned to carve a chair as skillfully as any master craftsman in Philadelphia? Was that a reasonable doubt for someone steeped in Sotheby's mania for provenance, or was it a racist's assumption?

I'd found someone named Tobey, but I still didn't know who he was. Or why he'd made that particular chair. Or how it had come into the hands of the Woodson family.

LOOK IN THE CENSUS, the MESDA curator had advised me. An enslaved man wouldn't show up by name in the census before the Civil War. But in 1870, as a free man, he would have been enumerated under his own name. His full name, including his surname.

When I first started working for Sotheby's, genealogical research was difficult, involving requests for censuses and county records on microfilm. I could still remember the frustration of searching the microfilmed records. The ache in my eyes and the ache in my back. I still couldn't believe how easy it had become to search the census.

Right away, I found a Tobias Woodson, Black, seventy years old, occupation cabinetmaker, born in Virginia, living in Memphis.

Was that Letitia's ancestor? Was that Tobey?

It was the easiest possible thing to keep going. To research Tobias Woodson's children. To trace the lineage to Letitia.

I'd done a fair amount of genealogical research. At Sotheby's, I'd joked that "we're good at spying on dead people." But this was different. I remembered the weariness on Letitia's face, a life that had aged her prematurely, and her distrust of me, which no amount of politeness could disguise.

I called Thomas. I heard a hubbub in the background. "Where are you?" I asked.

"I'm at a flea market."

"Finding anything?"

"Hope springs eternal. Is there something I can help you with?"

Maybe. "You were right."

A dry laugh. "I'm right about a lot of things. What in particular?"

"Tobey."

I heard the hitch of surprise in his voice. "Really? Where?"

"In Ezekiel Powell's will."

Another hitch, this one of sadness. "A slave inventory?"

"Yes," I said.

"What happened to him? Did you look in the 1870 census?"

I explained what I'd found. And that I'd stopped looking. "I don't feel right prying into Letitia Woodson's family history," I said. "She doesn't trust me, and I know why."

Thomas was silent, letting me hear the buzz of the flea market around him.

I said, "I think she'd feel better if someone who was an expert in Black genealogy did the research."

Another silence.

"Do you know anyone like that? Can you refer me?"

He said, "I've done a fair amount of African American genealogical research."

"I'd be glad to hire you as a consultant. I'd charge it to the estate appraisal. Pay you a reasonable fee."

"All right," he said slowly. "You know, if I turn anything up, we should loop in Letitia's brother and sister on this, too. Calvin is in Memphis. He's had a rough time, but he's doing well now. Working at Diamond Pawn. Ayesha's at Spelman. Basketball scholarship."

Sometimes the world was too small. I'd visited Adam's father at Diamond Pawn to get information on a guitar Gideon had found. Unknowing, had I run into Calvin Woodson when I was there? "Sure. What does Letitia do for a living?"

"She's an aide at a nursing home. She wanted to be a nurse, but a lot of things got in the way."

"The parents are gone?"

"Yes," Thomas said. "Blood pressure and diabetes, the scourge of poor Black people."

I allowed myself a small sigh for all the unfairness there, and for Thomas's dig at me. "Let me know what you find."

I CALLED ADAM. He sounded tired, like Josh did. When I said so, he told me, "I'm working much harder than I expected to at a law firm in Memphis." He sighed. "Sixty-hour weeks again to keep Holiday Inn happy."

"They're a client?"

"Our biggest." He brightened a little. "The corporate

guy I work with came over and saw the paperweight on my desk. Remember? The one I bought at your shop?"

"Of course I remember." I had an accurate memory for just about every object that had passed through my hands, an easier set of memories than the feel of Adam's skin.

"He admired it so much I gave it to him."

I laughed. "That's nice. It went back home."

"You really love old things, don't you? Like they were people."

"No, I know the difference. I'm sorry to hear they're working you to the bone."

"Me too. I still want to take you out to celebrate."

"Don't worry, it can wait," I said.

AFTER DEALING WITH THE HEIRS, Powell and Woodson, it was a relief to go back to the shop. To field questions about Elvis and occasionally, about W.C. Handy and B.B. King. To sell a surprising amount of tchotchkes and the occasional high-ticket item. A young couple came in. She was flushed and dazed. "We just bought a house!" she said. "We need a whole houseful of furniture!"

Glad to help out with that.

Dealers and decorators, friends of Jude's and Gideon's, continued to stop by. Sometimes all they did was schmooze, but sometimes they were interested in buying —or selling. Gideon knew a dealer who specialized in paper. Along with the prints and magazines, he sold sheet music and concert ephemera like posters and handbills, and he and Gideon traded information and sold each other merchandise. His name was Lymon Edger, and even among antique dealers, he was an odd duck. He was as pale as a grub, a feat in a climate like Memphis's, and even though he was in his late twenties, he walked with a pronounced, elderly stoop. He was painfully shy, unable to meet anyone's eyes. But he knew his stuff and Gideon trusted him.

I don't recall how it came up, but Gideon asked him about his own collecting interests, and he said, "I collect trolls."

Gideon and I looked puzzled, but Jude said, "You mean troll dolls?"

"Yes," he said, looking down at his shoes.

I asked, "I've never seen them. What do they look like?"

He said, "I have pictures." He showed us. They were the ugliest things I'd ever seen, plastic dolls about three inches high, with froglike features, short limbs, round bellies, and long tufts of hair. I told myself not to judge. Some people thought that Staffordshire china figurines were ugly.

Jude said, "I have some trolls."

Eagerly, he said, "The early ones? From the 1960s? With glass eyes?"

"I swear they all have glass eyes. I can bring them in if you want to take a look."

His pale cheeks suffused with color. "Tomorrow? I can be in Midtown tomorrow."

The next day, Jude brought in a cardboard box and set it on the counter.

"Goldsmith's?" I asked. Goldsmith's had once been the

biggest department store in Memphis, just down the street on Main. My mother had stories about shopping at Goldsmith's.

"I bought them at a garage sale, and I haven't taken them out of the box."

"The box is an antique, too."

When Lymon came in, Jude pulled out the box. His face lit up. She took a troll from the box, and he extended his right arm and laid it flat, near his elbow. She took out another, and he laid it next to the first, until he had six trolls lying on their backs, all balanced on his arm. He began to stroke their hair, one after another.

We'd all seen people get wrought up by an object. But this was something else. It was more than desire. It was lust, and seeing these ugly plastic dolls as the target for this kind of deviant passion jarred all three of us.

"What do you want for them?" Lymon asked, his voice throaty.

"Twenty-five each," Jude said. "That's market online these days."

He gazed at them, bedded on his arm. "I'll take all of them."

I thought, *You'll have to let go of them to pull out your wallet.*

He sighed and laid them on the counter. He didn't dicker or ask for a discount, and she didn't offer one. Without demur, he gave Jude $150 in cash. She kept a straight face as she wrapped them in tissue paper and put them back in the Goldsmith's box.

After he left, I said, "I've never seen anything like that."

Gideon said, "You've never sold a guitar."

"That's a different case for Dr. Freud." I said, "Those were the ugliest little things I ever saw, and I feel bad for what's going to happen to them when he gets them home."

Jude snorted. "We just sell the stuff," she said. "What they do with it is their business."

"Life's back to normal around here," I said.

Gideon asked, "Hey, how are you doing with the estate? Are they ready to think about doing a sale?"

"They aren't ready yet. They're still all worked up about the Philadelphia chairs."

"Raised their expectations, didn't you?"

"You know what it's like. You try to keep them reasonable, and the moment they hear a big number with three zeros in it, they're off to the races. My problem right now is something different." I thought of Letitia Woodson, too disappointed to have raised expectations. I said, "You have to keep this quiet. I mean confidential."

"Got it."

I told them about the Tennessee chair.

Gideon said, "You always worry that you see what you want to see, not what's there. You remember the guy who kidded me about Robert Johnson's guitar?"

"Now I know that no one has Robert Johnson's guitar."

"Good for you. You also know that people are crazy."

"If they can be crazy about trolls—"

Jude started to laugh. "I'll never forget that, as long as I live."

"If the Tennessee chair is right, it's really something," I said. "It's the only example of a fine Chippendale chair made by an enslaved craftsman whose name is known. And whose history may be known."

"Any leads on the history?"

"I'm working on it."

He said, "I know you don't want to be wrong about something and end up with egg on your face. But at a certain point, you know all you're going to know. And that's what you take to auction."

"For anyplace but Sotheby's, I'd agree with you."

He glanced at Jude, then at me. "Someday you'll have to let Sotheby's go," he said. "Like you'll have to let New York go."

I thought of everything I should be letting go. Some of it was still here in Memphis. "I will, after I get the highest price realized I can get."

I KEPT my phone on all the time and close by. I'd given out my cell number to anyone who might want to buy or sell. I'd given it to Letitia Woodson and both of the Powell heirs, so I knew who was calling me. Joyce called me all the time, the way she called her kids, to arrange for a time to meet me at the house to let me in. Owen had only called me to bug me. "How's it coming along?" he'd asked, meaning, *How much is the estate worth now?*

It was Letitia Woodson, who'd never called me before. And as soon as she heard my voice, she began screaming at me.

"What is it?" I said. Panic shot through me. The chair had been stolen. Or damaged. Or worse. She was so upset that I couldn't tell what she was saying. "Letitia, please. Take a deep breath. Tell me what's going on."

Panting with anger, she said, "Why did you tell that damn reporter about my chair?"

"Reporter?" I repeated, stunned.

"That damn blonde bitch from the *Appeal*. The one who wrote the other article. She knows about my chair!"

I said, "She called you?"

"She stood right outside my door and craned her neck to look inside. I slammed the door in her face. You told her! How could you?"

I felt anger along with the panic. "I didn't," I said. "As far as I'm concerned, it's confidential." I felt a twinge. Anyone who knew had been sworn to secrecy. Who hadn't kept it on the down-low?

"Someone told her," Letitia said. She was still furious, but she was losing steam.

"I'll call her," I said. I had a friend in Sotheby's PR department. I'd call her first and ask for advice on dealing with an overenthusiastic entertainment reporter who needed a good slap on the hand. I should call Josh, too.

"Can you give her shit?"

"I'll do my best," I said.

And not five minutes after I put down the phone, it rang again. This time it was Joyce, and she was just as mad as Letitia had been.

"You lied to us!" she shrieked. "Why did you lie to us? Why didn't you tell us you found the twelfth chair?"

5

THE HOUSEKEEPER

"Hey, Nat, is this a good time to talk?"

It was Josh, who knew the shop wasn't open on Mondays, but I appreciated that he asked.

"Sure. What's going on?"

He said, "Owen Powell just called me."

"Are your ears still ringing?"

"I'm all right now. I take it there's a bit of an issue with the appraisal."

"That's not news. I'm well aware that they're angry with me. They have eleven chairs, and they think I've found the missing twelfth. They think I've been holding out on them. Is Owen still pissed off?"

"I think I got him calmed down."

"Did he tell you that they heard about it because a reporter from the *Appeal* thinks she knows where the twelfth chair is? And went around town tattling about it?"

"Now you're the one who sounds steamed."

"I am. The people who own the chair are furious at me too. They think I called the reporter. As though I'd betray their confidence! I was about to call you to find out how we can put a stop to it."

"Shutting up a reporter? That may be out of my reach. If you come to my office to meet with them, I think we can get this straightened out."

Josh's office was on the tenth floor of an office building downtown, built in 1962 but elegant enough on street level, kitty-corner from a lovely old building in the Federal style that still housed the Bank of Tennessee. The law firm's offices were modern and pleasant but not country-club plush.

To my surprise, Josh's assistant was Black, a young woman with a friendly smile, dressed in a pantsuit. She led me to Josh's office, where Joyce and Owen sat at an oval table, looking like angry parents who'd been called into the principal's office.

As a kid, I'd never been called into the principal's office, and I wasn't going to start now.

Josh beckoned to me, and I took the empty chair. After pleasantries about parking and an offer of coffee, Josh pulled out a pen. He said to Owen, "So, tell me about these chairs."

As I'd suspected, they behaved better in Josh's office than on the phone with me. They talked with relative calm about the eleven chairs that were part of the estate, and they made it sound like I'd let them to believe there was a twelfth somewhere to complete the set. They were unhappy that I'd unearthed it and hadn't told them.

"Nat?" Josh asked. "Let's hear from you."

"That piece in the newspaper caught the eye of everyone in Memphis who has a Chippendale-style chair.

So this chair—this twelfth chair—isn't a match to the existing set."

Owen said, "How do you know that?"

I was about to say, *How do I know that an apple isn't an orange?* But I caught myself in time. I wasn't in New York, land of snappy answers to stupid questions. I was in Memphis, and everyone expected a veneer of Southern gentility over every exchange and every transaction. "There are some obvious differences. The woods. Your chairs are made of mahogany and yellow poplar. This one is made of black walnut and tulip poplar, which is a Tennessee wood. We know that your chairs were made in Philadelphia in 1773. This one has a date on it, 1838, much later. The design is similar. But it's not the twelfth chair in the set that belongs to the Powell estate."

"Then what is it?" Owen demanded.

"What I know for sure is what I've told you." I bit back the words: *I don't know enough to let you storm into someone else's house and take it home with you.*

"You don't dare say anything unless you have a provenance as long as your arm," Joyce said, with some bitterness.

"Provenance is difficult with a piece like this. The people who own it don't have the kind of documentation your family does."

Owen said, "We gave you everything in the safety deposit box. We let you go through everything in the attic. What more do you need?"

I heard the question again, in a more polite voice. My old boss used to ask me, "What are you missing, Nat? What more do you need?" I took a deep breath. "I have the impression that the Powells saved everything important, and documented it, too. I have a hunch that your mother had the same impulse. That she'd save anything significant to the family history and take good care of it. When I went through the papers in the attic I didn't find anything like that. I can't believe she threw any of it away."

"Then where is it?" Owen asked.

"Do you know if she donated anything to the Tennessee Historical Society? Or the county historical society?"

"We don't have a clue," Joyce said.

"She might have put it into storage. We didn't find any receipts for a storage unit, but that doesn't mean she didn't rent one."

Joyce now had a thoughtful look. "There's someone who might know. Ruth Anne."

Owen snorted. "Ruth Anne? I don't think she'd tell us how to get across the street."

"Who is Ruth Anne?" I asked.

"Mother's housekeeper," Joyce said. "She worked for Mother for years. She was there when we were growing up. She took care of everything in that house."

"How would I get in touch with her?"

Joyce said, "At one time she lived in the house. But she didn't stay there."

"Where did she go?"

"I don't know," Joyce said.

AFTER THEY LEFT, I lingered. "Josh, do you have a moment?"

"Just a moment."

"Close the door. What I have to say is confidential."

He shut the door and sat down at the table. "It stays that way. So what are you holding close?"

"I'm protecting the people who own the lookalike chair." I took a deep breath. "The lookalike chair has a maker's mark. The name is Tobey. It's not the name of a workshop. It's the name of an enslaved man who was listed as a carpenter in a Powell will from 1848."

Josh didn't reply.

"There's a connection, but I don't know what it is. And I don't want the Powells to hear about it and get the idea that this other chair, which clearly belongs to someone else—someone poor and Black, by the way—is really theirs. That's why I want to go looking for more family papers. If I can find those, I can look for the history of the Powell chairs. I can try to unearth more about the chair that's turned up, and I can try to find out what happened to the twelfth chair in their set."

"It's a long shot."

"It's a hunch, and I hate going by hunch. But it's worth a try."

"I'd agree with you."

"First I have to find the housekeeper. Didn't that strike you as strange? That they'd known her since they were kids and have such antipathy to her now? And that she worked for their mother for years—decades, probably—and just disappeared once Evelyn Powell died?" I said, "I saw Evelyn Powell's will because she kept it with the historic wills in her safety deposit box. I read it, but I didn't know to look for the housekeeper. Josh, I don't think she left anything to her faithful servant."

"I can tell you that she didn't."

"I guess I should go looking for the housekeeper to talk to her."

"Let me help you out with that," Josh said. "We have an investigator on retainer. This kind of thing will take him five minutes. He can get her credit report or her arrest record, if you like."

"I don't need her credit report or her arrest record. Just her phone number and her address."

I HAD to talk to Letitia Woodson. I didn't need a mediator, as with the Powells. I needed a guide. I called Thomas.

He said, "I've heard from Letitia."

"She has every reason to be livid. I'm furious myself."

"So is she. With reason."

"I'm aware of that. Could you help me a little?"

"Maybe."

"Just ask her if she'd hear me out. I have some ideas about where to go from here."

"Do the Powells really think that's their chair?"

"They can think whatever they like. Right now, it's Letitia Woodson's chair. I think there's a way to get more information."

"Schedule a séance?"

I ignored him. "There might be more family papers in storage somewhere. I'm trying to get in touch with the

Powells' former housekeeper, who may know where they are. They saved everything. I'd bet—oh, lunch somewhere nice, wherever you like—that they have stuff from before the Civil War."

He met me at the house in Orange Mound, and inside, we sat in the close little living room that felt humid despite the window unit's best efforts. Letitia had crossed her arms in a gesture that shouted, "I don't trust you."

I balanced myself on the uncomfortable chair she'd offered me. "The Powells never should have contacted the *Appeal*. And the reporter never should have bothered you. I'm sorry about all of it."

She glared at me. "Sorry is cheap," our housekeeper Mavis used to say to me when I tried to soften her up after I'd misbehaved or thrown a tantrum. "Can they take my chair away from me?"

"If they try, it's called theft, and the police take a dim view of it."

Letitia snorted. "Maybe out in Germantown or Cordova."

"It's your chair, not theirs, and I know how we can prove it."

Letitia was still crossing her arms.

"The Powell family saved the will. They saved the bill of sale on the original set of chairs. I bet they've saved a lot of other family papers."

"And how does that help you prove the chair is mine?"

"If we find the papers, we find Tobey. And the history of the chair. I know in my bones that those papers exist. I just have to find them." What was I saying? *I have a hunch.*

"You don't know where they are?"

"They're stored somewhere. I have to find out where."

"Good luck," Letitia said, her voice heavy with sarcasm.

Thomas didn't help me.

"I promise I'll find those papers," I said.

"You do that," Letitia said.

RUTH ANNE THOMPSON lived in Whitehaven. I'd been here before, researching the guitar. Some blocks in the neighborhood were run-down, with sagging, unpainted wooden houses piled with trash in the front yard. But Ruth Anne's block was lined with well-maintained brick ramblers. Her house had window boxes where petunias bloomed. The window trim had been recently refreshed. Planters bookended her front steps, bright with red geraniums.

Curtains obscured the picture window. No one in Germantown drew the drapes against the heat anymore, but I remembered how my grandmother pulled the curtains in the Shelby County house to keep the living room cool during the day.

As I hesitated on the steps, a neighbor opened her door, a middle-aged woman whose expression clearly said, "What are you doing here?" But she spoke to me politely. "Miss, can I help you?"

"I'm here to see Ms. Thompson."

The neighbor walked past me to knock on Ruth Anne's door, and the inside door opened.

"Ruth Anne?" the neighbor said. "There's someone here to see you."

A shadowy figure spoke through the screen door. "It's all right, I'm expecting her." She said to me, "Come in."

The air in the house was comfortably cool, and the a/c whispered from the vents. No groaning window unit in this house. Lamps burned to light the midday darkness.

Ruth Anne Thompson was small and fined-boned, with high cheekbones and a pointed chin. Her straightened hair, a silvery gray, framed her light-brown face. She wore a cream-colored silk blouse and navy trousers that had been tailored to her slender frame. Around her neck nestled a necklace of good cultured pearls, just like the one my grandmother Beardsley wore.

A sofa in the Hepplewhite style and two matching wing chairs graced the living room. In the dining room, a table in the Duncan Phyfe style filled the space, surrounded by six Chippendale chairs.

In miniature, it echoed the décor of the Powell house in Cordova.

None of the furniture was old. Everything was a good twentieth-century reproduction. Had she come to love the look of eighteenth-century furniture in her long employ with Evelyn Powell? Or had she received their castoffs?

She gestured to me to sit in the wing chair, and she sat in the middle of the little sofa, her spine too straight to touch the back. She said, "Ms. Raskin, what can I do for you?"

She hadn't offered me coffee or the usual beverage of

summer hospitality in Memphis, sweet tea. She didn't consider this a social visit, but neither did I.

"As I mentioned when we talked on the phone, I'm an antique dealer, but I'm also an antique appraiser. When Evelyn Powell passed on, her son and daughter inherited her estate, and they hired me to appraise the value of her furniture and artwork."

"I see."

"I understand you were employed as Ms. Powell's housekeeper for many years."

"Yes, I was."

"I'm in the process of appraising right now, and I had a few questions about the contents of the house. I thought you might be able to help me."

She inclined her head. "I might."

I glanced at the far wall. An oil painting in a gilt Victorian frame, a moody, moonlit landscape that looked like a Louisiana bayou, caught my eye. *1880s*, I thought. *The artist knew what he or she was doing.* I'd ask to take a good look at it later. I said, "I've gone through the papers that were in the attic, and I knew that it was in Ms. Powell's nature to save things. I've seen the papers in the safety deposit box, and I knew where she kept important documents. What I'm wondering is whether there were any other family papers, especially from the early years."

Ruth Anne Thompson lifted her chin. "Such as?"

"Letters. Diaries. Business records."

She considered this but didn't reply.

"Let me ask this a different way. Might she have put some of her papers in storage somewhere?" In the silence, I said, "As her housekeeper, perhaps you were responsible for moving some of her things into storage? Perhaps you arranged for the rental of the storage unit?"

Ruth Anne said, "If she had asked me, I would have done something like that."

What a circumlocution, I thought. "I thought you were the person to ask, since you were responsible for taking care of the house and of Ms. Powell herself."

"Yes, I took care of everything."

"But there's nothing in storage, as far as you know."

"As far as I know."

I knew better than to keep going and to pressure her. I said, "That's a lovely oil painting you have."

"Thank you," she said, but her voice didn't warm up.

"May I take a look at it?"

Another cool silence. I said, "I'm not here as a dealer today. That would be rude, frankly. I like paintings. I just want to look."

"All right," she said.

I stood back, taking in the whole image. Very atmospheric. Very Southern in tone. Very well composed. I moved closer. Loose brush strokes, but very controlled. Subtle use of color. A trained artist. I moved closer. Legibly signed. Henry Villere, 1888. American, then. He'd seen the Impressionists. Had he studied in Paris?

I said, "This is a lovely picture." I anticipated her silence. "How did you come by it?"

She stiffened. "I saw it in an antique shop," she said, her voice cool. "It was cheap, and I liked it, so I bought it." *How dare you suggest otherwise.*

"Do you know anything about it? Or about the artist?"

"No, I don't."

I said, "Well, it's a very nice thing, and if you got it cheap, I'm sure you paid less than it's worth."

"I'm not planning to sell it."

"Oh, no. Keep it and enjoy it."

"May I show you out, Ms. Raskin?"

I thought, *I'm done here.* "Thank you for your time, Ms. Thompson."

The air outside felt doubly hot and humid after the hushed cool of Ruth Anne Thompson's house. As I walked to my car, I felt my own temperature rise. Everything she'd told me was a half-truth meant to misdirect. She'd lied to me because I was white. I'd heard that before. But this was something different. Deeper and darker, like the bayou at night.

RUTH ANNE THOMPSON'S oil painting nagged at me. I couldn't do a thing about her intransigence, but I could research Henry Villere. I checked Davenport's reference guide, and Villere was indeed a listed artist. I searched online; a Villere portrait had sold a few years ago in New Orleans and had realized a few thousand dollars. *How dare you suspect me.* I ignored the feeling of guilt and called a friend at an auction house in North Carolina.

He was a native Southerner, like me, and we exchanged pleasantries about my move to Memphis and his gratitude that I'd referred someone to his auction house before we got down to business. I told him about the Villere, keeping quiet about the picture's owner. "I'm wondering if it ever came through one of your auctions. I already looked online." Their online sales records went back only a few years. "I didn't see it."

"We have earlier computerized records that aren't online. Now you've got me curious. Let me take a quick look."

I waited, shame seeping through me.

In a few minutes he said, "No, nothing at all."

"That helps. Thanks." This wasn't research. It was just spite.

AFTER MY RAGE at Ruth Anne cooled, it returned in full force, now directed at myself. How could I have been so stupid? I'd grown up in Memphis. I'd been back for months now. I'd just finished an appraisal where every Black person I'd interviewed had lied to me in self-protection. Why had I thought I could act like I was still in New York, where every conversation with someone Black wasn't darkened by the long reach of Jim Crow–era racism?

I needed someone to guide me through the rocky shoals of race relations in Memphis. I'd learned—the hard way, the embarrassing way—that not every Black person in Memphis knew every other Black person. But I also knew that communities defined by race or ethnicity in Memphis were small and tightly knit, and pulling on the right string would get me deep into the whole fabric.

I called my mother, who knew everyone in Cordova and everyone in the Jewish community in Memphis, and told her about my dilemma. "In New York I always knew who to call. Here I don't."

"I know people in Cordova, but I don't think that's what you need."

I sighed. "I need to talk to someone on the other side of the racial divide. I didn't think it would still be so hard in Memphis."

"You know, you might talk to Mavis."

"You're in touch with her?"

"We talk every few weeks."

"What's she doing these days?"

"She works for the Hilton downtown. She's done very well there. I've told her all about you and how well the shop is doing."

"Do you think she'd mind if I called her?"

"It would help if you told me what this was about."

I said, "I'm interviewing a woman who used to work as a housekeeper for the family where I'm appraising the estate. I thought she might know where some of the family papers were stored. I walked into a racial minefield, and I don't know why. I need to find someone who can fill me in on the history that's causing so much trouble. Do you think Mavis would be willing to help me?"

"Let me call her first and smooth the way."

I asked, "When Mavis worked for us, do you think she was ever angry with the way we treated her?"

"I'm sure she was. It happens whenever someone works for you."

"Did we act racist toward her? Because I don't remember that we did."

"We tried not to, but I know we made some mistakes."

She paused. "Once I offered her some clothes you and Josh had outgrown for her own kids. She shook her head and said to me, 'I can't take those, and you know why.' Oh, I did. I felt rotten. I said, 'I'm sorry, that was thoughtless of me.' It was in the eighties, and I should have known better."

I sighed. "So we're not post-racial yet in Memphis."

"Not by a long shot."

WHEN I CALLED, Mavis was gracious. She invited me to meet her at work, and I got the message. Despite her warmth, she wanted a business meeting.

I stepped from the elevator into a hushed corridor that smelled of fresh flowers. My feet sank into a plush carpet. A young white woman, dressed for the office, asked me, "Can I help you, ma'am?"

"I'm looking for Mavis Green's office. I have an appointment."

"She's right here."

The plaque by the door read "Executive Housekeeper." Through the open door, the top of a walnut desk shone. On it sat a sleek large-screen computer monitor. I glimpsed the edge of a glossy leather chair. An executive chair.

I tapped on the door and stepped inside.

The woman of my childhood memories had worn a print housedress and a pair of Keds. She covered her hair with a kerchief, and her hands were rough with house-work and dishwater. I didn't recognize the woman behind the desk. She wore an expensive tailored suit, and her black hair, perfectly straightened, gleamed in the light from the big plate glass window. She rose and extended a manicured hand with nails that shimmered a subtle pink.

I shook her hand and then held up my own as though I was at the manicurist's. "I like your polish," I said, testing the tease. We wore the same color.

At that she laughed, and I saw the resemblance between the woman who had once been the Raskin housekeeper and who had become the executive housekeeper for the Hilton. She scooted from behind the desk and hugged me. Smiling, she regarded me at arm's length. "It's so good to see you, Nat."

"Likewise. My mother told me you'd done well at the Hilton, but I see that congratulations are in order."

"You're doing well yourself. Your mother gives me all the updates on your shop. I keep meaning to come downtown to see you." She gestured toward the monitor. "Too busy."

"Please do. If you find something you like, you'll get the friends and family discount."

She sat at the table with an easy dignity, a woman used to leading meetings and managing people. She said, "Your mother told me a bit about why you wanted to see me. You're doing an estate appraisal, right?"

"Yes, for the Powell family out in Cordova."

"What's the situation? How can I help?"

"I'm looking for some family papers that aren't in the house. I'm pretty sure they went into storage somewhere. Evelyn Powell employed a housekeeper, and I thought she'd taken care of the storage unit. I went to talk to her, and she wasn't forthcoming. It wasn't about the storage unit. It's some history I don't know. I'm trying to find out what it is."

Mavis nodded.

"My mother recommended you as someone who's well connected. She thought—I thought—that you might help me find someone to enlighten me on the background here."

She hesitated. She steepled her hands. "Powell family? Is this Ruth Anne Thompson?"

"Yes, it is."

She hesitated again, and I had a sinking feeling. But she said, "Well, you don't have to go very far to find someone who knows about the situation."

I waited.

"Sometimes Memphis really is a small town. Ruth Anne Thompson belongs to my church. I don't know her well, but I know her. And a lot of people know about her history with the Powell family."

"So there's a history."

"The story of her relationship with the Powells is common knowledge in the Black community."

I took a deep breath. "Is it something you're willing to share with me?"

She laid her hand on my forearm, and the subtle pink of her nails glowed against my skin. I met her eyes and she sighed. "Oh, Nat," she said, old South and new mingling in her voice.

I waited to hear whatever she would tell me.

"Ruth Anne worked for the Powells for decades. Her mother worked for Evelyn Powell's parents. The relationship was so strange in this day and age that people talked about it. It's like they were stuck in some weird reenactment of slavery. The Powells probably thought to themselves that she was like a member of the family. And Ruth Anne actually started to believe it. Did the Powells leave her anything in the will?"

"Nothing."

"She spent her life working for Evelyn Powell, hoping for a reward, and she ended up with nothing. Is she bitter?"

"Yes, and she doesn't like me because I'm working for the Powells myself."

Mavis nodded.

I said, "I don't really need her to like me. I just want to find the family papers. I'm sure they're in storage somewhere. It would be easier if she told me, but there must be another way to find out."

"Storage? You know, her nephew owns a storage company. If she's stored anything belonging to the Powells, it's probably in one of his storage units."

"What's his name?"

"The company is Five Star Storage. He's Curtis Thompson."

6

THE KEY

FIVE STAR STORAGE HAD AN OFFICE BUILDING WITH A limestone façade, and behind it, a gated yard full of units with blue doors. Everything was neat and well-tended. Inside, the building smelled of an industrial pine scent, like a car deodorizer. The place sold an array of mailing supplies and greeting cards, surprisingly tasteful.

When I walked in, a burly man was saying to a skinny kid, dressed in a hoodie despite the heat, "You clean out that unit yet?"

"Not yet."

"Get going. I want to rent it. Pull up your pants and put on a belt. You ain't in prison anymore."

The kid slunk off, the hoodie obscuring his face.

The man behind the office counter was more than burly. He had the build of a linebacker and the demeanor of a man who said no a lot. He wore a blue shirt, tight in the shoulders and the arms, with "Five Star Storage" embroidered on the pocket.

I said, "I'm looking for Curtis Thompson."

"You found him. How can I help you? Are you looking to rent a unit?" I recognized that tone. It was like my retail cheer in the shop, not my natural self.

"Not today, thank you. I'm an antique dealer, and I'm working on an estate appraisal. We think the family put some stuff in storage. I want to find out if they rented a unit here."

"You got a name?"

"The surname is Powell."

He said, "I can take a look, but before I do, I've got to tell you, I can't let you into the unit unless your name is on the lease."

"Could you look first, please?"

He tapped on the keyboard and scrutinized the screen. "No, I don't have a record of it."

I asked, "How about Thompson?" When he didn't reply, I said, "Ruth Anne Thompson?"

He said, "What is this about?"

"I wonder if Ruth Anne Thompson rented a unit for her former employer, Evelyn Powell. We think there may be items from the Powell estate in there."

He said, "I get this kind of thing all day long. I'm the husband. The wife. The brother. The sister. The friend. The appraiser, that's a new one on me, but I've got to tell everyone the same thing. I'm sorry, if your name isn't on the lease, I can't let you in there."

"Would it make a difference if one of the Powell heirs asked you?"

"Not if their names aren't on the lease."

"I'm sure there's stuff belonging to the Powell estate in there. Is there any way I can get in?"

He gave me a long look. An appraisal of his own. "Well, you could get a warrant, but that won't make anybody happy."

As I leaned against the counter, stewing, he said, "A key or a warrant. That's all I can tell you."

I SAT IN MY CAR, feeling hot, tired, and irritated. I turned on the air conditioning and shook my head. I called Josh. "How do I get a search warrant?"

"Excuse me?"

"Ruth Anne Thompson has a storage unit. I'm sure it's full of Powell family stuff. The guy who owns it just told me I can't get in there unless she unlocks it for me. Or unless I get a search warrant."

"Jesus, Nat. You don't get a warrant like you're ordering a bagel at the coffee shop. Do you have any reason to think Ruth Anne Thompson stole the stuff? Or that she has illegal substances in there? That would give you probable cause."

"No, I don't think she stole it." Reason returned, and with it, a headache started.

"Whose name is it under?"

"Hers." My headache worsened. "I'm pretty sure she put the stuff in storage at her employer's request. She took care of it, like housekeepers do."

"Evelyn Powell might have been infirm by then. Or ailing. All the more reason for Ruth Anne to handle it."

"Did you ever meet Evelyn Powell? Do you know what kind of shape she was in?"

"No, I didn't. I wasn't at the firm when the will was made. I inherited her as a client when one of the partners retired. So no, I never met her, and I can't say anything about her health. Couldn't the heirs tell you?"

"They hadn't seen her for several years. There was some kind of estrangement. They couldn't tell me, either." Through the headache, reason was clearer than ever. "It's likely that Ruth Anne was her sole caretaker at the end of her life. Besides being her housekeeper."

"I'm not surprised."

"Josh, I'm thinking about the will again. That Evelyn Powell didn't leave anything to Ruth Anne. It seems odder than ever, now that I understand what the relationship was. It sounds like she pushed her children away and kept Ruth Anne close. But she left everything to the kids and didn't do anything for Ruth Anne."

"Nothing I see in a will surprises me anymore."

"I'm wondering, though. If Evelyn Powell left all this stuff for Ruth Anne to store while she was around, what did Ruth Anne plan to do with it after Evelyn died?"

"What she's doing now, evidently."

"Sit on it because she's unhappy with the Powell family?"

"That's what it looks like. Nat, if there's all this bad feeling between the Powells and Ruth Anne Thompson, getting a search warrant is the worst thing you could do."

I sighed. I had ibuprofen with me but nothing to wash it down, and I hated to dry-swallow a pill. "I guess so."

"I know this isn't pleasant. But the best thing you can do is to try to talk her into opening the unit for you."

He was right, but I didn't feel any better. After he

disconnected, I started the car to find a convenience store to buy a bottle of water.

WHAT WAS I going to do? I thought wildly about breaking into the unit myself. Maybe Gideon, who had a checkered past, knew someone who could help me.

That was all I needed. An arrest warrant for B&E. A new low in the evaluation and appraisal business.

I decided to call Joyce. I told her about the storage unit and my futile effort to get Ruth Anne to open it.

"What does she want?" Joyce asked. "Money?"

"I don't think so."

Joyce said, "I'd walk through hell before I gave her a damn thing. Not a dime. Not a word of apology. Not after the way she treated Owen and me. She wouldn't let us see Mother. And at the end, she wouldn't even speak to us. She'd just hang up if we called. I went out there once, worried about Mother. She cracked open the door and told me to go away. I told her I'd get Social Services in the house if she didn't let me in. She laughed, in the nastiest way I've ever heard, and dared me to try it. Then she slammed the door in my face."

"Maybe an apology would help."

"Apology for what?"

"I don't know. I thought you might."

Her voice rose. "What are you talking about?"

"I don't know. You tell me." I was too tired to watch my tone.

At that she shrieked at me, as she'd done when she

thought I was holding out on the twelfth chair. "How dare you lecture me about charity! Christian charity! Someone like you!" It was a statement that demanded an old-fashioned slam of the receiver. The soft click when she disconnected me wasn't enough.

I CALLED RUTH ANNE FIRST, leaving her a message that I was coming by, and I drove to Whitehaven in the heat. I reminded myself that I'd dealt with difficult clients before. I tried to think of Ruth Anne Thompson that way. I took a deep breath before I left the cool of my car to plunge into the soupy heat.

I rang the bell and the inner door opened, and as on my first visit, she stood in its shadow, the screen door a barrier between us.

She said, "I told you not to come back here."

"I went to Five Star Storage," I said. "I know about the storage unit."

"That's none of your business."

"No, but it's the estate's business."

It didn't matter that I hadn't mentioned the Powell name. Her voice rose. "I've had enough trouble with the Powell family," she said.

"I understand," I said.

"No, you don't." Her voice shook a little. "You have no idea."

I said, "Let me take it from here. Let me empty out that storage unit. Shut it down. Close the account. Let me take it from you."

Silence.

"Would you take me over there? Or give me the key?"

"Go away," she said, but her voice was shaky. "Leave me alone." She shut the door.

I walked back to my car, damp with sweat and itchy with frustration. What was in that storage unit? I thought of the ring we hadn't found. I thought of the baseball. Maybe I could get a search warrant.

I shook my head. In the car, I ran the a/c and wiped my face before I drove away.

BACK AT THE SHOP, the electronic bell jangled, and I looked up, readying myself for my retail persona. I had to work harder than usual, since I was so preoccupied with the problem of getting into Ruth Anne Thompson's storage unit, and no closer to any way to do it.

Curtis Thompson walked in. He came up to the counter and leaned against it, spreading his hands on the glass. I hadn't noticed it when I visited him in his facility, which was scaled so much bigger than our shop, but he had the handspan of a former quarterback.

"Mr. Thompson! Can I help you?" I asked.

His face, which he had made so pleasant at his own place of business, was now dark with displeasure. "I hope so."

Gideon, who had been closing a case, moved closer to the counter, where he could keep an eye on our customer.

My skin began to prickle with discomfort. "What can I do for you?" I asked.

"My aunt Ruth Anne called me the other day. She said you came to see her again, after she told you not to. She was very upset."

I wondered who was the one to overreact here. "I didn't mean to upset her. I just wanted to ask her about getting the key to the unit. As you suggested."

"I didn't tell you to harass her!"

Gideon was paying close attention.

"I'm sorry I upset her," I said, hoping that apology might help.

It didn't. He leaned his bulk harder against the counter. "She's had enough grief from the Powell family. She doesn't need any more."

"It wasn't my intention to cause her any trouble."

"Then it won't be hard for you. Leave her alone." He stepped back from the counter, and he took in Gideon, standing to my side. "You understand me?"

"I believe I do," I said.

"Don't bother her again. Or you'll regret it."

"Excuse me," I said. "What do you mean?"

He looked at me, his gaze a further warning, and he shook his head. Then he turned his back on us both and left the shop.

I'D BEEN THREATENED BEFORE, and I knew what it felt like. Last time, I didn't have a name to give to the police. This time I did. But this wasn't a matter for the police. I thought of Josh's investigator, and I called him.

I told the investigator what had happened and that I was uneasy about Curtis Thompson.

He said, "You want a background check."

"You can bill me for it."

"The basics? It will take me an hour. The retainer will cover it."

I asked, "How do you find all that stuff?"

He laughed. "How do you look at an old piece of furniture and know what it is and how much it's worth?"

"You have to know where to look."

"Bingo," he said.

"If you don't mind my asking, what did you do before you went private?"

"I was with the FBI."

"A G-man?"

"Yes, they taught me how to shoot and all that stuff, but what I did for them was forensic accounting. I have a BA in accounting."

"Follow the money."

"You got it. Are you in a hurry to get this?"

"No, especially since you're doing me a favor."

"I should have something for you in a couple of days."

WHEN HE CALLED ME BACK, he said, "I just emailed you the report, but I can give you the salient points over the phone."

"Go ahead."

"He's an upstanding citizen. Owns a business with solid financials, has a family, volunteers as a deacon at a church in Whitehaven. Just a little blot on his record. Spot of B&E as a young man. It went to court. Evidently the judge gave him the choice between going to prison or joining the army. From there he went straight. Reenlisted several times, exemplary service, honorable discharge."

"What's your take? Should I worry about him, or treat him like a disgruntled customer?"

"I went to Five Star Storage to meet him. Maybe I'll need a storage unit sometime. He's a big tough guy, and he's used to being in charge and telling people what to do. But he hasn't broken the law since he was eighteen, and he has a lot more to lose now. My take is that he's very protective of his aunt and he overstated his case when he talked to you."

I shared the results with Gideon, who said, "Your investigator is an optimist."

"He's a forensic accountant at heart."

Gideon snorted.

"Should we worry?" I asked.

"We won't worry, but we'll keep our eyes open."

"I still have to get into that storage unit, and I don't know how I'm going to do it." Half kidding, I asked him, "You want to help me break into it?"

Jude teased, "His B&E days are behind him."

"You did B&E?"

"Of course not. Can't you tell she's pulling your leg?"

I leaned on the counter with my elbows, like a bad kid at the table, and rested my chin in my hands. "I'm stumped," I said.

Jude said, "Sleep on it. Something will occur to you."

I threw Gideon a pleading look. "You won't reconsider?"

"You'll figure it out."

—⁂—

IT WAS two in the morning when the phone pulled me from sleep. I stared at the screen, and fear caught in my throat. Our security company was calling.

"Ms. Raskin?" The voice was female and soothing. "The alarm's been triggered at your property. There's been a break-in."

Stunned, I said, "Oh."

"The police have been notified."

"I'll be there right away."

I sat up, unable to think straight. A break-in. *You'll regret it.* I took a deep breath. Hysteria later. I held the phone in my hand.

I called Gideon.

He said, "I'll meet you there. If you get there before I do, wait in your car."

"Okay."

Adrenaline kicked in as I dressed, got into my car, and drove over to the shop. At two in the morning, South Main was quiet. I drove past the shop. The door was ajar. And the big plate glass window had been shattered. No police car.

I pulled into the parking lot and sat in the car. I was shaking. *Leave her alone.* Gideon pulled up next to me, and we both got out. He said, "How are you?"

If I talked about it, I'd give in to hysteria. "Never mind," I said. "Let's see how bad it is."

"I saw the door. And the busted window."

"What should we do? Should we wait for the police?"

"They may not be here for a while."

As we walked through the yard, we heard the siren, and they pulled up as we approached the broken door.

There were two of them, a burly man and a sturdy woman, both white. They were heavily armed. The sight of those guns bothered me. What good would they do?

The man said, "Let us go in first."

We stood on the sidewalk, and in the balmy night air, I began to shiver. Gideon shucked off his leather jacket. "Here."

I put it on.

The cops made their round and came back. The woman said, "It's clear. Come in and look around. See if anything's been stolen."

I stepped inside and looked around. I groaned. The floor was covered with shards of china and glass. The Lenox pattern I'd always disliked was visible on the bigger pieces, and flakes of crystal glittered among them.

We stepped into the shop and looked around. The front case, full of silver, was intact. So was the jewelry case. None of the cases had been smashed or forced open.

Just smashed china and glass, and it was everywhere.

I said, "I don't see anything missing. Nothing of value, that is." I gestured toward the floor. "Besides this. What happens now?"

"We'll file a report," the man said. "And if you discover

that anything's been stolen, you can file a stolen property report, too."

I said, "The one that goes to the pawnshops." I'd visited the pawnshop that Adam's father ran. I thought of Ben Levy reading the police report in his office at Diamond Pawn.

"Right. Do you have any idea who might have done this? Anyone suspicious coming through in the past week or so?" he asked.

Yes. Gideon put his hand on my shoulder, to silence me as well as steady me. "We have everything on video. We'll take a look at it, and we can send it to you, too."

He said, "We see this kind of thing all the time. Drug addicts looking for stuff to sell. It's unlikely we'll be able to find much to work with."

I looked down at the floor, speckled with china and spangled with glass, and I felt like hell.

Gideon didn't move his hand from my shoulder. His voice was as calm as though he was thanking a customer. "We'll do what we can, and we know you will, too."

After the cops left, I said to Gideon, "It's such a mess." My voice sounded small and weak.

He rubbed my back. "Hey, Nat. Rite of passage for a retailer. Now you've gone through it. It's going to be all right."

"What do we do now?"

"Call the glass company for an emergency board-up. And the locksmith for the door."

"How can you sound so calm?"

"We were broken into twice at my old shop. One was a smash and grab, like this, and one was serious. They disabled the security system, and they stole some valuable guitars. I know the drill."

"Were you scared?"

"No. I was mad. Mad as hell." He reached into his pocket for his phone. "I'll call the glass company and the locksmith. I can hang around until they get here. You want to go home? Get some sleep?"

"I'll never get back to sleep tonight. Besides, I have the company credit card." I didn't sound like I was making a joke. I sounded shaky.

He touched my shoulder again. "Hey, Nat. You always hated that china set. Thought the best thing would be to smash it."

I laughed but there was a sob in it. "I did."

"Well, someone took you at your word. Broke it right up for you."

I put my hand to my face. "I've got to sit down."

"Let's find you a chair and sweep all the glass off it."

I said, "Curtis Thompson. He meant it."

"We don't know that," Gideon said. "We'll look at the video tomorrow."

THE NEXT MORNING, both Jude and Gideon came in early to help me clean up the mess. Jude said, "It doesn't matter how careful we are. We'll be finding shards of glass for days." She picked up a broom and sighed.

Once the worst of the mess was gone, Gideon downloaded the video footage. All three of us watched it. I winced as the skinny kid shrouded in a hoodie ran through the shop, throwing china on the floor.

Gideon said, "He was a punk, but he wasn't stupid. He made sure we couldn't see his face."

"I saw a kid just like that working at Curtis's storage facility."

He said, "A kid in a hoodie? How many kids in Memphis dress like that?"

"This kid just got out of prison."

Jude said, "Nat, I know you're upset."

"Upset doesn't begin to cover it."

Gideon said, "It doesn't make sense. Why would Curtis Thompson be involved? I really don't see him risking his own business for something like this. This is just a rotten coincidence."

"I wish I believed you," I said.

Jude said, "That isn't a South Main business owner talking. Do you know who you sound like?"

I did. Embarrassed, I admitted, "My grandmother, Eleanor Beardsley." To Gideon, I said, "That's the rich, racist side of the family."

Gideon said, "Miss Minerva, are you angry enough to think about doing something stupid?"

"Not that stupid." Last time I'd let my temper get the better of me, I'd created a rift in my relationship with my father that hadn't healed yet. And he was likely to forgive me, sometime. My relationship with the Thompsons was strictly business. Forgiveness wasn't on the agenda.

Did I believe that Ruth Anne had taken the ring? Did I believe that Curtis had masterminded the break-in?

I didn't like the part of myself that could think like that.

THE NIGHT OF THE BREAK-IN, it had been too late to call Adam. We didn't yet have the kind of relationship where I could wake him at two in the morning. When I came home that day, after talking to the insurance company and arranging with the glass company to replace our plate glass window, I was so tired I didn't have the energy to change my clothes. I poured a glass of wine and put on music. It didn't help. Last night's fear and anger returned. I called Adam.

He said, "Nat, you sound like hell. What's wrong?"

"We had a break-in at the shop last night."

"Why didn't you call me?"

"At two in the morning? I called the cops."

"You didn't go there alone!"

"Gideon met me there. We talked to the cops together."

"How bad was it?"

"Nothing seems to be missing. We got it on video. Some kid who got mad when he didn't see anything he could boost easily. He broke some ugly glass and china, and he shattered our plate glass window, too. I was on the phone most of the day, getting that taken care of."

"I wish you'd called me."

"There was nothing you could do."

He was a little sharp. "Moral support, maybe?"

"Be nice now, please? I'm dead tired, and I'm in pain

from finding out how much it will cost to replace the window. Even with insurance."

He was contrite. "Oh, Nat. I'm sorry. Do you want me to come over?"

I wished we had the kind of relationship that would let me say, *Please do.* "Thanks for offering, but I'm beat. I just want to crawl into bed." I heard what I'd said, and I went on, "And not in a fun way."

He said, "That's a good sign. Sardonic humor." He sighed. "Take it easy. I'll call you tomorrow. See you soon?"

"As soon as I feel better."

"Nat, take care of yourself."

"I'll do my best."

I WATCHED the video from the break-in again, and I knew who I'd show it to. I'd keep my promise to Curtis. I wouldn't bother Ruth Anne again.

When I walked into Five Star Storage, Curtis stood behind the counter. "What do you want?" he demanded.

"I have a question for you."

"You're not getting into the storage unit."

I met his rudeness with my own. "It's not about the storage unit."

"If it's not about the storage unit, then you've got no business here."

I heard her before I saw her. "Curtis, are you dissing a customer?"

"She's not a customer," Curtis said, as a curvy woman

in a bright peach-colored pantsuit, her hair in a long curly weave, her lips bright with red lipstick, emerged from the back office.

She assessed me with a smart, weary gaze. "Who is she?" she asked Curtis.

"That appraiser I told you about. The one who's working for the Powells. The one who's been bothering Ruth Anne."

I said, "I'm not here about that." I leaned against the counter, even though I didn't have Curtis's ability to intimidate. "Someone broke into my shop not long ago. We have it on video. That's what my question is about." I laid my phone on the counter and pulled up the video. "Take a look."

He looked.

I said, "That kid in the hoodie. Does he look familiar?"

"Could be anyone," he said.

"Isn't there a skinny kid like that who works for you?"

"Not anymore. I fired him." He said, "You can't prove a thing by that video."

"Maybe I'll show it to the police and let them figure it out."

He said, "If you think you'll get into the unit by threatening me—"

The woman said, "Curtis, if you didn't hire jailbirds, you wouldn't have to worry about what they do when they aren't working for you."

"Georgina—"

She looked at me, then at Curtis. "You know perfectly well what this is about. You and Ruth Anne have gotten her tangled up in your family feud with the

Powells. It's been going on for years. I'm tired of it, Curtis. Sick of it."

Curtis looked even darker.

She continued, "And what's in that unit? It's a lot of junk that Ruth Anne has no reason to hold on to."

He gestured toward me. "Her name isn't on the agreement—"

She looked at me again. "Can you get a letter from the estate lawyer? Letting us know you represent the estate?"

"Would that be enough?"

"Georgina, let me—"

She cut him off. "Yes, it would."

"That's no problem, since the lawyer is my brother."

Georgina said, "You bring that in and hand it to me, and I'll give you the key. Let me give you my cell number so you can call me first." She glanced at Curtis. "So I can be here."

"Georgina, you leave this alone and stay out of my business," Curtis said, but for the first time since I'd met him, he wavered.

"It's my business too," Georgina said. "Since my name is on those tax returns, right next to yours."

Now it was clear who was large and in charge at home.

She asked me, "You're an appraiser?"

"Antique dealer and appraiser."

She said, "You know, we have stuff that people abandon in the units. Most of it is junk, but there are things that might be worth something. Maybe you could help us out. Let us ask you about them before we auction off the whole unit."

I was shaking, but I wanted to laugh. This was familiar

territory, just like New York. Quid pro quo, and the same timbre as in Brooklyn or Queens. "Sure, I can do that. If it's just a quick look, a rough valuation, and some advice about where to sell it, stop by the shop or send me pictures. I do that for free."

She said, "Hear that, Curtis? She'll help us out. For free."

Curtis turned to me. "After you get into that unit, I never want to see you again."

"Once you get that letter, call me," Georgina said.

7

THE STORAGE UNIT

I called Joyce and Owen to let them know I had the key to the storage unit with their mother's stuff in it. They agreed to meet me there. Gideon told me he'd bring his truck. "If it's full—whatever it's full of—we'll need it," he said.

We met outside the unit. I took the key from my purse. Such a little thing, smaller than my house key, and I still couldn't believe how difficult it had been to get it into my hand. As I held it in my palm, Curtis Thompson walked by, giving me a look of disgust.

"What was that about?" Gideon asked. "Why is he giving you the stink eye?"

"He doesn't like how I got the key."

"I thought it was on the level."

I put the key in the lock. "It was, but I don't feel good about it." I'd been underhanded and manipulative, and along the way, I'd thought the worst of everyone in the Thompson family.

He shook his head.

I opened the door, and we peered inside. The unit was filled with piles of old clothes, pieces of broken furniture, heaps of old crockery, toasters and blenders with frayed electrical cords.

"It's junk," Owen said.

"It's hard to tell," I said.

Joyce looked like she was going to cry. "I don't have the heart to go through it."

Jude put her arm around Joyce's shoulders to reassure her. "It's all right. We've done lots of estate sales. We've cleaned out hoarder houses. This is nothing. We'll get through it in no time at all."

I envied Jude's ease with Joyce.

Owen said, "I don't have time to help you."

Gideon said, "That's all right. We'll load up the truck and take everything back to Cordova. We'll sort out the good stuff from the junk for you."

"Good luck," Owen said.

Joyce dabbed her eyes. "Maybe the baseball is in there."

Or the ring. "Who knows," I said, and both of them left, Owen to go to work in Germantown, Joyce to Cordova to unlock the house for us.

The three of us were left to pull everything out. "Don't sort it now," Gideon said. "We'll take everything back to the house and go through it there."

I was too disheartened to make a joke about Miss Varina's letters.

We unearthed a fondue pot from the 1960s in its original box, browned and battered, and a set of fondue forks. We pulled out a push mower so badly rusted the blades wouldn't turn. We found a set of dish towels that had mildewed.

In no time, we were all sweating and filthy. I said, "I thought Evelyn Powell was a curator, but I'm beginning to revise my opinion."

"Maybe she was really a hoarder and this is where she put the mess," Jude said.

Once the unit was half-empty, we saw the banker's boxes. Stacks and stacks of them, not as pristine as the boxes in the attic. I couldn't stand the thought that we'd found more ancient phone bills. I reached for the nearest box.

"Nat, don't go through them here," Gideon said.

Jude looked over my shoulder as I lifted the lid. The neat labels and the careful handwriting were familiar. Jude reached for a folder labeled *School pictures*. She opened the folder and pulled out one of Owen and the other of Joyce, elementary school towheads. "Look, Nat. They were so cute when they were little!"

I pulled out a folder labeled *Birthday cards* and opened the topmost card. "Mama, Happy birthday! Love, your son, Owney."

Jude and I looked at each other. "It's the personal stuff," I said. "The stuff that was missing from the house." I had a terrible yearning to go through the boxes on the spot. Had Evelyn Powell, with her archivist's soul, saved the detritus of earlier generations? Had she kept the antebellum equivalent of class pictures and birthday cards?

"Nat, hang on," Gideon said. "Once we get back to Cordova, we'll touch everything in every one of those boxes. We'll do it in air-conditioned comfort. Let's not stand here in the heat to satisfy your curiosity." He wiped his face with his arm, which left a streak of dirt on his forehead. His T-shirt, clean this morning, was now streaked with dirt and sweat.

I stared at the boxes and made a swift count. "A hundred," I said. "I'll get in my share of toting today. What my grandmother calls schlepping." I wiped my hands on my shorts. "And shmutz."

Gideon preceded us in the truck, and when Jude and I arrived at the Powell house, he had already pulled into the driveway. I got out of my car, and the heat hit me in the face like a fist. Jude and I helped him unload.

He said, "It's all right with Joyce if we leave the worst of the junk in the garage. She'll take a quick look and let us know if we can call the junk company for a pickup."

"What about the boxes?"

He said, "I have a dolly."

"Thank God," Jude said. "I want to take the clothes inside."

"They're pretty disgusting to take inside," I said.

"If I go through them out here, I'll get heat prostration."

"I have a tarp," Gideon said.

"Were you a Boy Scout?" I asked.

He snorted. "No. Just the hired muscle for an estate sale."

Inside, Jude dumped the clothes on the tarp and began to go through them, checking the pockets. "They're not even good enough to give away," she said. "These are all going on the toss pile."

"What are you looking for?" I asked.

"Money, illicit correspondence, jewelry—"

"Rings?"

"Baseballs… Help me out, it will go faster."

She found $30.57 and an old Timex watch.

"Does it work?" I asked.

She tried to wind it and shook her head.

By the time we'd wrapped the clothes in the tarp and dumped them in the garage, I felt wrung out. I was too filthy to lie on the pristine sofa, so I stretched out on the pristine carpet instead. I closed my eyes and let my conscience bother me. Curtis's words echoed again. *You'll regret this.* I was still regretting the invasive destruction of the break-in. I hadn't realized I'd rue the revelation that I was capable of thinking like a racist jerk. I thought I'd rooted that stuff out of myself in New York, but it had come right back in Memphis, as vigorous and lively as kudzu.

Gideon squatted on the floor next to me. He smelled sweaty and musky, but I found I didn't mind it. "You feeling all right, Nat?"

I sat up. "Just dehydrated."

"Well, that we can take care of. Let me run out and get us some lunch, and we'll dig in all these boxes afterwards. Any requests?"

"Potato chips," Jude said. "I need salt."

He rose. "Sweet tea. I need sugar."

"Low-cal sweet tea for us!" Jude was laughing.

"I know. Wasn't a girl singer in Nashville who would drink the real thing!"

After lunch, I felt better. Even though Gideon said, "We have a shitload of these things to go through," I felt the boxes call to me. I'd done a fair amount of wrong for the promise of provenance. Now I wanted to find it.

We split up and lifted the lids at random. Gideon said, "Whoever packed these up was organized as all get out."

"That was Evelyn Powell," I said. "An archivist's soul, and a lot of free time, since she never saw her children or grandchildren."

Jude was immediately entranced by the contents of the first box she touched. "Look, Nat," she said. "I bet this is Evelyn as a debutante."

The sweetheart neckline of her dress enhanced her fragile-looking collarbones, and her pageboy hairdo softened the sharp features she'd passed to her children. "She looks pretty," I said.

"All debutantes look pretty. Like all brides do."

I said to Gideon, "I was invited to the Memphis Cotillion Ball when I was in high school."

Jude laughed. "I remember."

"Did you go?"

I said, "Jude did. I didn't."

Gideon said, "Jude, stop fussing with the folders! We're just sorting today. Let's get a move on."

But she couldn't help herself. She opened another folder. "Oh, an album," she said happily, paging through it. "From someone's school days, circa 1900. All her friends signed it, and she pressed flowers into it, too." She looked at me. "I can't help it, I just love this sentimental Edwardian stuff."

"Jude," Gideon admonished.

"All right!" She tucked the album back in its folder.

Gideon began to open boxes and sort them.

"What have you got?" I asked him.

"Business records. From the 1890s, it looks like."

"Their cotton brokerage, right? Those were the boom years. When they bought all the pretties that ended up in this house."

"Ledgers and correspondence. Boxes and boxes worth."

I uncovered a box to find the social equivalent of the brokerage records: calling cards, dance cards (they really did fill up their dance cards!), and another photo album. A quick look revealed a photograph of a baby in a long white dress, and another of a boy, presumably the baby grown older, hugging a spaniel. There were grocer's bills as well. "Hey, guys. The Powells saved their receipts in the 1880s, too."

"Move it along, Nat," Gideon said.

I sighed and pried the lid from the nearest box. No folders, just something bound in leather, spines out. Old, deteriorating leather, the kind that left a brown stain on your hands, like dirt. More ledgers. How old were they?

I carefully removed one and opened it with care. The pages were brittle. On the first page, I read: "Commencing January of 1823." I felt hot and cold at the same time. "These are really old," I said.

Jude came to peer over my shoulder. "What is it?"

The handwriting was hard to read. And familiar. I'd seen it before, on Ezekiel Powell's will. I worked to decipher it. "It's a list. A bushel of salt, a hundredweight of nails, ten pairs of shoes, and a hat for someone named Silas."

"Another grocery list," Gideon said.

"But this one is from 1823."

"Who was Silas?" Jude asked.

I thought of the slave inventory in the will. "I think I know."

"What have you got?" Gideon came close enough to see.

I showed him. "It's a plantation ledger. Ezekiel Powell's plantation ledger." I closed it and rested my hands on the spines of the rest. "A whole run of them, it looks like."

I laid the flaking leather volume on the lid of the box, careful of the carpet. I picked up another ledger at random and read aloud. "Commencing January 1836." I laid it down and picked another. "Commencing January 1848."

We found another box of ledgers, the last one commencing in January of 1859 and ending in December of 1860.

Still more boxes. Jude left the Edwardian era to help me look. She lifted the lid and smiled.

She eased something from the box. Too small to be a ledger. "Oh, look at this. Such a pretty cover."

"A diary. A lady's diary," I said. "Small enough to fit in her dress pocket."

Jude handed it to me and watched as I opened it. The handwriting inside was clear and beautiful. "Do we know whose it is?" Jude asked me.

On the flyleaf, in a careful, rounded hand, was written: *Amelia Powell*. I showed Jude, and Gideon came to look, too. "Ezekiel Powell's wife. They were the first generation of the family to live in Tennessee. The couple that moved from Virginia shortly after they got married."

"There are more," Jude said.

I looked inside the box. It was full of folders, and every folder held a little diary. One a year? More? I sat back on my heels, feeling light-headed. "It looks like a full run."

"Check the last folder," Gideon said.

I did. "1860."

"Where's the Civil War stuff?"

I thought of everything that was missing. I was so tired I laughed. "Where's the twelfth chair?"

ADAM KEPT his promise about treating me to dinner. The restaurant he chose wasn't far from the shop, but I drove there, not wanting to wilt in the heat that hadn't acceded to evening yet. The server took me through the restaurant to the patio.

At the edge of the patio, gardenia shrubs grew, suffusing the air with their strong, sweet scent. Citronella candles burned, an old-fashioned, astringent bug repellant. The scent of garlic and barbecue wafted from the kitchen. The sound of traffic was a distant hum here. The laughter from the tables was low and the speech was soft. The server threaded her way through the tables. Adam sat in a secluded corner, and he smiled as I arrived.

The crisp linen of the tablecloth brushed my knees as I sat. The napkins were a bright red gingham that reminded me of the backyard barbecues of my childhood. I relaxed into the old-fashioned ladderback chair. The slightest breeze caressed my face, reminding me of the relief that would come once the sun set.

"This is lovely, Adam."

"Yes, it is," he said.

There was the faintest crease between his eyes, his old expression of concern. "Nat, did you ever hear from the police?"

"About the break-in? No. I don't think we ever will."

"I've been a little worried about you."

"Oh, there's nothing to worry about in broad daylight, and I'm never alone in the shop. And it's unlikely we'll get hit again. I bet the word is out that we don't have anything easy to boost and fence. You know the worst of it?"

"Besides replacing the window?"

"Don't remind me. We're still finding bits of glass and china everywhere. I cut myself on a shard yesterday."

"Let me see." His eyes were full of sympathy.

"There's nothing to see."

"Give me your hand anyway."

I laughed. "Oh, you just want to flirt," I said, and I extended my hand to him.

He cradled it in his own and pretended to examine my fingers for cuts.

I said, "You can't even find it."

He smiled, then he bent and kissed my palm. At the touch of his lips, I felt a powerful throb of desire, as though he'd kissed a much more intimate spot. "Better?" he said.

Blushing, I said, "I think so."

He laughed. "Tell me what you found."

I told him about the wills and the diaries. "Diaries are wonderful," I said. "The best kind of personal record. Worth something in their own right, too."

"Have you had a chance to look at them?"

"Not yet. But I can't wait to get my hands on them."

Our server stopped at the table. "Can I get you anything to start?"

Adam asked, "Do you have champagne by the glass?"

She took us in and smiled. "Are you folks celebratin'?"

Adam reached for the wounded hand he'd kissed. "Yes," he said, and I laughed softly as I met his eyes and nodded.

When the champagne came, he raised his glass to me with his free hand. "Here's to provenance," he said.

I felt the desire return as I looked into the dark pools of his eyes. I thought about the body beneath the white shirt, feeling a hunger as plain and obvious as hunger for food. For the first time in a long time, I was free of the anxiety that came from grief and guilt and doubt. I let myself admit, *I want you.*

I raised my glass. "And to us," I said.

WHEN WE GOT up to go, desire shimmered between us. He walked me to my car. In the parking lot, the scent of gardenia was even stronger than on the patio. We both hesitated.

He said, "I want to kiss you, but not in a parking lot."

I said, "Would you come back to the shop with me? I want to show you something."

"In the shop?"

"In the backyard."

"A surprise?"

I thought of standing under the live oak, its branches shading us. "Yes."

When we both arrived in the parking lot, the sun was beginning to set, and as the light faded, the air cooled, too. I led him into the backyard to stand under the sheltering branches of the live oak.

"Why are we here, Nat?"

I waited and I heard it, her low hooting call. "Look up," I said.

The owl sat low enough for us to gaze at her and for her to gaze back at us with her huge yellow eyes. I whispered, "She lives in the tree."

He moved close to me. "Minerva's owl," he whispered back.

I moved closer to him. This wasn't like our first time, when we were both surprised. This kiss was slow, passionate, mutual. We kissed and kissed. If the owl called again, I didn't hear it. When we came up for air, he said, "Don't even ask. Of course I remember."

I stood in his embrace as though I'd always belonged there. I smiled. "What do you remember?" I asked, very softly.

"How we wanted our first time together to be right," he said, his palm warm on my skin. "And the trouble we took to make sure it was."

"Yes," I said.

"We were smarter than we realized. This time, things should be right, too."

I smiled. I said, "Come to my place for dinner on Friday, and we'll do it right. We'll take it sweet and slow. Very sweet, and very slow."

8

THE ENSLAVED CARPENTER

I called Thomas. "Is Letitia still mad at me about the reporter? Does she still want to pull off my arms and legs?"

"Just your fingers and toes."

"Thanks for the vote of confidence." It didn't come out as jocular as I hoped. I still didn't feel at ease with Thomas. "I found the antebellum papers. A full run of plantation ledgers, and diaries, too. I haven't gone through them yet."

"I was about to call you. I've been able to trace the family tree."

I waited for the rest.

He said, "I want to tell them."

"All right," I said, but I was surprised at how much it felt like a slight. He didn't trust me, either.

"You should be there. You should tell them about the ledgers. I'll call Letitia and see when they can meet."

I was still smarting. "They?"

"She wants her brother and sister to know, too.

Calvin's here. Ayesha's in Atlanta. We can Skype her in. I'll bring my laptop."

Because neither of the Woodsons, save college student Ayesha, had one. I was a little tired of having my white privilege rubbed in my face, even though I deserved it. But this wasn't the moment to argue with Thomas.

When I arrived at the little house in Orange Mound, Letitia answered the door. She was smiling, even though I knew she wasn't happy to see me. Thomas was already there, seated at the dinette table, and so was a young man who rose when I walked in.

"This is my brother, Calvin," Letitia said.

He was broad-shouldered and muscular, and like Letitia, he looked older than his years. He shook my hand as Thomas introduced me. I tried to put him at ease. "Call me Nat," I said. But he was uncomfortable with me, as I was with him.

Thomas's laptop sat on the coffee table, and we arranged ourselves on the sectional around it.

Ayesha's image filled the screen. She had her brother's coloring and a lean, rangy look like her sister's. She wore her hair in long braids, caught in a clasp, which made her cheekbones stand out. Behind her, on her dorm room wall, was a Spelman pennant, and she wore a Spelman sweatshirt, too.

Smiling and animated, she said, "Uncle Thomas, it's so good to see you. And Calvin! How you doing? You getting along all right?"

"I got a raise at work," he said.

"That's great! Tish, what's this about that old chair? Is it really something special, like we always thought?"

"I hope so," Tish said, holding her little girl on her lap. She said, "Wave at Aunty Ayesha, sugar." The little girl looked confused.

Ayesha laughed. "She's too little to understand Skype," she said.

Thomas introduced me, and Ayesha said, "Tish told me. You're the antique dealer? And the appraiser?"

I ventured a little joke. "Are you a collector?"

She laughed. "No, but one of my roommates lives in a fancy house full of stuff they had appraised for insurance."

Ayesha was the only member of the family who looked her youthful age, and Spelman had clearly exposed her to a different universe than the one her brother and sister lived in.

Thomas said, "Calvin, Ayesha, I don't know how much Letitia told you about the chair and the situation around it."

Letitia said, "They know bits and pieces. Go ahead, tell them the whole thing."

Thomas explained about the chairs in the Powell estate and how they had led to the discovery that the Woodsons' chair was made later by a man enslaved by the Powell family.

Ayesha said, "I read in the *Appeal* that those white people's chairs are worth a pile of money."

Thomas turned to me. "Nat?"

"They might be. I know the estimate that an auction house would put on them if they came to auction. But you never know what something will actually sell for."

"What about our chair?" Calvin asked.

I turned to Thomas. "That's what we're trying to figure out."

Thomas said, "The chair is marked with the name of Tobey. Before the Civil War, the Powell family owned a man named Tobey. And there was a free Black man named Tobias Woodson living in Memphis in 1870, and he had a cabinetmaking shop. But we don't know how everything fits together."

"Is Tobias Woodson related to us?" Ayesha asked.

Thomas said, "That's something we can know for sure. I traced the family tree. You're directly related. He's your ancestor."

Ayesha asked, "How did you find him? Since enslaved people weren't in the census as people with names before they got emancipated?"

Thomas said, "Both of the Powells who held Tobey in slavery left wills. They inventoried their slaves, and they recorded them by name, in family groupings. And after the Civil War, the formerly enslaved showed up in the census. I made an educated guess."

Letitia said, "Tobias Woodson. Was he the ancestor who made the chair?"

I said, "Tobey was. Was Tobey the same person as Tobias Woodson? We don't know for sure yet."

"Isn't it close enough?" Calvin said.

"Not for a major auction house. They need proof. Evidence. Provenance." I took a deep breath. "It's worth the trouble. If this chair is as unusual and special as I think it is, it could be worth even more than the Powell family chairs."

"How much more?" Calvin asked.

"David Drake," I said to Thomas, who nodded. To the Woodsons, I said, "There's a South Carolina potter named David Drake who was enslaved most of his life. He made all kinds of practical pieces, pitchers and storage jars. Beautiful shapes, beautiful glazes. We know for sure, because he signed and dated his work. Before he was free, he was called Dave. He was more than a potter. He was a poet, too. About forty of his pieces included a rhymed couplet. Some of them were sly and funny, and some of them were oblique observations about slavery. Here's the thing. A piece by a free white potter in antebellum South, nice shape, nice glaze, can go for as much as $10,000 to $20,000 at auction. A piece by David Drake? Add a zero."

Ayesha said, "$100,000 to $200,00?"

"Yes. Because he's the only known enslaved potter who signed his work."

Ayesha said, "Dave was his slave name and David Drake was his name after slavery?"

"Yes."

"Tobey," she said slowly. "Tobias Woodson." She stared at me from the screen. "How do we find out if they're the same person? For sure?"

"The Powell family saved everything," I said. "They have plantation ledgers dating back to the 1820s."

Ayesha said, "I've seen ledgers like that. Some planters wrote down every time they whupped a slave!"

I thought of the glimpse I'd had of Ezekiel Powell's ledger. Salt, nails, slave shoes. "I don't know what's in there. But the family has agreed to let me look at them." I glanced at her and at the rest of them in the room with me. "We go looking."

After we left, we stood on the sidewalk, in the summer dusk. I said to Thomas, "I'd appreciate your help in looking at the ledgers."

"Heading me off at the pass, are you?"

"You'll see things I wouldn't. And the work will go faster with two, even if one of them doesn't know what she's looking for. You'd be a consultant to the appraisal. Like with the family tree."

"I'd be glad to help you."

"You won't like the Powells much."

"White people who won't like me. As though that would be a novelty."

I CALLED Joyce to tell her that I'd be bringing along a colleague, a fellow dealer who was an expert in African American material culture.

"All right," she said, sounding distracted.

"I've hired him as a member of the appraisal team, and he's bound by the same rules of confidentiality and ethics as I am."

"That's good," she said, listless.

"Joyce? Is there a problem?"

"I just want to get this wrapped up," she said.

"Is Owen upset again?"

She gave a tiny, ladylike snort. "Owen's upset a lot these days," she said.

"About the baseball?"

"And the ring, too."

"We're still looking," I told her.

Thomas was resplendent on the day we met at the door of the Powell house. "You look like an English gentleman," I said.

"That's the idea."

But Joyce stared at Thomas with confusion on her face. With alarm.

I reminded her, "Joyce, this is my colleague Thomas Waverley. The expert in African American history and culture."

She had to shake his hand and invite him in. But I could read her expression, even if this was the new South, where no one said it outright. *Why did you bring a Black man into my house?*

No coffee for us, not today. She looked askance at Thomas again as she left.

When the house was empty, he said, "I thought she'd tell me to keep my cotton-picking hands off her family papers."

The racial splinter, still under my skin, suddenly hurt a lot. "I warned you."

He glanced at the dining room table, which had been covered with a cloth to spare the finish. Then he gestured to a chair. "These are the famous chairs? May I look?"

"Of course," I said.

But he was already kneeling to examine the carving. Done, he rested his hands on the brocade seat and gazed at the backsplat. He rose. "The spitting image of each other," he said, smiling. "Where are the papers?"

I'd ordered archivists' gloves, and I gave Thomas a pair. "I just can't touch paper that old with my bare hands," I said.

He pulled them on. "They don't match my outfit," he said ruefully, and I had a glimpse of the gay self he might show when he felt at ease. I wanted to see more of that. I'd gotten used to being surrounded by gay men in New York, and I missed it in Memphis.

I joked, "We'll match each other. Archive chic." I gave him the earliest ledger.

He handled it carefully and opened it gently, a man used to archival protocol, and glanced at the first page. "What am I looking at?"

"The plantation records of a man named Ezekiel Powell, a transplant from Virginia who settled in Shelby County shortly after it was opened to white settlement. That's the oldest one we found. It's dated 1823."

"Is there anything else you're looking for, besides Tobey and his chair?"

"I don't know. You know the context better than I do. I defer to you."

He bent his head slightly, as though he was embarrassed by a compliment. "I'll do what I can."

As he began to examine the ledger, I retrieved the oldest diary from its folder and laid it before me.

"What's that?"

"A diary kept by Amelia Powell. Ezekiel's wife."

"Parallel narratives," Thomas said, smiling a little.

VIRGINIA, *April 1821*

Ezekiel and I are leaving tomorrow morning, starting our journey to the land he has purchased in Tennessee, and I do not know whether to be glad or sad.

The wagons are packed with the things that will be difficult to purchase there. We're taking the chairs that my father-in-law so graciously gave us as a wedding present. I do think it's a conceit to travel with a dozen mahogany chairs. They have a wagon to themselves, and I don't know where we'll put them when we get there. The letters that come from Shelby County describe rude little log houses. Perhaps the chairs will have to live in the barn.

I dwell on the chairs because it is so hard to admit that I will be saying goodbye to Mama and Papa and my sisters, perhaps for the last time. It pains me to look around the countryside of Westmoreland County and to say goodbye to everything dear and familiar. Yesterday I stood in the side yard, my hand on a tall pine tree, and I wept to think that I would never see it again.

We're not leaving everything familiar behind, thank goodness. My maid Harriet is coming with me, as is a man named Tobey, who has a talent for carpentry and cabinetmaking. The two of them live as husband and wife, and I'm pleased they can be together. My father-in-law has given us five more slaves to work in our fields and our house. He told us we should put them in chains, against their running away, but Ezekiel thought that was cruel. They will ride unchained in the wagon with us.

I LOOKED UP. Thomas said, "I'm seeing something interesting."

"Me too. What have you found?"

"Tobey. He was in demand, not just on the Powell place but all over the county. Ezekiel Powell leased him out to his neighbors."

"Leased? How did that work?"

"It was a common practice to lease out an enslaved person. Not so different from renting out a horse. The enslaved person did the work, and the enslaver kept the fee."

"Did the enslaved people ever see any money?"

"I've seen cases where they did. But it was at the enslaver's whim. It wasn't typical." He said, "Tobey was never paid."

"What was he doing?"

"Making furniture. Ezekiel Powell recorded what he made. A clothes press. A desk. A cabinet. Chairs."

"So he was well-known all over the county as a skilled cabinet- and chairmaker."

"It seems so."

"Do you have a date for one of his stays with the neighbors, making furniture?" I held up the diary. "I wonder if Amelia Powell mentions it."

He looked at the page. "Check April of 1826. He was gone for nearly a month, working for the Beardsley family."

"Did you say Beardsley?"

"Yes. Why?"

I felt my cheeks grow hot. "That's my mother's family."

"I thought you were Jewish."

"On my father's side. My mother's people settled in Shelby County in the 1820s." My face got hotter. "Before the war they were cotton planters. Slave owners."

Matter-of-factly, he said, "You can't change that."

"No. But I can feel embarrassed and guilty about it. Which I do."

"What does Amelia Powell say?"

I picked up a diary and paged through it, looking for entries from April of 1826. I said, "I found him." I read the entry aloud.

April 17, 1826

Yesterday, at church, Mrs. Beardsley pressed my hands and told me how glad she was with the loan of our cabinetmaker Tobey. He has been making chairs for them, and she says that she is delighted that they are so sturdy and so pleasing to the eye. She says that his is a gift from God. She is more religious than I am.

I miss having Tobey at our place, and I know that Ezekiel does as well. His character is like his furniture: steady and pleasant. I will be happy when he comes back to us.

"That's a lot of consideration for an enslaved man," I said.

"He earned them a lot of money."

"I know. But it sounds as though they liked him, too."

Thomas shook his head. "They didn't have enough consideration to free him, did they?"

"Could they?"

"Yes, they could."

I turned my attention back to Amelia's diary. Thomas returned to the ledger.

When we broke for lunch, I asked Thomas if I could pick anything up for him.

"No, I brought lunch," he said. I should have known. He'd brought a Thermos full of coffee, too.

I'd also brought lunch, even though I'd discovered every bakery and sandwich shop in driving distance.

We moved into the kitchen to sit at the breakfast bar, far from the documents. As we unwrapped our sandwiches, I laughed. We'd both made ourselves turkey and Swiss sandwiches on whole wheat bread. "We're sandwich twins," I said.

He nodded as he chewed. His table manners were as elegant as his bow tie and his manicure.

I said, "We've never had a chance to talk, and I don't know anything about you. Are you from Memphis?"

He put down his sandwich. "Yes, I am. I grew up in Orange Mound."

"Where did you go to school? You must have left Memphis for that."

"I attended Oberlin College in Ohio. I got my first job there, in the university archives. That led to a job with the state historical society in Columbus." He picked up his sandwich and took a genteel bite.

I waited until he swallowed. "Why did you come back to Memphis?"

"My mother wasn't well. She needed my help." He held the sandwich in midair. "She's gone now."

"I'm sorry," I said.

"It was some time ago, but thank you." He took a bigger bite and finished it off. "There's something I've wondered about you."

"Ask away."

"What made you leave New York? I would have thought it was just the place for you."

I took a swig of my iced tea. "I realized that I was still a

Southerner," I said. I thought of my fury at Ruth Anne and my blame for Curtis. "It seems I've never stopped being a Southerner."

Thomas said softly, "I know. It's home, isn't it? Despite everything about it."

By the time I left, New York had no longer been home to me. "Yes, it is," I replied.

9

A LIVING THING

THOMAS LEFT AROUND TWO, BUT I STAYED IN THE HOUSE. I'd never been alone here, in the cool hush that was scarcely disturbed by the a/c.

I was curious about something. I checked the ledger that mentioned a hat for Silas, and I searched through Amelia's diaries for an entry.

JANUARY 6, 1823

Mr. Beardsley, who had gone into Memphis, delivered the items we'd asked our factor to buy for us in town. Among them was a new hat for Silas. Upon receiving it, his face broke into a broad smile. He immediately clapped it on his head and announced that he was now so fine that no woman in the county would refuse to walk out with him. It takes so little to make these people happy, and I am glad that Ezekiel is kind-hearted enough to indulge them a little.

. . .

EZEKIEL'S LEDGER was the bare bones of life on his plantation. Amelia's diary fleshed it out.

I left the ledgers for Thomas, with his keen eye and sharp sense of injustice, and I read what Amelia had written in her clear, easy hand.

SEPTEMBER 2, 1821

I'm going to have a baby—thank goodness, it survived the trip to Tennessee—and at five months along, I'll have to let out my dresses. Ezekiel is delighted and hopes for a boy. He suggests that we call him something grand, like Octavian or Augustus, instead of naming him after his grandfather Jonathan. My maid Harriet is expecting, too. We will increase together, which pleases me.

I READ ALL THE ENTRIES. Some were prosaic, about doing the wash or making pies for supper, and some were disgusting to a modern reader, like the account of slaughtering the pig. The Powell family's enslaved people were vividly described: Silas, who was a hard worker; Luke, who cut himself with a hoe, and was so sick Amelia despaired of his life; Harriet, whose pregnancy was difficult; and Tobey, who was often gone on his cabinet-making work elsewhere. "Tobey is gone for the month, and we all miss him," Amelia wrote.

JANUARY 22, 1822

When my baby came, his father insisted on naming him

Lucullus. I looked at him, sleeping in his cradle and thought, Such a big name for a wrinkled little thing.

I had an easy time of it, only four hours in labor. Harriet, who went into labor two weeks after Lucullus arrived, did not. She labored for a long time, and I sat with her, bathing her forehead and holding her hand. I prayed for her, although God knows that I am not as religious as I should be. But the baby finally came, to the relief and joy of everyone in the birthing room. Her name is Rosetta. Tobey told me that she was named after his mother.

THE DIARIES HAD A RHYTHM. One was the daily rhythm of the cotton crop: plowing, planting, chopping, picking, baling. Another was a seasonal rhythm, of setting the hens in the spring, tending the kitchen garden through the summer, and slaughtering the pigs in the fall. There was a weekly rhythm, too, just like the old saying: "Wash on Monday, iron on Tuesday, mend on Thursday, churn on Thursday, clean on Friday, bake on Saturday, rest on Sunday."

All the children on the place grew, too.

FEBRUARY 16, 1828

I am worried about Lucullus. He had a temper from the moment he was born, but it hasn't lessened as he's grown. I'm afraid that he has a streak of meanness in his heart. Rosetta came to me crying and dragged me into the kitchen, where I found him tormenting the cat, tugging on her tail until she howled.

I separated him from the poor creature and said to him, "It's wrong to hurt the cat like that."

He was very sullen. "It's only a cat."

I was surprised at how quick and strong my own anger was. "She is one of God's creatures. It's very wrong to hurt any of God's creatures."

Of course, that wasn't the end of it. The next time, Rosetta cried for the hurt he had done to her, tugging on her hair. I was rougher with him that time. "Don't hurt Rosetta."

"She's just a slave."

"They're God's creatures, too. You'll treat them with kindness."

THE PLACE PROSPERED. No doubt the ledgers listed the cotton baled and the bushels of corn harvested, but in 1832, Amelia noted:

WE HAVE DONE SO WELL with the cotton crop that Ezekiel has bought five more slaves to work the fields and has decided to build a bigger house! I am so glad. We'll have a proper dining room, big enough for the twelve chairs we brought from Virginia. I can't wait to see them in the new house, taking pride of place!

THE CHILDREN CONTINUED TO GROW, and she talked about the two who were closest to her.

.   .   .

*T*OBEY'S *little girl is growing up. She is a comely little thing. Why shouldn't she be? Both Harriet and Tobey are comely people, even though their skins are black.*

Lucullus is old enough to go away to school. Ezekiel has decided to send him to an academy in Nashville. Ezekiel says that he must learn to govern his temper and that the discipline of the academy will improve his character.

I worry for Lucullus, whose temper flares so hot. It isn't a seemly trait in a boy, and even less so in one who will grow into a man who needs to govern others as well as himself.

THE COTTON CROP. The weekly round of household work. And this:

*M*ARCH *22, 1834*

I lost another baby. I had such hope this time. Oh, how my heart aches so.

THE REST of the page was blank, except for a water spot. A tear. I touched the page with my gloved hand as tenderly as I'd touch a sister's cheek, and I felt the familiar ache in my abdomen.

After my second miscarriage, the ache was so painful and so persistent that I made an appointment with my OB. She reassured me that nothing was wrong with me physically. In a gentle tone, she recommended a therapist who specialized in complicated grief, and offered to prescribe an antidepressant. I refused both.

Now I felt the pain again, so acute that I pressed my hand to my abdomen. As the tears came, I turned away, careful of the diary even though I hurt so much, in sympathy for a woman over a hundred years dead. *It aches so.*

THE NEXT MORNING, I took up Amelia's diaries again, as Thomas read through the ledgers. He was the one to look up to say, "Here's something odd. It's from the summer of 1838."

"The year the chair was made."

"Tobey was working on a neighboring plantation. He was leased out for two months to make some furniture. Ezekiel Powell writes that he regretted ending the lease early, but he brought Tobey back to the Powell plantation in the summer of 1838 to make a chair." Thomas looked up. "Not just any old chair. He wrote, and here I quote, 'to match the other Chippendale chairs.'"

"What's the date?"

"June 8, 1838."

I began to search.

June 3, 1838

Lucullus has come home from the academy in Nashville for the summer. I do not like the company he keeps. He spends time with the Beardsley boys, who are older than he is, and who encourage him in riding too hard and drinking too much.

I found him in the alcove near the butler's pantry. He had pressed Rosetta against the wall, and there was no mistaking his intention. He was fumbling with the buttons on his trousers.

I dragged him away. "What are you doing?" I shouted.

Rosetta sobbed as she ran.

"I'm a grown man, and she's a slave," he said.

"I'll let your father handle you," I said.

Ezekiel thrashed him. He used the cane, as they would at the academy, but he applied it with enough force to make Lucullus cry out. I could hear it, behind the closed door of the study.

When Lucullus emerged, limping, he wouldn't raise his head to look at me. He left the house without a word.

He reappeared at dinner that night. He was disheveled and drunk. He sat down gingerly because of the beating, and Ezekiel said, "You won't sit at the table like that."

"Like what?"

"Drunk!"

At that he rose from the chair. He gripped the top rail. He looked at me, then at Ezekiel, with such fury that I was afraid. "You care about that n— Tobey and his family more than you care about me!" he shouted. He lifted the chair and flung it at the far wall. I gasped as I heard the leg crack at the impact.

He grabbed the chair and ran from the house. I hurried to the window as he dropped the chair in the side yard and retrieved the ax we kept there to chop kindling. As I watched, he attacked the chair with the ax, chopping it into pieces. I cried out. The chair, a wedding present, our connection with Virginia, cherished all these years in the wilds of Tennessee.

I didn't move from the spot. I couldn't. I watched as he assaulted the chair as though it were a living thing and he hated it with all his heart and soul.

The next morning, Ezekiel sent Lucullus away to Natchez, and I don't know if he will ever be welcome back.

———

WE GOT the Woodsons together again, Letitia and Calvin in her living room and Ayesha Skyping from Atlanta, and they listened to the story in astonishment.

Calvin said, "He whupped his own son for that?"

"Yes," Thomas said.

"And the son got so mad he chopped the chair to bits?"

Thomas nodded.

"And the family was so upset they took Tobey off his work somewhere else to make them another chair?"

"It seems so," Thomas said.

Letitia said, "So we got the story from those old papers, like you said. What happens now?"

I'd readied myself for this moment, but my mouth was dry. "Do you remember, when I first talked to all of you, that I told you I thought this chair was unusual and special?"

"I remember," Letitia said, and both Calvin and Ayesha nodded.

I said, "It is, and it's worth even more than the Powell family chairs."

"How much more?" Calvin asked.

"You remember what I told you about David Drake the potter?"

"Add a zero," Ayesha said, like the good student she was.

"Right. The Powell chairs are worth $25,000. Each."

They stared at me in astonishment. Calvin was the one to say, "Are you telling us that our chair is worth a quarter of a million dollars?"

"If I were still at Sotheby's, and I had to stake my career on the estimate, that's what I'd put on it."

They were dumbstruck.

I said, "You'll want to insure it right away. I'll give you a formal appraisal for the insurance company. Don't worry, I'll only charge you a dollar to make it binding. I can talk to my brother, who's an estate lawyer. He can recommend an insurance company who specializes in objects of value like this."

They were still stunned.

"I can understand if you don't want to sell it, because it's so precious to the family. But if you do, I'd recommend that you contact a major auction house."

"Like Sotheby's," Letitia murmured.

"Sure. I'd be glad to use my contacts there. But Christie's would be just as interested."

Ayesha found her voice. "I don't think we should sell it. I think we should donate it to a museum."

I said, "Here's something to think about. A piece like this, something as historically and culturally significant as this, would be of great interest to a museum if it came up for auction. Museums like the Metropolitan Museum of Art in New York or the National Museum of African American History and Culture, which is part of the Smithsonian, would be very much interested in it. And they rely on rich patrons to buy items like this at auction, which they then donate." I leaned forward to address myself to Ayesha's image on the screen. "You'd have the best of both worlds. It would go to a museum—one that could really do it justice—and you'd have the money."

Letitia covered her mouth, and Calvin leaned forward and said softly, like a prayer, "Well, shit."

I said, "It's a big decision, and it's up to you. You can take your time thinking about it. But I'd move quickly on insuring it. And I'd think about storing it somewhere secure, too."

10

TAKE IT SLOW

I STOOD BEFORE THE MIRROR, AS I HAD SO MANY TIMES, looking at my reflection. I was dressed only in the black lace bra and panties I'd bought earlier this week in anticipation of Adam's visit. I shivered, even though I kept the a/c at an eco-conscious 74 degrees. My chill was internal. It had been a long time since I wanted a man to look at me with a seductive light in his eyes. In my marriage, sex had become a low flame, and when the baby-making began, an obsession fraught with anxiety. The betrayal had doused the flame altogether.

Would Adam remember me as I'd been at eighteen, before life and gravity had made their marks on my body? I remembered him all too well. I'd known every inch of his adolescent skin. Of course he'd changed, as I had. I thought of finding out how, and I shivered again.

I thought of the way I'd felt before our very first time. Excited and nervous. I remembered my adolescent certainty and marveled at it. Now I knew that nothing would ever be so sure again. There had been too much pain and loss since.

I looked again at the black lace, intended to seduce, thinking ruefully of our high school relationship, when neither of us felt any need to work at seduction.

The black lace didn't seem like a tease. It seemed like a dare, as in, *Did I really dare to do this?*

I put my hand on my hip, not a sexy pose but the reassurance I'd give myself in a dressing room at my father's boutique. *You look good, Nat.* Then I put on the dress I'd already chosen, pretty rather than provocative, even if the neckline was a little lower than I'd wear in the shop, keeping the layer underneath as a secret and a surprise.

I walked into my living room, savoring the fact that the house smelled of lemon polish and rosemary. I'd worried about dinner, as about my appearance, but I'd planned a meal that could grace my parents' table on Friday night, a secular form of Shabbos: roasted chicken with rosemary, risotto, asparagus. I'd light candles, not for religious reasons, but as my mother did, for ambiance. I was just about to sit in my big armchair, to try to breathe deeply and wait, when the doorbell rang.

Adam stood on my porch, casually dressed in jeans and a crisp linen shirt, his hair damp and curly in the humidity. He held a bottle of wine in his hands.

"It's so good to see you," I said, beckoning him in. "You didn't have any trouble finding me?"

In high school, Adam's disorientation had been a running joke. His sense of direction was so bad that he could get lost on the familiar streets of Germantown.

"I'm better about that," he said. He held out the bottle. "I thought you'd like this."

I took it, and the chill felt good in my hands. "Thank you."

"You can open it now, or whenever."

"Let's open it now. Follow me into the kitchen."

"Will you give me the tour?"

"En route to the kitchen, you'll get the tour, which is a misnomer, because you can see everything but the bedroom from here."

He said, "Is the bedroom in the mission style, too?" He was teasing me.

I wasn't ready to tease back in the same way. I gave him the decorator's answer. "All this furniture was in the house, and I bought it from the owner. But the bedroom is different. All mine."

"Sorry. That didn't come out right. I meant the decor. Let me try that again." It made me feel better to know he was nervous, too. He looked around the room. "What I can see is lovely, Nat," he said. "It looks like you're really at home here."

"I am," I said, grateful to Jude and my mother, who had helped me settle in.

Melancholy flickered over his face. "I never liked my ex's taste," he said. "All that chintz. But it was home, living with her. And now it isn't."

With an antique dealer's insight, I realized that for Adam, home would never be a place, or the things in it, as it was for me. Home was a relationship, and when he got divorced, he had become homeless. "I promise there's no chintz here, not anywhere," I said.

Once in the kitchen, he leaned against the counter as I rummaged in a drawer for the corkscrew. I was suddenly shaky. The certainty of eighteen had deserted me completely. As I drew the corkscrew out, my hand trembled.

"Can I help you with that?" he asked.

I put the corkscrew down on the counter to face him.

"Are you nervous, Nat?" he asked, his voice soft.

Can I do this? Will it be all right? "I can't deny it. Are you?"

He put his hand over mine, stilling it. "Do you remember?"

Our motto. "What?"

"What you said to me before our very first time?"

"Remind me exactly what."

"That we could be terrible at this together?"

"Yes, I remember," I said. "I'm surprised you do."

He smoothed a lock of hair from my face, and I savored the sweetness in his touch. "It's like that, again," he said.

The past isn't past… I pressed his hand to my cheek, a sweet but not seductive touch. "It is, and it isn't."

"Let me open the wine." He uncorked and I poured. He lifted his glass. "To however things go tonight," he said, his eyes twinkling with warmth and desire.

Suddenly the black lace against my hips seemed to generate its own heat.

At the table, I saw the melancholy flicker over his face again. "You've made Shabbos," he said.

"The secular version," I said. "The Raskin version."

I didn't say the prayer over the candles, but I lit them,

and I lifted my eyes to see him watching me, his expression full of yearning. Had his wife been religious, or not? What was he thinking of, and what was he missing?

He sighed as he tasted everything with a satisfaction that was about more than food. "This is wonderful, Nat," he said.

I said, "Food. The other Raskin love language." I blushed as I realized what I'd said.

He laughed. "I know what you meant." He put his hand over mine. "All of it."

"I'm still a little nervous."

"So am I."

After dinner, we cleared the table together. As I put away the food, he stacked the plates.

"There's dessert," I said.

"Can it wait?"

"Yes," I said, and I put my arms around him, savoring the embrace as he'd savored dinner. *How I've missed this.* We met in a kiss that was so slow, but so sweet, that I began to tremble with anticipation instead of worry. I tangled my hands in his hair. I whispered, "Do you want the tour of the bedroom?"

This laugh was a low rumble of pleasure. "Show me."

We sat on the bed, held each other, and caressed each other everywhere we could reach. I thought, *If you don't hurry up I think I'm going to die of longing,* and he pulled back and smiled as though he'd heard me speak. He began to unbutton my blouse, just as I'd imagined he would, and at the sight of the black lace, he grinned.

"What's so funny?"

"You'll see."

He unzipped my skirt and laughed at the sight of more black lace. "Now it's your turn," he said.

"Will I find out why you're laughing?"

"Yes," he said, his eyes bright.

I unbuttoned his shirt and eased it off him. He was no longer the slender boy I remembered. His shoulders had broadened and his chest had hardened with muscle. I ran my hand down the black hairs that ran down his belly and he looked at me with eyes bright with anticipation. I unzipped his jeans and pulled them away.

Smiling, teasing, he eased the jeans off. Underneath was a wisp of a brief, silky and black to match my own.

He'd dressed to seduce me, as I had for him.

Our eyes met, and we both burst into laughter. We clung to each other, laughing, until our mutual fears melted away. Gasping with laughter, wiping my eyes, I said, "We might be all right after all."

He reached behind me for the hooks on my brassiere. "Now I can't wait to take this off," he said, his breath warm in my ear.

I curled my fingers around the edge of the sleek black garment that left nothing to the imagination. "Likewise," I said, leaning close to lick his earlobe.

Naked, we fell backward on the bed, twining together to start a new dance of anticipation and desire. I thought, *This is the present, and I want to stay in it.*

THE NEXT MORNING, when I woke, the sun glowed through my curtains. I propped myself on my elbow and watched Adam sleep. I bent to nuzzle his shoulder, relishing the musk that overwhelmed his natural scent of cinnamon.

His eyes fluttered open, and he smiled at me.

I touched his cheek. "So it wasn't a dream. You're really here."

He laughed and rolled over to embrace me, chest to breast, belly to belly, his legs tangling with mine.

"We can try again, just so you're sure," he said.

And we did.

I murmured to him, "You always were good at this."

"And I've learned a few things since."

When we were still, he brushed the hair from my face and whispered, "When can I come back?"

"Tonight."

THE NEXT MORNING, in the shop, Jude knew right away. "You're glowing," she said, but she didn't sound happy about it.

"Is it that obvious?"

"Don't tell me it was Adam."

"Yes, it was."

She sighed. "Oh, Nat," she said.

I flushed because my internal voice supplied the rest: *What were you thinking? What are you doing?* "I'm happy for the first time in a long time," I said. "Don't try to spoil it."

She leaned close. "Just be careful," she reminded me.

All that day, Gideon was quiet. He wasn't curt or icy—I knew the signs of anger—but he was distant. We were too busy all day for a talk, but after we closed, I asked him, "Walk me to my car?"

In the yard, we stopped under the live oak tree. "Is there something bothering you?" I asked. "Did Jude say anything?"

"Your love life ain't none of my business. But if you get hurt, that is."

"Did Jude say something to you?"

"She didn't have to." He walked away, his shoulders hunched as though he felt cold, even though it was ninety degrees out and the air was so humid it was hard to take a breath.

NEITHER JUDE'S warning nor Gideon's worry spoiled my pleasure with Adam. It was bliss, and doubly sweet because I'd forgotten what bliss felt like. The food and the wine were part of the foreplay that made sex so hot and so sweet. In bed, we didn't take it slow, and his eagerness —and mine—restored my self-esteem, which had taken such a beating in the divorce.

Whenever we touched, I thought, *Do you remember?* Without any effort, we slipped back into the power of our adolescent connection, fueled equally by friendship and sex. I marveled at how easy it seemed and how good it felt. The pleasure wiped out even the memory of pain. I hoped I'd never feel the loss or the grief again.

I was wrong.

We'd made love, and I fell asleep in a haze of pleasure, wrapped in Adam's arms. And I woke to pain more acute than it had ever been. I laid my hand on my abdomen and breathed deeply, trying to relieve it.

It didn't help.

I didn't want to wake Adam, so I got up, slipped on my bathrobe, and made my way to the living room, thinking that I might feel better sitting up. I eased myself into the Morris chair, leaned back, and rested my hand on the sore spot.

That didn't help, either.

At the soft sound of footsteps, I opened my eyes. It was Adam, a shape in the darkness. "Nat?" he asked softly. "I wondered where you'd gone."

"I got up. I had a cramp," I said, but it came out as a gasp.

He knelt on the rug. He'd been in such a hurry to find me that he hadn't bothered to cover himself. "Are you all right?" he asked, resting his hands on my knees, his voice soft with concern.

"Just a cramp," I repeated, sounding no better than before.

He slid forward, moving his hands to my thighs. "That's more than a cramp."

I looked up, even though I couldn't see his expression in the darkness. "It's nothing serious."

"You're sure?"

If I didn't feel so awful, I would have appreciated the sight of a nude man kneeling at my feet, his hands on my thighs, his face full of worry. I took another deep breath, even though it didn't help. "I'm sure. It's nothing. It's psychosomatic."

"Psychosomatic still hurts. What's wrong?"

"I'm fine. It's emotional."

"Nat, if you don't tell me what's wrong, I'm taking you to the emergency room."

I leaned back, and I didn't have what my Raskin grandmother called the *koyekh*, the strength, to lie to him. "When I was married, I wanted kids more than anything. I had two miscarriages, trying. After that my husband divorced me. Now it hurts."

"Oh, Nat," he said, his voice low, pained, breathless, because he knew all about being punched in the gut by divorce. He leaned forward to put his arms around me, and I leaned into the embrace.

He said, "Where does it hurt? Show me."

I lay back, taking deep breaths against the pain, and I showed him.

I thought he'd lay his hand there, as my ex-husband had when I was pregnant, but he didn't. He kissed it, very softly, and he laid his cheek on my belly instead. The stubble on his skin rasped a little, but his gesture was full of tenderness. I tangled my fingers in his hair, and he raised his head. "Does that help?"

I breathed deeply again, this time against the way my eyes stung. "Yes. It does."

"Come back to bed."

He rose and gave me his hand. When I stood, he took my arm, and slowly, tenderly, he led me back to the bedroom.

On the bed he lay beside me and wrapped his arms around me, enfolding me without a word, and the pain ebbed away.

11

THE BLUE CAT

THE WOODSONS' APPRAISAL WAS CONFIDENTIAL, BUT THE history I'd found in the Powell papers wasn't. I owed the Powells a report, and I wasn't looking forward to it. I wanted Josh to help me handle it. I started with the easiest task. I called him, and after we exchanged pleasantries about the shop and his family, I asked, "Josh, can you recommend an insurer who handles antiques?"

"Is this about the Woodson chair?"

"I appraised it for them, so there are things I can't tell you."

"It's worth enough to insure?" he asked.

"I didn't say a thing." I knew he'd drawn a conclusion, as I had when he kept Owen Powell's finances from me.

"Sure, I can give you a recommendation. I'll email you a couple of names."

"Thanks."

"Did you find anything that isn't confidential?"

"Sure, about the history of the piece. Now we know more than when it was made. We know why."

"What's the story?"

I thought of Lucullus in a destructive rage, using an ax on the chair as though he were flaying a human body. I thought I'd keep that confidential for a while, too. "The original chair was badly damaged in 1838, and the Powells set their enslaved cabinetmaker to make a replacement. The Woodsons are descended from that enslaved man. We don't know how the chair came into their hands, but it's been theirs for decades."

"Does any of that new info affect the value?"

"No exact numbers, Josh. I really want to protect the Woodsons."

"Have the Powell heirs been causing you more trouble?"

"You know what they're like, and hearing a number is going to make it worse. I'm afraid it will encourage them to stake their own claim to the chair."

"They can claim anything they like. Right now, it belongs to the Woodsons. Can the Powell heirs prove it's theirs?"

I thought of the 1861 will, which mentioned twelve chairs, and the 1893 upholsterer's bill, which named eleven. "That's the provenance question."

Josh said, "Without proof of ownership, you have three options. You can buy it, you can sue for it, or you can steal it."

"I'll let my bias show here. Isn't it awfully mean-spirited for a rich white family—who used to own slaves before the Civil War—to say that a poor Black family, descended from one of those slaves, isn't entitled to the only object of value they have? To accuse them of having stolen it?"

"I'd certainly think so."

"But they could sue?"

"Personally, I think it would be a waste of their time and money, and I'd tell them so. But we both know you can sue anyone for anything."

I was quiet. Josh said, "You know, this isn't part of the original appraisal you contracted to do for them. If they want to give you tzuris about this, let me help you out."

"Believe me, I will."

"How's the appraisal coming along?"

"We're done. I've finished the catalog. I'd like to send it to them and invoice them."

"There's a 'but.' Something's bothering you."

"You're good," I said, teasing him.

"Lifelong experience," he said, teasing back. "What is it? Anything I can help you with?"

"I'm really uneasy about the two items we can't find. They have financial and sentimental value. One is a baseball that reminds Owen of his father, and the other is a Victorian ring that Joyce thought she'd inherit. Believe me, they'll notice that those two things are missing."

"You've made a good faith effort to find them?"

"Of course. We didn't stop at looking everywhere in the house and in the storage unit. We checked for receipts, to see if Evelyn Powell had sold them, and I talked to her insurance agent to see if she'd ever filed a claim. I even checked with the hospital to see if she'd left the ring there. Those two items are truly missing."

"Here's what I'd suggest. Attach an addendum to your

report, listing them as missing and giving a rough appraisal—can you do that?"

"Sure, no problem. I can do a good estimate on the value without having them in hand."

"And document your good faith effort to find them."

"I'll do that. But we both know what the Powells are like. They're awfully quick to assume that someone stole something."

"Nat, if they get hot about the report, they can come into my office and I'll talk them through it and take the heat."

I wasn't reassured. "Crank up the a/c in your office."

IT WAS SUNDAY, and Sunday mornings were a little slow, between the churchgoers, who had to finish brunch before they went shopping, and the tourists, who'd been out late on Saturday night. Gideon was sharing shop duty that morning, even though he'd had a late night himself on a gig. He'd kept his word. He hadn't said a thing to me about Adam. He wasn't distant with me, but he was wary. Since ending his career as a session musician in Nashville and becoming an antique dealer in Memphis, he'd worked as a bouncer. Since I'd gotten involved with Adam, Gideon was in his bouncer mode with me, not expecting trouble, but ready for it.

When the electronic bell jangled, just after we opened, I looked up, ready to smile and say, "Welcome! Have you been here before?" Then I recognized the dark-skinned, broad-shouldered man who'd just walked in.

It was Calvin Woodson, who looked around with wide eyes.

I greeted Calvin and introduced him to Gideon. Even though I'd told both Jude and Gideon that I'd appraised the Woodson family chair and the details were confidential, Gideon had never met Calvin, and he welcomed him as a brand-new customer, nothing more.

I asked Calvin, "Are you looking for anything?"

"No, I just came to look around," he said. "I wanted to look at old stuff that's good. The pawnshop gets some old stuff, but it's not much."

"Look around to your heart's content. Ask if you have questions, and let us know if we can open a case for you."

He looked. He lingered. When he was in the back of the shop, out of earshot, Gideon whispered to me, "Woodson as in Woodson chair?"

"Yes."

"It'll stay confidential," he whispered back.

Calvin returned to the counter. "There's something I want to ask you about," he said. "It's in back."

That case was full of my stuff, and I retrieved my key. "What can I show you?"

"That blue cat." He pointed, as they always did, as though I wouldn't find it otherwise.

I opened the case and carefully removed the figurine. "You have a good eye," I said. "It's French, from the 1870s. Theodore Deck, one of their best potters, and the director of Sevres in the 1880s and 1890s. Egyptian influence. It's a lovely thing." I held it out to him.

"It's really something," he said, his face softening as he looked at it. "Can I touch it?"

"Of course! We're not a museum. Just handle it carefully."

He took it gently, admiring it, and he began to hand it back to me.

I said, "Look at the bottom. Look at the mark."

He turned it over. "Where?"

I showed him.

He saw the price tag, too. "$3,800 for this little kitty-cat," he said.

I kidded him. "Worth every dime."

"Not if I drop it." He gave it back to me. When it was safely in my hands again, he joked, "If we sell that chair, I might come back to get it."

"You're still thinking about it? All of you?"

"Yes, we are," he said, and he sighed softly.

"Take your time," I said. I was still holding the Sevres cat. "Did you talk to the insurance agent?"

"Letitia called him. We just can't afford to insure it."

I shook my head.

"Man, I like this thing," he said. "But even if I could afford it, I couldn't keep it in my place. My roommates aren't careful with anything. They'd break it."

I had an idea. I locked the case and went to open another. "Take a look at this," I said. "Another cat. Also French, same time period, and this one is indestructible."

"It's heavy," he said, hefting it.

"It's a bronze, by a sculptor named Alfred Barye. He was known as an animalier, a specialist in animal figures. Most of them are kind of disgusting. Lions eating antelopes. Stags fighting. But this is sweet."

"Another kittycat," he said, turning it in his hands. "Does it have a mark?"

He was a quick study like his sister Ayesha. "It does. Right here, by the feet. The artist's name."

As he looked, I said, "It was popular in its day, because it was small and the subject was appealing. A lot of them were cast and they come up pretty often. So it's not very expensive."

He upended it to read the price tag.

"What do I have on it?" I asked him.

"$175." He let it rest in his hands. Its heft reassured him. He gazed at it with affection and respect. I knew he wanted to own it.

I fibbed because I wanted him to have it. "It's been here for a while. I can do $85 on it."

"Really? That won't put you out?"

"Not a bit."

"I can manage that," he said.

After he left, Gideon said, "That piece came in not two weeks ago."

I said, "Either I'll make it up to the consignor myself, or I'll call her and give her a sob story about a deserving young collector who fell in love with it and couldn't live without it. Whatever I feel like."

Gideon said, "If the family sells their chair, he can come back to buy the Deck figurine."

I was glad to hear him tease me about business. "You don't know what that chair is valued at, and don't try to guess," I said.

I SENT each of the Powells a copy of the report, along with the invoice, and I didn't have long to wait for the response. Josh called me.

"Did they tell you what they're upset about?" I asked.

"They mentioned a baseball. A ring. And a chair. Like you thought they would."

"So I'm going into the principal's office again?" I said.

He sighed.

I wasn't looking forward to this meeting. It wouldn't be about the appraisal, which had unearthed an estate of items great and small, fine and trivial, worth close to $750,000. It would be about the two things we hadn't found, and the one thing we'd found that wasn't theirs—the Woodson chair, which had a value I was honor-bound not to share.

Josh himself came to bring me back to his office. As we walked there, I asked, "How are they?" When he hesitated, I said, "Don't spare me. I need to know."

"Spitting mad," he said.

"Did they tell you I lied to them?"

"We haven't gotten that far yet."

"Saving it up for me, no doubt."

Josh settled me at his oval guest table and offered coffee, which I refused. Joyce and Owen sat side by side, across from me, and they were as angry as they'd been when they accused me of lying to them about the Woodson chair in the first place.

Before I could say anything, Owen said, "What's this business about missing items?"

I stifled my impulse to say, "The ones we know about." I said, "I'm well aware of the importance of those two items. Believe me, we've done our best to find them. I explained it in the catalog. I've done everything I know to do. We can't find them. They're missing."

Owen said, "How do we know you didn't take them? Or those people you brought in to work with you?"

Joyce gasped and put her hand on Owen's arm, but he shook it off.

I said, "I understand that you're upset. I realize the things we can't find have a lot of sentimental value in your family. But an appraiser who took anything from the estate wouldn't last long in the appraisal business. And the same goes for anyone who works for me. Their reputations are at stake, just as mine is."

I dare you to try to sue me, I thought, my head starting to ache.

Owen scowled. Joyce grabbed his arm and said, "Be reasonable, Owney."

He ignored her and said to me, "What about that damn chair? The twelfth chair?"

I glanced at Josh, who calmly explained, "Even though that isn't part of your estate, Nat has some information to share with you."

Appreciating Josh's reminder, trying to emulate his calm, I reiterated the story of the damage to the original twelfth chair and Tobey's work in making a replacement.

Owen leaned forward. "Cut the crap. What's it worth?"

"I did a formal appraisal for the Woodsons. That's confidential."

"Bullshit," Owen said. "I bet you told them what our chairs are worth."

I kept my voice level. "The *Commercial Appeal* made

that public information," I said. "Everyone in Memphis knows what your chairs are worth. I didn't tell them."

Owen said, "If she won't say, I'll bet it's worth a lot." He stared at me. "Is it?"

I didn't reply.

Joyce said, "Wait a minute. Didn't you say their slave made that chair?" She looked at Josh. "Didn't it belong to his master?"

"At the time, yes," I said.

"So it's ours."

Josh said, "No, it's currently in the hands of the Woodson family."

"Because they stole it from us."

Josh said sharply, "It's in their hands. They don't have to prove they own it. If you want to claim ownership, that burden of proof is yours."

"But it's ours!"

"Not at the moment," I said, in concert with Josh.

She gave me a hateful look. "I can't believe you care more about that family of n—"

Josh said, "If you use the n-word in this office, I'll have to ask you to leave."

"I'll say what I like," she said.

"Not in this office."

She glared at me again.

Josh said, "The appraisal that you contracted for is finished. I believe Nat has invoiced you for it."

Owen said, "I don't give a damn about the appraisal. I never wanted to hire you. Don't expect us to pay you. You're fired." He rose. "That chair is ours, and we'll get it back."

Josh showed them out and returned to sit with me at his oval table. I'd never been fired from anything, not even a part-time summer job. My face burned with humiliation. I felt so sick I didn't even want a sip of water.

Josh said, "I may fire them, too. They can take their business to another partner in the firm. Someone who doesn't care if they use a racial slur." His color was high.

I said, "If they don't pay me, can I sue them?"

He recovered enough to snort. "I'll give you the same advice I'd give them about suing for the chair. It looks like hell, and it's not worth the time or money."

"They owe me $22,500," I said, trying to get angry.

"Nat, believe me, they'll calm down and they'll pay you."

I clenched the edge of the table and stared at my hands. "Well, there goes my career as an appraiser in Memphis," I said.

He rested his hand on my shoulder. "I'm really sorry. I never expected things to work out like this."

"Me neither."

IT WAS NEARLY CLOSING time when I returned to the shop, and Jude had already left. Gideon leaned against the counter, filling out the daily sales report. He looked up. "We did good today. $3,000. Sold some of those pictures you have on consignment. Those landscapes."

I nodded. I didn't care. We could have sold out the contents of the shop and I'd still feel sick to my stomach.

"The Powells give you a hard time?" he asked.

"Let's close up."

At five in the afternoon, it was still unbearably hot. Outside the cocoon of the shop's a/c, the heat was like a fist, squeezing my chest. As we walked through the yard to the parking lot, the owl called, and we both stopped under the live oak, hoping to catch a glimpse of her. Gideon said, "She's still there."

I nodded.

He said, "You look puny. You need something to drink before you take yourself home?"

"No, I'm fully hydrated." The heat shimmered in the air. The headache was still pounding. I rubbed my temple.

"Exactly how did the Powells give you a hard time?"

"All right, it's business, so I can tell you." I felt another wave of nausea at the memory of the words *You're fired*.

"Go ahead."

"I've made a mess of this appraisal job, the Powells just fired me, and I don't think I'll ever see the money they owe me. They'll talk trash about me all over town, and I'll never get another appraisal job. I feel like such a failure."

His laugh was low and soft. "Failure! I bet you felt like a failure if you got a B on a paper in high school."

"How did you guess?"

He asked, "Was there alcohol involved here?"

He'd had a drinking problem in Nashville, and he still drank more than he should. I laughed, sounding shaky. "Just a little after hours."

"Drugs?" His problem with cocaine had been more serious. He'd left that behind in Nashville, too.

"Does ibuprofen count?"

"Anyone go to rehab?"

That I didn't know about. I wondered if he had. "No," I said.

"Anyone get arrested?"

"No."

"Anyone's heart get broken? Any families busted up?"

I met his eyes. "How much of that happened to you?"

He didn't reply, and we both listened to the owl, making her evening call, her sweet, high-pitched hoot. He watched as she took flight. Softly, he said, "They fly without a sound." I looked up to follow her path in the evening sky.

In the silence between us, he began to sing, also softly.

"I'll Fly Away" was a hymn that every white Baptist knew, full of longing for heaven and the release from earthly pain. Gideon's singing voice had a gravelly, bluesy edge. He sounded as though he'd known all the failures he'd named for me, and they lingered for him like the owl's call in the evening air.

I said, "That was beautiful." I didn't know how to console him, so I said, "If you made a record like that, I'd buy it."

"There ain't a producer in Nashville who would agree with you, but thank you," he replied.

"It still hurts, doesn't it?" The musician's career he'd given up, and all the other losses.

"It always will."

The owl called again, and he said, "Let me walk you to your car."

In the parking lot we both hesitated. If I had a grain of sense—or courage—I'd fold my arms around him and hold him close and tell him that his life wasn't over yet and he had time to make things right again. But I didn't. Not because of Adam.

He smoothed a lock of hair from my forehead, his callused fingers gentle on my skin, as Adam had, but this felt different. "You take care of yourself, Nat," he said, as I got into the car. He watched, keeping me in his sight, as I drove away.

12

MISSING ITEMS

THAT EVENING, DESPITE GIDEON'S REASSURANCE, I DIDN'T feel much better about what had happened with the appraisal. Adam was coming over, and I had no energy to worry about dinner. There was a good bottle of Italian white in the refrigerator. We'd start with that.

When he arrived, he looked tired, too. He'd taken off his jacket and tie, but he didn't look comfortable. He slumped onto the loveseat and sighed.

"Rough day?" I asked.

"They all are."

I was too preoccupied to ask, "Anything in particular?" Instead, I said, "I had a rough day myself."

"What happened?" he asked, without moving.

"My appraisal clients fired me."

He shook his head and sat up. "Fired you?"

I explained what had happened.

As I talked, he didn't give me his full attention. I'd become used to that interested, sympathetic, seductive gaze, and I was surprised to see him staring somewhere past me. When I finished, he said, "It's no big deal. You'll be fine, Nat."

Had he listened? Disappointed, I said, "It's not the end of the world, but it upset me."

"I'm beat, Nat. Can we talk about this later?"

This was like the conversation after the break-in. "Just a little sympathy, maybe?" I asked. I didn't like the way I sounded. Plaintive.

He sighed and touched my cheek. "I'm sorry, Nat. I just can't right now."

I thought of Gideon's consideration for me. *That's not fair*, I told myself. "All right," I said, hurt but not wanting to show it.

But as soon as I'd poured him a glass of wine and offered him cheese and crackers, he said, "I thought I liked IP law in Nashville. But this job is just killing me."

It wasn't the first time he'd mentioned he wasn't happy at work. Today, with work problems of my own—real ones—I felt irritated. I tried to be sympathetic. "I've always wondered why you took that job," I said. "It sounds like you knew from the beginning you wouldn't be happy there."

"It was something my father said to me after I'd been back for two weeks, sitting around the house feeling sorry for myself. Didn't I tell you?"

"I don't remember that you did."

"He said, 'There's always a place for you in the business.'"

I was startled. "But he never wanted you to work in the pawnshop!"

"Oh, it wasn't an invitation. It was a kick in the rear.

The next day, I got up, cleaned up, and started networking for a job at a law firm." He sighed. "I'm in touch with my old boss at Warner, but they're not in hiring mode. And he thinks they won't be for a while."

I tried to sound light. "It's temporary," I said. "You won't be working for Holiday Inn for the rest of your life."

"No, it just feels that way." He rested his chin in his hands. I remembered that posture from high school, when he felt tired of the burdens of youth group leadership.

"Oh, poor Adam," I said, teasing to cover how irritated I felt.

"Are you making fun of me?" Now I heard his irritation, too.

"No. You always were the kvetch in our relationship. I can stand to hear a little of it, not a lot, and I get to kvetch, too."

"Are you tired of hearing me kvetch?" I heard the barb: *Tired of me?*

"No. I just want to move you in a different direction."

He sounded unhappy, even a little sullen: "I'm afraid you'll have to take me as I am."

I thought, *If we keep this up, we'll have a fight.* I was much too tired to fight. "You're fine," I said, skating too close to an outright lie. "Just be nice to me."

"Oh, Nat," he said, now contrite. "I should take better care of you."

Yes, you should.

He leaned forward to kiss me.

"That helps, but it doesn't make it all better," I said.

He cupped my face in his hands. "Let me try harder."

I let him show me. For the first time since we'd come

together, sex had an uneasy undertone. It didn't make everything better.

ON A SLOW THURSDAY AFTERNOON, when it was so hot outside that I felt it when I put my hand on the window, the bell jangled, and Joyce walked into the shop. I'd seen her tired and harried before, but today she looked downright disheveled. Her hair, ordinarily flat as a helmet, flew away in damp wisps around her face, and her eyes were red-rimmed, as though she'd been crying in the car as she drove here.

I leaned against the counter, letting Jude and Gideon know that this one was mine to handle. "Joyce!" I said, in my cheerful retail mode, as though I was glad to see her. "Is there something I can do for you?"

She came closer, but she didn't lean on the counter or rest her hands on it. "There is," she said.

"It must be important if you braved traffic all the way from Bartlett," I said.

"Is there someplace we can talk?" She waved her hand toward the back door. "In the yard?"

"We don't make anyone stand in the yard in weather like this," I said. "There's a back room that's cool." I turned to ask Jude and Gideon, "Can you two hold the fort for a bit?"

Jude gave Joyce a look that had some sympathy in it. "Sure."

I ushered Joyce into the back room and showed her to

a chair. "Can I get you something to drink?" I asked. "There's sparkling water."

She sank into the chair and wiped her forehead with her forearm. "That's fine, thanks."

I wished she'd called, because I would have let it go to voicemail, but she had taken the trouble to drive here. I sat down, and the retail cheer left my voice. "What can I really do for you, Joyce?"

Her voice shook. "I am so sorry for the way Owen talked to you."

You weren't an innocent bystander, I thought.

"He shouldn't have talked about firing you."

I didn't reply, letting the silence pressure her, a consultant's trick.

"I can't write you a check, not right now, but I'll talk to him again about paying you."

I thought of the way Josh had been coy with me about Owen's finances. I no longer had to be tactful. "Is Owen in any financial trouble?"

She looked up with a jerk. "Did Josh tell you?"

"Josh hasn't said a thing. He's bound by professional ethics, too. It's just that I've seen clients under financial pressure before."

She hesitated. When she looked up, I saw all the evidence of her distress. "You can't tell him I said anything."

What was one more secret? "Of course I won't."

"I don't know the details, but I know he made a bad investment and lost some money."

"Was it business? Or was it personal?"

"I don't know the details," she said, her red-rimmed eyes glistening.

I said, "You could call the estate sale company today and have the sale in less than a month. You could put the house on the market. Wouldn't that help?"

Her voice rose. "Of course it would!"

"Why is he focusing on the baseball and the ring? I get the sentimental value, but the market value on those two items is less than $10,000. What's he so mad about?"

She stared at the water bottle, then she looked up at me. "He wants to go to the police."

I expelled a breath. "Is this about Ruth Anne?"

"Yes," she said.

I didn't reply.

She said, "We can't talk to her. She'd slam the door on us."

"She doesn't like me any better," I said. "And neither does her nephew, Curtis, after the way I leaned on both of them to get the storage unit open."

"I don't know what to do," she said. She was good at playing the helpless Southern belle.

That didn't get to me. But I could see the pain in the pallor of her cheeks and the lines etched around her mouth. "Look, I don't work for you anymore. I can't offer you any professional advice. But I can give you my take as an informed bystander."

She said, "You know you're more to us than that."

"Don't flatter me, Joyce, I'm not in the mood for it."

"You don't like us much, either."

"Right now, I don't."

She asked, "Doesn't it bother you that we couldn't find the baseball or the ring?"

She wasn't helpless or stupid, even though she was good at pretending to be both. She'd landed a jab into my professional pride. As an appraiser, it made me crazy that we hadn't found the missing items. "I have a thought for you. Josh's firm keeps an investigator on retainer."

"A detective?"

"He specializes in financial investigation. He can do a quiet background check on Ruth Anne without bothering her. If he finds anything to look into, he can let you know. And if he doesn't, that tells you something, too."

She was staring at the water bottle again.

I asked, "Can you sell this idea to Owen?"

"I can try."

"Try as hard as you can."

AFTER JOYCE LEFT, I pulled Jude in back to ask if she had time for a drink after work. "Adam?" she asked.

I nodded.

After we closed, Jude said, "I'm taking Nat out for a drink."

"Without me? You're going to E&H without me?"

"It's girl talk, Gid."

His eyes flickered over me. "Some other time, then," he said.

It was so humid outside that the a/c in E&H wheezed as it struggled to cool the interior. The air smelled of beer and grease, and not even the low light could make the place feel cooler. The server, who knew us both, greeted us. "Beer or bourbon tonight?" she asked.

"I have to drive home," I said. "Just beer. But with onion rings to make up for it."

She nodded and left. Jude asked, "So what's going on?"

"I'm sorry I haven't told you much. I just don't want to talk about Adam in front of Gideon."

Jude gave me a sideways look. "That's tactful of you," she said. "It must be killing you."

I said, "Discretion in my professional life wears me out. I hate keeping a lid on my personal life, too."

Our drinks arrived, and Jude took a swig from the bottle. "Go ahead," she said. "Don't worry, it stays between us. I want to be tactful around Gideon, too."

I sighed.

"So what's going on?"

"The sex is great," I said.

"And?"

"Everything else, not so great."

She took a swig from the bottle, settling herself to listen. "How so?"

"You were right about the charm. He was courting me. And now—" I felt disloyal to say it. And foolish.

"Just spit it out, Nat."

"Nothing awful. Just that he spends a lot of time talking about his problems. Complaining about them. He's not happy about his job, and he's still upset about his divorce." I said, "Believe me, I know what it's like to feel lousy after a divorce. I can sympathize. But that's all he wants to talk about."

Jude nodded.

"I can't get a word in edgewise. I don't want to complain. I just want to talk about my own life occasionally. And he won't give me a chance."

"You're surprised."

"I am. I don't remember him being so needy when we were in high school."

Jude snorted. "He was always the needy one. You were just so gaga over him you didn't see it."

"Was I?" I remembered the high school relationship as an idyll.

"He clung to you like kudzu clings to a wall. And why wouldn't he? He needed a lot of stroking and propping up. And you were happy to do it."

"It didn't seem like that. I loved him, and I thought he loved me."

"At eighteen. Now that you'll all grown up, do you still think so?"

I shook my head. "That's not how adults love each other," I said. "They're friends who take care of each other." I thought of Gideon, quietly putting his jacket over my shoulders as we waited for the police after our break-in, and waiting until the locksmith and the glass company had finished their work to secure the shop. It wasn't a fair comparison. Gideon and I were friends who worked together. Maybe he was awful in his personal life.

"I'd bet that's how Adam's mama always loved him," Jude said.

"Mrs. Levy? She always liked me."

"No wonder. She saw you'd pick up where she left off." Jude took another swig. "I always thought he was a spoiled brat."

That was my first impression of Adam when we were in religious school together. In high school, his newly acquired charm had dazzled me so much I'd forgotten about the snot he'd been. "I thought he might have grown out of it by now."

"Why? Self-centered mama's boy who thinks any woman in his life should love him the same way his mama did? What went wrong in his marriage?"

I said, "He told me she was selfish."

Jude said, "Is that what he'd say about you if you stood up for yourself? Insisted on equal time in this relationship?"

"I wonder," I said.

JOSH'S INVESTIGATOR was glad to oblige the Powells. When he finished, he called me. "I'll talk to them myself, but I wanted to give you a heads-up. Since the task of wrangling them seems to have fallen to you."

"I'll be ready when they complain to me. What can you tell me?"

He said, "You keep siccing me on the Thompson family and all I can find is that they're model citizens. Ruth Anne Thompson was paid a decent salary for a housekeeper, and she was frugal with her money. She saved enough to buy her house, which she owns outright. She's invested some of her money, too, and done well with it. The only thing of interest about her income was that she seems to have gotten a bonus from her employers twice a year, once in the middle of the year and the other at the end. The amounts varied, but that isn't unusual for a bonus that depends on personal largesse."

"What did she do with her windfalls?"

"The same as with her income. Saved some, invested some. She declared it all as income and paid taxes on everything that was taxable."

"Anything else?"

"No. Not even a traffic ticket. Her record is as clean as a whistle."

"Nothing to suggest she may have brought something home that wasn't part of her bonus?"

"If there's that kind of funny business, there's usually a pattern. And with her, there isn't."

"I visited her. She had a lot of nice furniture—not old, but nice—and a good oil painting. She told me it had been a bargain in an antique shop. I researched it. As far as I could tell, it was the truth."

He said, "It sounds like you have nagging doubts."

"I spent fifteen years as a professional skeptic at Sotheby's."

"We have that in common."

I sighed. "But at Sotheby's I never needed to get a search warrant for a client."

"In this situation? I don't recommend it."

"Josh doesn't either, and I agree with both of you, even though those missing items bother the heck out of me."

He said, "Some things just get lost. Evelyn Powell might have dropped the ring down the disposal and been too ashamed to admit it. And Ruth Anne Thompson might be unhappy to say so, either. Especially if she knew that Joyce expected to inherit it."

"That's all plausible."

He said, "I'll talk to the Powells and let them know what I've told you. But you'll be aware if they call you."

"They may."

He said, "Some clients are harder than others."

"You said it."

I CONTINUED to be nagged by doubt. Ruth Anne hadn't stolen anything—I was sure of that—but she was defensive and tightlipped for a reason. Whatever it was, she wasn't willing to unbend to share it with a white stranger.

I'd recently researched a vintage guitar that had sent me into a tangled web that involved my own family, and that's how I'd met John Ivey, a retired detective on the Memphis police force. He appreciated that I called on his expertise and his memory as a detective, and he'd come to like me. We'd developed a relationship that would let me ask a question with painful racial overtones, but he was a Black man as well as a former police officer. I never knew how he'd answer.

I called him and explained that I had a situation that didn't need investigation, but I'd appreciate his point of view.

After he heard me out, he said, "Ruth Anne Thompson? She belongs to my church."

"That perspective would help, too."

"Come out here to see me."

"Will I get better answers?" That was a running joke

between us. Early in our association, he'd told me that was why he'd always sent his men in person.

"I can't guarantee that. But I'll have the pleasure of your company."

Ivey was a massive man with a tough guy's presence. He had a big, affectionate family and a supportive church community, but he still missed his former life as a police detective since he'd retired. He now savored any opportunity to exercise his investigative talent. He'd never said it outright, but he missed his old cronies on the force, too. He'd rather have a heart attack than admit that he wanted to see me because he was lonesome.

"I'll be there."

I drove out to Whitehaven and parked before the well-kept brick rambler. Mrs. Ivey, wiry and active, opened the door before I could ring the bell. "Come on in. I have to run. I'm late for volunteering at the elementary school."

"What do you do?"

"I tutor the kids in reading. I'm glad you're here. John is really glad to see you."

I said, "That sounds great. Why doesn't Mr. Ivey tutor the kids at the elementary school?"

She laughed. "A classroom full of little kids? They'd drive him crazy," she said. "There's coffee and cake and you two help yourselves."

He sat in a big lounge chair, a contemporary version of mine, and unlike me, his big body filled it. He let me pour my own coffee into one of his wife's fragile cups. "So you've got a situation," he said.

"I have some items missing from an estate. I have someone who's likely to know where they are but won't talk about it. I can't figure out how to connect the dots here."

"You're being cagey," he said, taking a piece of coffee cake. "Just tell me what's going on."

I sighed. "It's the usual Memphis interracial mess."

"That's nothing new," he said. "Just lay it out."

I told him about Joyce and Owen. About Ruth Anne and her long, strange relationship with Evelyn. About the struggle to get into the storage unit. About the missing items, both the Powells' suspicions and my doubts.

I hadn't realized how much I'd been holding in. It was the kind of thing I used to tell my father, before we had an estrangement about the secrets I'd turned up in researching the guitar.

Ivey said, "You've been carrying a lot around."

For a moment I wondered if I could trust him with my doubts about Adam, too. I knew I shouldn't. As much as I craved paternal kindness, I needed his detective's acumen more. I nodded. "I know I'm not seeing something. What do you think?"

He picked up another piece of coffee cake and ate it to fill the silence. When he finished, he wiped the crumbs from his fingers and sighed, not in satisfaction but in frustration. "It's not about the stuff," he said. "It's about the family."

"The family history. And the rest of the history that we both know about."

"I have a hunch," he said. "And I could sit here for a long time, telling you a story based on my hunch. I'm like you. I want proof. I don't see how to get it."

Now I was silent, and I was too full for another piece

of cake to hide the silence. Finally, I sighed too. "I'm beginning to think the investigator was right. He couldn't find a thing. He said he was pretty sure that Miss Evelyn lost the ring down the disposal. But I don't think so."

He hesitated, but he finally said, "Neither do I."

"Any proof, Detective Ivey, or just an investigator's hunch?"

At that he smiled, a subtle look on his face. "I didn't say a word," he said.

I smiled back. "And I heard you loud and clear, not saying a word."

13

MAKE AN OFFER

I was at home, getting ready to go into the shop, when Joyce called me. Without any preliminary, she said, "I heard from that investigator."

Too mad for manners, I thought. "I take it you weren't happy about it."

"We think he should look harder."

"For what, Joyce?"

Her voice was cold. "Ruth Anne took that ring. I bet she stole the baseball, too. We should call the police."

"Can you report a burglary in a situation like this? When it's so far in the past?"

"That shouldn't make any difference."

"Joyce, be reasonable."

"Don't you tell me to be reasonable."

"Do you really want the cops to get a search warrant? You may not like what happens."

"Is that a threat?"

I felt very tired. "Of course not. I just meant that

nothing good can come of sending the cops in. I don't think the police will give it much attention. And you'll just make the Thompsons more upset."

"The police will do their job." Her voice was icy.

"If you call the police, you'll never get those missing items back," I said.

"You're a fine one to talk." She hung up.

I WAS ALARMED enough to call ex-Detective Ivey, who was happy to hear from me. "It isn't such great news," I said. "And I'm sorry that I can't come to see you to talk about it. It's time sensitive."

"The Powell family acting up?"

"You got it." I told him about Joyce's call.

He snorted. "I wouldn't worry much if I were you."

"Are you trying to cheer me up or are you serious?"

"Let me tell you, the department can barely keep up with last week's burglaries. Something like this? What's there to go on? It's right at the bottom of the priority list."

"You know for sure?"

"I know pretty well. But I can put in a word in the right place, if it would make you feel better."

I knew that he meant, *I can call my son.* "It would."

He chortled. "You rest easy."

I sighed. "Next time, I'll come to see you in person, I promise."

I didn't feel any better.

A FEW DAYS LATER, Calvin came into the shop, sighing with relief when he shut the door behind him. "How hot is it out there?" I asked him.

"It's not the heat. It's just that it's so nice here. I always feel better when I come here."

Gideon said, "We like it when customers say that. How's your little bronze? You find a safe spot for it?"

"I did. My housemates don't mess with it."

I said, "Do you want another one? You know what they say. Once you have two, you have a collection."

He smiled, and it took away the years that trouble and hard living had etched in his face. I wondered how bad the trouble had been. "I want to see that blue kittycat," he said.

"Give me the key," I said to Gideon.

Calvin followed me, and as I stood before the case, key in hand, the pleasure drained from his face. He hadn't come here to pine after the cat figurine. He dropped his voice. "Letitia's been getting calls about our chair."

"Who's been calling?"

"The Powells. The sister called first."

I groaned. "Joyce," I said. "What did she want?"

He leaned close enough for me to smell his cologne, strong and sweet. "She offered to buy the chair off Letitia."

"How much?"

At that he snorted. "$1,000."

"And what did Letitia say?"

"Laughed and told her she was crazy. Then hung up on her."

"Good for her," I said.

"Then Tish got another call. This time from the brother."

"Owen called her?"

"Yes, he did. He upped the offer. He offered her $10,000. That got Letitia's antenna up. They want that chair, and they know it's worth something. It didn't change her mind. She said no to him, too."

I said, "I can't tell you how much it bothers me that they're calling you." I thought briefly about telling him that they had been ready to send the police to Ruth Anne on the thinnest pretext. They hadn't, since I would have heard from an enraged Curtis Thompson. Instead, they'd decided to pursue the item that wasn't theirs no matter how much they wanted it.

"They can call every day. They can offer more every day, too. We aren't selling it."

"Let me know if they do that."

He nodded. "I guess I want to see the cat after all," he said.

At that I smiled, unlocked the case, and extricated the piece for him. This time, he knew to handle it carefully, admiring it from every angle. He checked the mark again, and the price tag as well. "Still can't afford it," he said.

"At that price, it won't move fast. It should be here for a while."

"I'll have to look for it when I come back."

"We'll make a collector of you yet," I said, putting the cat back in the case.

A FEW DAYS LATER, when the unfamiliar number showed on my phone, I answered anyway. Every call could be business, whether for the shop or (I was still hoping) another appraisal. It was Calvin, who hoped he hadn't caught me at a bad time.

Oh, the South, where even convicted felons had good manners.

I began to worry before I could say, "Of course not. What's going on?"

"Letitia got another call."

"Joyce or Owen?"

"Owen. He wasn't as polite this time. Said he'd given her a reasonable offer last time. When she told him it wasn't, he got mad. He said, 'Why? What is your chair worth?' She wouldn't tell him, and he kept after her. 'More? A lot more?' She hung up on him."

"I really don't like this. You and Letitia should think about putting that chair somewhere secure." Then, ashamed, I said, "Is Letitia worried? Does she feel safe?"

"She didn't sound worried. She said he didn't sound threatening, just mad."

"Maybe you could store the chair at the pawnshop. I know the owner, and he says they have security as right as a bank's."

"I already thought of that. I asked Mr. Levy himself. He knows me. He hired me."

"What did he say?"

Calvin said, "He told me it wouldn't be covered by his insurance unless I pawned it."

"Well, it would be safe there. Isn't that the main thing?"

Calvin was suddenly very upset. "I didn't even talk to Letitia because I know what she'd say. We'd never pawn our chair! We can't do that!"

I had to bite my tongue not to argue with him. He was a client, and I owed him the same respect I'd give a rich client who refused to do the intelligent or obvious thing, at least by my lights. "I understand," I said, but I worried. I called Thomas.

When he answered, for once I didn't hear the hubbub of flea market or a show on the other end of the line. I told him that the Powells had been calling Letitia about buying the chair and I was concerned. "About her, too, but I don't think there's anything I can do to help. But that chair should be safe in storage somewhere. Would you be willing to split the rent on a climate-controlled storage unit? I'd be happy to reimburse you if it's a financial burden."

Thomas said, "Are you still appraising the Powell estate?"

"I finished the appraisal. I invoiced them. They haven't paid me yet."

"Then you shouldn't be involved in this at all. Not at all." He hung up.

I fumed. Why did Thomas make it so hard for me to help? I felt I had an obligation to protect the Woodsons and their chair, both personal and professional. Why did Thomas object so much to my doing that?

THE NEXT MORNING, I sat in my living room chair to drink coffee and plan a day when the shop wasn't open. The sun slanted through my front windows and the a/c whispered a cool song, but I felt itchy and hot. New York would be only a little cooler than Tennessee in midsummer, but I wished I was back in Manhattan, far from the complications I'd created for myself in Memphis.

My phone rang. It was Josh, and I sighed. The best I could hope for was an invitation to a backyard barbecue. Josh was troubled by my estrangement from Dad, and he'd offered more than once to make overtures to mend the rift. The worst—well, Josh was the lawyer for the Powell estate, and I'd been uneasy about the Powells since Calvin first told me they'd offered to buy the chair.

We chatted a bit. He asked after the shop—business, the Raskin love language—and I asked about his kids, whom I hadn't seen for a while. Finally I said, "I bet you've called me on business. Legal estate business."

"I have."

"Is it the Powells?"

"As a matter of fact, it is."

I said, "Do you know that they've called Letitia Woodson a couple of times? They made offers for the chair. Lowball offers. Letitia turned them down."

"Yes, Owen told me. They're really interested in buying the chair. He and Joyce want to meet with the Woodsons for a serious conversation. I thought you should join us."

"Even though I can't disclose the value of the chair."

"Nat, how far off was the last offer? The ten thousand?"

"It was laughable, given the appraisal value."

"Whatever you tell me is confidential, you know that."

"Not privileged."

"Confidential," he insisted.

I caught myself before I said, "Can I trust you?" This was Josh, who'd supported and championed me since we were little kids together. "Okay. I made a conservative estimate, because there are no direct comps, and there's a gap in the provenance that would bother an auction house. I appraised the chair at two hundred fifty thousand."

He said, "A quarter of a million dollars?"

"Conservative estimate."

He didn't reply. I wasn't sure whether he was stunned or trying to get me to say more.

I said, "I'd stake my professional reputation on it."

<hr>

I CALLED LETITIA, and a few days later, Calvin, Thomas, and I met at her house, where the window a/c unit struggled against the heat, wheezing softly like an asthmatic. The carpet had wrinkled in the humidity and felt damp underfoot.

The chair was gone. I knew it must be somewhere safe, since no one was worried about it, but I had to know. "Where is the chair?" I asked.

Thomas said, "I rented a storage unit."

"Why didn't you tell me?"

"Because there was no reason to."

I tamped down my irritation. "Is the unit climate controlled?"

"Yes," Thomas said, his voice dripping sarcasm. "Secure and climate controlled."

I smarted at Thomas's tone, but I wasn't here to argue with him.

Ayesha joined us on Skype, greeting her brother and sister, smiling at Thomas, and waving to me. "Tish told me all about those calls from the Powells," she said. "I hear they dropped the zero."

"Worse than that," I said.

Calvin said, "What do they want now? They got a better offer for us?"

"I don't know. All I know is that they want to meet to talk about buying the chair."

"Are they on the level?" Calvin asked.

I looked from one Woodson to another, and I betrayed a confidence. I told them how the Powells had treated Ruth Anne in their search for the baseball and the ring. "And she was someone who worked for the family for decades."

They listened, their expressions impassive, as though it didn't surprise them.

I said, "You're in charge here. This is your decision. What do you want to do?"

Ayesha said, "About selling it? Or selling it to them?"

"Both."

Calvin said, "We haven't made up our minds yet, have we? Tish? Ayesha?"

Letitia looked at her brother and at Thomas before she turned to me. "I've always loved that chair," she said.

"Always respected its connection to the family. It reminds me of my mother and my grandmother, who knew how special it was. Knowing about Tobias just makes all those feelings stronger. I'm not sure I want to let it go."

Calvin reached for his sister's hand and clasped it. "I know how you feel. But think of the money, Tish."

"I do think of the money. What all of us could do with that money. That's why it's so hard."

I said, "If you decide to sell it—that's a big if—I want you to get what it's worth. And I want to see it go to someone who will cherish it and respect it, like you have."

Ayesha said, "You mean send it to an auction, like at Sotheby's."

"That's a possibility, yes."

Ayesha said, "I've been thinking about what you told us. That a museum might want it. If we send it to an auction, anyone could buy it. The Powells could buy it."

I said, "I doubt they could afford it."

Ayesha leaned forward, and her face filled the screen. "Why couldn't we sell it to a museum ourselves? The African American museum at the Smithsonian?"

I sighed, thinking of the dance between museums, patrons, and auction houses when it came to major acquisitions. "It's unusual for a museum to buy directly from a private individual. When it comes to acquiring something important and valuable, either they go through an internal process to allocate their budget or they approach a well-to-do patron willing to buy it and donate it. Either way, they prefer to work with an auction house."

"They wouldn't take it from us?"

"Not unless you were donating it."

Ayesha said, "You already talked me out of that."

"If we want to sell it," Letitia reminded them. Her eyes slid to the spot where the chair used to sit, as though she were missing it like a relative who'd passed on.

Calvin said, "I think we can agree that we don't want to sell it to the Powells."

"As a private seller, working with a private buyer, you can certainly do that."

Ayesha flung her braids over her shoulder. "They don't deserve to have it!"

Thomas smiled, not a pleasant smile.

I asked, "Do you want to meet with the Powells at all? Or just let me tell them the chair isn't for sale?"

Calvin leaned forward. He was smiling too, and it wasn't pleasant, either. "I want to meet them to tell them face-to-face."

I asked, "Are you sure? I've seen these people act vindictive before."

Letitia's eyes gleamed with emotion. "I want the satisfaction of telling them no, too. Face-to-face."

WHEN I WALKED into the waiting area at Josh's office, the Woodsons were already there, perched uneasily on a banquette. Calvin rose, but I said, "No, sit," and I joined them there.

Calvin knotted his hands together, and Letitia sat up straight, her eyes wide with nerves. As we waited, not speaking, lawyers emerged from the back to greet clients. One of the firm's Black attorneys, dressed in an impeccable navy suit, greeted her white clients with a smile, and led them back to her office.

Letitia whispered to Calvin, "Did you see her?"

He whispered back, "Public defender hires Black lawyers, too. I had one."

So his trouble had involved a lawyer and a court appearance.

Josh came out, and I made the introductions. He shook their hands and said, "I asked you to come a little early. I want to get you settled before the Powells arrive."

In his office, he sat them at his round table and asked if they wanted any refreshment. They both shook their heads.

Josh said, "I can tell this is uncomfortable for you, both of you. But I want to remind you that no one is in the hot seat here. This is just an exploratory meeting. We're going to see where you are, and where they are, and if there's reason to proceed with any negotiation. There may be, and there may not." He looked from Letitia to Calvin. "Both Nat and I are here to run interference."

Letitia nodded, the smallest of gestures, and Calvin ducked his head, restraining himself from the doubt of shaking it.

Josh's assistant tapped on the door and showed the Powells in. Owen frowned as he stepped into the room. Joyce followed him, her face creased and tired.

When everyone was settled at the table, Josh recapped for the Powells what he'd told the Woodsons about exploration and negotiation. Owen tapped his fingers on the tabletop as Josh spoke.

When Josh paused, Owen said, "That's enough lawyer

talk. We came here to make an offer for the chair." He looked at Letitia. "A good faith offer. We're willing to pay what one of our chairs is worth. Twenty-five thousand dollars."

Calvin shook his head. I knew what he was thinking: *They dropped a zero.*

I said, "I'm afraid that the chair isn't for sale at that price."

Owen tapped his fingers harder on the table. "Everything's for sale at the right price." He stared at me. "What is it? And don't give me any guff about confidentiality."

Calvin glanced at Letitia. To me, he said, "Tell him."

I said, "Two hundred fifty thousand."

Owen balled his hand into a fist. "That's crazy! Just crazy!"

Josh said, "Nat, can you explain how you arrived at that figure?"

I caught Joyce's eyes. She shook her head, a small gesture. Owen stared at me, his eyes narrowed, his lip curled. *Little lady, how in hell do you know?* I thought of every angry, contemptuous client I'd ever faced at Sotheby's, and I summoned my consultant's tone, cool and dispassionate. *In God we trust. All others bring provenance.*

Owen wasn't listening. He interrupted me. "That's all bullshit," he said. "You pulled that number out of—"

Joyce laid her hand on his arm in warning.

"—thin air. You're highballing us." He looked at Calvin like he'd look at an intruder on his block in Germantown. "Cut the crap and give me a reasonable number."

"That is the reasonable number," I said. This was

familiar, feeling the indignation and the anger but showing only the calm.

Owen's voice rose. "That chair is ours," he said. "We shouldn't have to buy it from anyone. This is all bullshit!"

Joyce grabbed Owen's arm. "Owen, stop it! Schedule the estate sale and put the house on the market. That's two million. Isn't that enough for you?"

Now Owen stared at Joyce with venom, too. "That chair is ours, and we'll get it back."

Joyce said, "I won't stay to listen to this." She rose and left the room.

I was trembling and my gut was in knots. As I searched for the right words, Calvin spoke.

"We aren't interested. We aren't selling."

Owen said to me, "Did you know that? Was that the plan all along?"

Calvin said, "We aren't selling to you."

Josh said, "Please, all of you. We're here to talk reasonably. We came here to try to find common ground. Mr. Powell, you've heard the asking price and you're not satisfied with it. Mr. Woodson, Ms. Woodson, you're having second thoughts about putting the chair on the market at all. You're very far apart here. I don't think it's worthwhile to proceed at this time."

Owen rose. He spat out the words. "I won't stay to listen to any of this, either."

Josh said, "Let me see you out."

"Don't bother." Owen slammed the door as he left.

Letitia broke the ensuing silence. "What happens now?"

Josh said, "Is the chair somewhere secure?"

"Yes," Calvin said. He began to laugh, and he forced himself to stop. "I know this ain't funny."

Nerves, I thought. "Josh, I don't think we've heard the last of this."

Josh sighed. "I don't either, but we'll handle it."

I said, "I wish I had your faith."

Josh looked around the table. Letitia was now limp with the aftermath of her nerves, and Calvin was still stifling laughter as though he had the hiccups.

"It's not faith. It's professional experience."

DAYS WENT BY. A week passed. When I didn't hear from Joyce, Owen, or Josh, I began to think that I'd worried for nothing.

Then Calvin called.

I was in the shop, but I had no retail cheer for him. I felt a rush of nerves as I asked, "What's up?"

"Well, now we know why the Powells have been so quiet."

I'd never heard him sound upset like that. My heart began to pound. "Did they call?"

"Letitia got a letter from their lawyer yesterday."

"What did the letter say?"

"They want to sue us for the chair."

I drew in my breath.

"How is Letitia doing?"

"She's in shock. Doesn't know what we'll do."

"You need a lawyer, too," I said.

Calvin spat out the words. "Like we can afford one!"

I felt awful. I felt responsible. "Talk to Thomas," I said, because it was the only way I could help.

Calvin let me hear an anger he'd never allowed himself before, not with me. "Accuse us like we're criminals! Say we stole it! Make us prove we didn't!"

14

TAKE A DEEP BREATH

ONE EVENING, NOT LONG AFTER OUR NEAR-FIGHT, ADAM and I lay together after making love, my head on his shoulder, his hand resting on the curve of my hip. "I feel so good," he said, his voice low and drowsy.

"I feel good too," I said. That we could agree on.

"I've been so happy, being here with you."

"Likewise."

He shifted a little. "Does your family know about me? Have you told them?"

"Not yet."

"Why not?"

"I just wanted to keep it quiet for a while." *Until I know where we're going.* "What about you? Have you told your family?"

"Just that I'm seeing someone. My mother's excited about it. 'We'd love to meet her! Invite her here for dinner.'"

I raised my head to look at him. "That's not such a good idea."

"Why not?"

I sighed. "You know why not. It will be all over Temple Israel right away, and in fifteen minutes they'll have us engaged and under the huppah."

He was smiling. "And is that such a bad thing?"

I turned to face him directly. "No, not if we both agree that's where we want to go."

He asked, "Where do you want to go?"

My chest began to feel tight. "I'm fine where we are right now. We have a good time, we enjoy each other's company, and we're helping each other get over a divorce." I propped myself on my elbow, which meant pulling away from him. I asked the question I'd been dreading. "What about you?"

He looked down.

"Adam?"

"More than that," he whispered.

I said, "I think you're way ahead of me, then."

He looked up and touched my cheek, and for the first time since we'd gotten back together, it didn't feel like a caress. It felt as heavy as a vow. His voice was very soft. "Nat, I can't lie to you. Or to myself." His eyes met mine, so dark and so bright at the same time. "I love you."

There was more. I let him say it.

"It's as though I never forgot how to love you."

The tight feeling in my chest grew worse. "Adam, what do you want?"

Still touching my face, he said, "I want the chance to try again. To get it right this time."

The nineteenth century had the perfect response for a situation like this. *Oh, sir, your proposal does me such an honor. But I'm afraid that I must refuse.* It was a lot better than the contemporary version: *Sorry, I don't feel the same way.*

I put my hand over his and resisted the impulse to pull it from my cheek. "We're very far apart on this one," I said.

His face grew soft. "That could change."

"If we both want it to." I moved my hand.

He sighed. He caressed my cheek and let his hand slide away. "I surprised you," he said. "I dumped it on you. I'm sorry."

I nodded.

"Is it something you'd think about? Something we can talk about later?"

"I'd like some time to think about it."

He put his arms around me, and I thought again about the nineteenth-century lady who would have removed her gloved hand from her would-be suitor's, smiling as she did so. I moved close to reassure Adam I still cared about him. I did, but now I was full of confusion, and our embrace was fraught with my ambivalence.

THE WOODSONS' legal trouble weighed on me, too. It wasn't enough to call Josh to ask for his reassurance. I wanted to see him, and he met me at a Vietnamese restaurant near his office. Their pho was as comforting as my grandmother's chicken soup, and as soon as I ordered it, Josh asked me, "What's wrong, Nat?"

I hadn't realized how much I'd missed the ready

sympathy of my family. "It's personal," I said. "Can I dump it on you?"

"Sure," he said, and I thought of everything he'd ever done for me as a loving big brother.

"I've been seeing someone, and it isn't going well." It hurt to let myself admit it. "I don't think it's going to last."

He reached for the hand that wasn't holding a ceramic spoon and covered it with his own.

I said, "When I decided to open the business and buy a house, Dad kept asking me if it was a rebound thing. This is definitely a rebound thing."

"I'm so sorry, Nat."

Thank you for not asking who it is. I said, "There's a business question, too. A legal question."

He smiled. "I can't promise I'll have an answer for that, either."

"I just need to talk about it."

He squeezed my hand and let it go. He wasn't the lawyer yet; he was still the concerned big brother, worried about me. "Spill it."

"The Powells are suing the Woodsons over the chair."

"I'm not the least bit surprised."

"Did you know?"

"No. I'm not involved in this, and neither is my firm. They've retained someone else. I have no idea who."

"Could you find out?"

"I could nose around, sure. What's going on?"

"Letitia got a letter from the Powells' attorney."

"A demand letter?"

"All I know is that it outlined their intent to sue."

Now he was the lawyer again. "A demand letter is a

shot over the bow to get someone to sit down for a negotiation. That's it. But it's very effective in intimidating people who don't know the legal process."

"Letitia's very upset. And so is Calvin, who knows too much about the legal process. I don't know why, but from his reaction, I suspect he was convicted of something. He's in a panic."

"Even if this goes to court, it's a civil suit. The Powells want the chair, or they want damages. No one is going to prison over this." He frowned. "Have the Woodsons retained a lawyer?"

"They're looking for one." I thought of Thomas.

He shook his head. "I couldn't get involved in this, even if I wanted to."

I nodded.

"And you shouldn't be, either."

I sighed. "If you find out who's representing the Powells, will you let me know?"

"There's no harm in that."

I was surprised to hear from Josh the next day. "I have something for you."

"The Powells' lawyer? How did you find out?"

He laughed. "Networking," he said.

"Who is it?"

"A guy named Bradley Sexton. Civil litigator. Good old boy, even though he's a little young for it. A big smile on the surface and an alligator's jaws just underneath."

"How well do you know him?"

"I met him once at an ABA function. It was memorable, let me tell you."

"Why? What did he do?"

"He gave me a big aw-shucks grin and said, 'Raskin? Isn't that a Jewish name?' I said to him, 'Why would you ask that?' He said, 'Just making conversation. Don't take it the wrong way.' I gave him the coldest stare I could manage. 'I'll take it as it's meant. As an anti-Semitic slur.'"

"He just walked up to you and said that?"

"Yes, and you can bet he remembers me for it, too."

"I can guess how he feels about Black people."

"Oh, it's the full neo-Confederate ball of wax."

"I see why the Powells like him," I said, feeling queasy. "It's not good news, but thanks for letting me know."

"Nat, I know you feel responsible for the Woodsons, but let them find their own lawyer and let their lawyer fight it out with this guy. Please."

WHY WAS everyone telling me to leave this alone like it was a darkened basement in a horror movie? I decided that "leave it alone" meant "don't try to hire the Woodsons a lawyer or give them legal advice." It didn't prohibit me from calling them to offer moral support.

I decided to call Calvin, but he beat me to it. He came into the shop early on Saturday morning. He looked so tired and worried I wanted to cheer him up, if only a little. I said, "The blue cat is still here."

He didn't smile.

"How's it going, Calvin?"

He glanced at Gideon, who sat behind the counter, next to me, keeping an eye on things. He said, "I guess I'd like to take a look at the cat after all."

I took the key with me, but when we stood before the case, out of Gideon's earshot, Calvin said, "We started looking for a lawyer. We're still looking."

"Did you talk to Thomas? Is he helping you?"

"He says he might know someone. I don't know how we're going to pay a lawyer, even if he finds one." He rubbed his face. "I don't want to go into court, not ever again."

I'd been right. "This isn't the same."

"Judge is a judge. Courtroom's a courtroom. Nothing good ever happened to me in a place like that."

It wasn't right to ask what had happened. "See what Thomas finds out," I said.

He stared into the case at the blue cat.

"Do you want to take a look at it?"

He shook his head.

AFTER CALVIN LEFT, Gideon asked me, "You all right, Miss Minerva?"

"I'm fine. I'm worried about Calvin. About all the Woodsons."

"Anything else on your mind?"

I wanted so badly to talk to him freely again. "Nothing you want to hear about," I said, a little too sharply.

"I can tell it's making you crazy," he said.

"Well, as you keep telling me, my love life ain't none of

your business, is it? Don't ask me about something you don't want to know about."

He tensed up, as though I'd touched a sore spot. He hesitated, weighing his words, and finally he said, "How well do you know the Bible, Miss Minerva?"

"Some of it, pretty well."

"Are you acquainted with Proverbs 26:11?"

Gideon's grandfather had been a preacher, but I was in no mood for a Scripture lesson. "Not off the top of my head."

"Go home and look it up."

I took my headache and my attitude home with me, and as soon as I shut the door behind me, I made a beeline for the bookcase. I'd received a copy of the Jewish Publication Society version of the Old Testament when I was bat mitzvahed, but the one I kept on the shelf—the one I swore by—was the King James version. I fell into my big armchair, the only embrace I liked right now, and riffled through the pages, looking for the verse Gideon had pointed out to me.

"As a dog returneth to his vomit, so a fool returneth to his folly."

I slammed the book shut, my face hot. Had Jude told him? How did he know?

Another verse came to me, from the Testament that I hadn't read every week in Temple, but had somehow sunk into my bones, growing up as a Southerner. I didn't know it by heart; it came to me a paraphrase. I thought, *When I was a child, I spoke as a child, I understood as a child, I thought as a child: but when I grew up, I put away childish things. For now we see through a glass, darkly; but then face-to-face.*

With the full benefit of adult hindsight, I saw how young I'd been at sixteen, when I fell in love with Adam. I'd been overwhelmed that I had caught the eye—and the heart—of a prince. I'd spun myself a fairy tale, about a pure and perfect love, two souls and two bodies in seamless harmony.

When I grew up... But it hadn't been like that. Jude, whom I'd thought was stupid for being a cheerleader, had been able to see through Adam's veneer of charm. Beneath it, he'd needed constant love and reassurance, and he'd found it in me. I'd been so happy to act as his right hand in youth group. But there, as in the rest of our relationship, I'd done all the work, propping him up and making him look good as he took all the credit.

It couldn't last, and it hadn't. My acceptance letter from Columbia University had been enough to threaten it. We'd seen our relationship in black and white. Tennessee or New York. Together forever or torn apart. He'd pleaded, and I'd run.

I saw through a glass, darkly... I'd never let myself think about why I'd run. Now I confronted it, face-to-face.

Adam had seen our future with unshaken confidence, a clear path strewn with rose petals. Our college romance, a happy continuation of the one in high school. Our marriage, full of connubial bliss. He'd assumed that I wanted what he wanted, and he'd done everything he could to manipulate me into coming with him. Into staying with him.

I shook my head as I lifted my coffee cup. I was hardly going to break up with Adam again because he'd used and manipulated me when we were in high school together. I took a sip of coffee. It was cold and bitter.

If I broke up with Adam as an adult, it was because he'd used and manipulated me in the present. He wanted me back, this time for good, and he'd teased me and flirted with me and seduced me to get me there. He'd shamelessly pulled on the string of the past. *Do you remember…*

His words echoed in the morning quiet. *I love you. I never stopped loving you.*

Why had I thought that Adam and I could see each other again, that we could evoke the past with each other, and that we'd remain no more than friends, having a good time together? My desire for him had returned as though it had never gone away. He'd revived feelings much deeper and more dangerous than that.

I want to try again and get it right this time.

I'd grown up. The glass had cleared, and I saw through it clearly. I came face to face with the truth.

This was the twenty-first century, not the nineteenth, and I could say what I meant. *This isn't right for me. This won't work out for either of us. We can't stay together. I'm so sorry, Adam.*

THAT WEEK, in addition to the usual humidity, thick clouds descended over Memphis, and when it wasn't storming, the promise of a storm hung in the air and made the air too thick to breathe. Feeling worse than ever, I called Thomas. Unusually for him, the call went to voicemail. I left him a message. It took him a day to return the call, and when he called back, I was at the shop. "What is it, Nat?" he asked, sounding harassed and tired.

I wished that he'd allow me to ask if he was all right. "Do you have some time to talk?"

There was no background noise, and I wondered if he was at home. "This is as good a time as any."

"I've been worried about the Woodsons, that's all. Calvin stopped by the shop yesterday, and I know he's concerned. I wondered if they'd found a lawyer yet."

Thomas said, "I'm well aware that they need a lawyer."

"Are you—"

His voice was sharp. "Let me handle that."

"Is there anything I can do—"

He cut me off. "No."

I felt my temper rise. "I know it isn't any of my business, but I like Calvin and I feel bad for all of them, and I just wanted to know if you're making any progress in finding someone to assure they get to keep something that's theirs."

"You're absolutely right, it isn't any of your business."

"I don't like unfairness either. Or racism. I want things to come out all right for the Woodsons. Do I get to feel that way?"

He didn't raise his voice. He was coldly angry. "We don't need you to save us. Let us handle this ourselves."

I struggled to reply and realized that any rejoinder would only make him angrier. His ice was worse than rage. "I understand," I said. It was meaningless; it was just something to say instead of cutting him off.

"I wonder if you do." He hung up.

Now I felt worse than before. With pain, I thought of the Thomas I'd glimpsed when we worked together—the impish gay man beneath the self-made connoisseur. His accusation—that I was a white savior, getting in the Woodsons' way—hurt me more than anything the Powells had said to me. I couldn't explain that I was the granddaughter of a Jewish civil rights advocate in Memphis, or that my grandfather's sympathies had given me an uncle who was half Black. Thomas would hear any protest from me as more savior talk.

I thought of him sitting at home, surrounded by his collection of racist memorabilia and brooding over racial injustices, big and small. I missed the attitude of Black people in Manhattan. None of this politeness until they exploded from keeping it in. They were in your face, like any other New Yorker.

I leaned against the case. I needed to sit down. I wished I could lie down. I called to Gideon, "I'm going in back for a minute."

In the back room, I sat down and laid my head on the rickety little table, feeling the metal cool against my cheek, trying to catch my breath. I couldn't.

I don't know how long I stayed like that, but Gideon's voice roused me. "Hey, Miss Minerva, you all right?" he asked.

I lifted my head. "Just tired." A little too tired to say, *You were right.*

He opened the refrigerator and took out a bottle of water. "Would this help any?"

"You'd do that for me? After quoting Proverbs at me?"

He flushed. "I was out of line," he said.

I wished I could tell him he'd been right. "Okay," I said.

He handed me the bottle.

I uncapped it and took a drink. "That helps," I said. "Thanks."

He sat down. "I know your love life still ain't none of my business."

"Apology accepted," I said.

He hesitated, as though he wanted to say more, but I shook my head.

"This is appraisal business." Letting him back in. Friends and business associates again.

"Is it the Woodsons? Something going on with the Woodsons?"

I was so miserable that I didn't care he'd eavesdropped on Calvin. "The Powells are suing them for the chair."

"That's got to be a mess."

I stared at the table. My head felt too heavy for my neck. "Everyone's told me to leave it alone," I said. "I can't do anything, and I feel like hell."

"Hey," he said. "Why is it up to you to fix it?"

I knew what he meant, but I thought of Adam, too. I raised my head. "Thomas just reamed me out for that. Handed my white savior ass to me."

He said, "Got him in a sore spot, didn't you?"

"He's all over sore spots."

Gideon gave me the ghost of a grin. "I know him." He touched my arm. "If there's anything I can do, anything Jude can do, let us know. We'll do it."

I nodded. My head was starting to ache. "I wish I could think of something. If I do, I'll ask both of you."

He put his hand over mine, as Josh had. Josh's fingers

were soft, but Gideon's were callused. I'd forgotten how warm his skin felt. "There's always hope," he said. "Sorrow may last for the night, but joy comes in the morning."

"I know that one. It's from the Psalms, too, isn't it?"

"Psalm 30, verse 5. They say it at every Baptist funeral."

Bad as I felt, that gave me a ghost of a smile, too. "Some cheerer upper."

He tightened his hand over mine. "We take what we can get in this life."

"Hope? Or love, too?" I thought of Adam again, and the truth I owed him.

"Both."

AT NINE IN THE MORNING, I was still in my bathrobe, sitting in my Morris chair, letting a cup of coffee cool by my elbow. For the first time since I'd opened the shop, I wasn't enthusiastic about going in. I looked around my pleasing living room without pleasure.

I thought of my admission to Josh—that starting a business and buying a house in Memphis had been decisions I'd made on the rebound. I'd been so sure they were the right ones. This morning, doubtful about Adam, shaken by Thomas's rebuff, I was no longer sure.

I sighed. I was just about to get up to take a hurried shower when the phone rang. Caller ID showed an unfamiliar number, but I picked up. It might be a customer. It might be a client for an appraisal, as though I needed one.

Like a hole in my head, as my Raskin grandmother would say.

An unfamiliar voice said, "Ms. Raskin? My name is Kenya Davis, and I'm an attorney in Atlanta. I specialize in civil litigation, and I'm working with the Woodson family in Memphis in the matter of their antique chair."

So Thomas had found them a lawyer. "How did you get my name?"

"From Letitia and Calvin Woodson. They told me about your role in appraising their chair, and in working with the Powell estate as well."

Her voice was low-pitched and confident, the accent smoothed away. I couldn't place her. "And why are you calling me?"

"I understand you're a licensed appraiser with expertise in early American decorative art. I'm hoping to talk to you about the chair and about the situation related to the Powell family's intention to sue."

I said, "Have you talked to Thomas Waverley?"

"I have, since he brought the Woodsons' situation to my attention."

"Then you know that he's very protective of the Woodsons. And that he's a prickly individual in his own right."

She said, "Yes, I've seen that." She didn't permit herself to laugh, but there was a note of humor in her voice. "I've dealt with him before. Is there a complication?"

"He and I have a business relationship, since he rents case space in my antique shop. He was the one who connected me with the Woodsons. But now that I've finished the appraisal on their chair, he has strong feelings about my involvement. He's asked me not to inter-fere, to put it bluntly."

She said, "It's hardly interfering if I ask you to provide your expertise."

"In what way?"

"Your expertise in researching an object's ownership."

"What we call provenance."

"As I'm learning, Ms. Raskin."

I hesitated. I'd been flattered in every possible way. This was subtle.

She said, "I don't want to ruffle Thomas, either. This isn't the first case he's referred to me, and I hope it won't be the last. I think we both need him, and we both want to preserve a working relationship with him. I believe we can work together on that. Among other things."

She was presuming, not so subtly now. "What are you suggesting, Ms. Davis?"

"I'm going to be in Memphis in a week or so to meet with the Woodsons in person. If you're amenable, I'd like to meet with you."

As I hesitated, she said, "Just an exploratory conversation."

"My brother is a lawyer. That's what he says as he reels them in."

At that she laughed, and I heard her background in it, Southern and Black. "So you know just what you're in for."

I wasn't ready to laugh, not yet, but I said to her, "Yes, I'm pretty sure I am."

15

KENYA DAVIS

I looked Kenya Davis up. She worked for a big law firm in Atlanta, as white-shoe as you could get in the new South, and on the website, hers was a lonely brown visage among the white faces. An Atlanta native, she'd done her undergrad at Howard University, but she'd made the leap to do her law degree at Harvard. Glossy black hair, straightened and bobbed, brushed the shoulders of her dark gray suit. In her photo, she smiled, but she stood before a big glass window with her arms folded. A combative posture, but oddly reassuring: *I'll fight for you.*

As I put my phone away, the shop door opened, and Thomas came in, carrying a box.

Jude greeted him with a smile, saying, "New merch?"

The face above the crisp white shirt and the jaunty bow tie was unsmiling, even though his voice was pleasant. "Yes," he said.

"Anything good?"

"I hope so." He set the box on the counter and said to me, "I hear Kenya Davis talked to you." Still pleasant, but cold, as he'd been cold the last time we talked on the phone.

"Yes, she called me. On Calvin's suggestion, I understand."

He rested his hands on the counter, his slender, well-kept, scholar's hands. "And I hear you're going to meet with her when she comes to Memphis."

"Yes, she said she wanted some background on the situation."

"I would have been glad to fill her in," he said, and grievance tinged his voice.

"I'm sure you could have, and I'm sure she knows that. She decided to ask me."

He tilted his head and asked Jude, "Could I have my key, please?"

Jude rummaged for his case key and handed it to me. I handed it to him.

He picked up his box and walked to his case without thanking either of us.

A WEEK LATER, I opened the door to Kenya Davis. In person, she was as polished as the photo on her law firm's website, but without her arms crossed, she looked cordial rather than confrontational. She wore a black wool suit, beautifully tailored, and she carried an expensive leather shoulder bag. Once inside, she shook my hand. Despite the heat, her palm was cool and dry. "It's a pleasure to meet you, Ms. Raskin."

"Call me Nat."

She smiled and looked briefly around the shop. "This is a lovely place," she said. "How long have you been in business?"

"Not long. Since the beginning of the year. We're doing remarkably well. Are you a collector?"

"No, but I'm always on the lookout for unusual things. I know what I like."

I imagined her in a luxury condo in Atlanta or a trendy loft. "You're welcome to look around, if we have time."

She said, "I'm afraid that will have to wait."

"Conflict of interest?" I said.

"I can't afford even the appearance of conflict of interest," she said.

I said, "There's space in back to sit. It's not as nice as out front, but no one will knock on the door and ask if we're open."

At the table in back, she sat, pulled a yellow pad from her bag, and politely declined my offer of a bottle of sparkling water. "How did you get involved in appraising the Woodson family's chair?"

I told her about Josh and his referral to the Powells. About the initial appraisal and the discovery of the Thomas Tufft chairs. About the way the Woodsons' chair surfaced, and how I'd done a formal appraisal for them, with the valuation that stunned the family. About the Powell family's assumption that the Woodson chair belonged to them, and their rage that it did not.

She said, "It's helpful that you have a relationship with both parties."

"And complicating."

She nodded. "You worked for Sotheby's Auction House in New York, right? Tell me about that."

I gave her the LinkedIn summary. I explained about provenance at Sotheby's. "When I wasn't managing clients —I'm sure you know what that's like—I spent a lot of my time researching history of ownership. At an auction house, that's especially important for marketing purposes. You don't want to mislead or exaggerate. But if you have bills of sale and wills that show the chain of ownership, the asking price goes up."

"Did you ever get involved in a case of disputed ownership?"

"No. Most of the pieces I researched had been in the same New England or Philadelphia family for centuries. But I have friends who worked on establishing ownership of Nazi-looted art. That's quite a thorny problem."

"You mentioned bills of sale and wills as—well, for lack of a better term, evidence—in establishing provenance. What have you found so far?"

"The Powells have family papers that go back to their roots in Virginia in the 1770s. Bills of sale, business papers—plantation ledgers, I'm sorry to say—and diaries. The Woodsons have nothing like that. The chair itself and family lore."

"And you haven't found anything to prove transfer of ownership?"

"No, but I wasn't looking for it the first time I went through the Powell family papers. I need to go back to look again. My friends who are archivists have told me more than once that the evidence is often hiding in plain sight. You just need to look for it with fresh eyes."

"Can you fill me in on the Powells?"

"Old money. Old South. The estate is worth a lot. The older brother, Owen, has been acting strange for someone who could realize a pile of money if he scheduled the estate sale and put the house on the market. He's gotten fixated on a couple of heirlooms we can't find. And now he's focused on the Woodson chair."

"What's your take?"

"I have the impression that he's under some financial pressure. I don't know the particulars. But there's some family issue in there, too. And that I don't have a clue about."

"What about the sister?"

"Joyce? She goes along with him until he overdoes it. Then she pulls him back. But she's been back and forth—upset about the heirlooms and eager to get things settled."

"Have you met the Powells' lawyer?"

"No, but my brother has. He told me quite a story. Evidently Bradley Sexton walked up to Josh at an ABA function and in lieu of an introduction, made an anti-Semitic remark."

"In a roomful of lawyers? That takes some chutzpah." I laughed, and she said, "You pick it up at Harvard Law."

Yiddish, along with self-confidence.

She stopped taking notes. She said, "So there are two problems here. One is finding the proof of ownership. The other is handling the Powells, who sound like they have some strong and irrational feelings about this chair."

"Yes, that's exactly it," I said.

"I'm curious about something that I saw in your

report. The Powells owned the Woodsons' ancestor. Does that figure in?"

"Ghosts of the past," I said. "I see you're a Southerner yourself."

"Born and raised in Atlanta, which is an oddball corner of the South. But my relatives are from Augusta, which is a stone's throw from South Carolina. I know exactly what you mean."

I asked, "What got you interested in taking this on? Besides Thomas's powers of persuasion?"

She said, "I'm interested in taking on cases that make restitution for slavery. This is a good way to flex those muscles." She laughed. "And there's quite an irony here, watching the descendants of former enslavers try to sue the descendants of the people they enslaved."

"More an injustice than an irony, I'd think," I said.

She smiled at that.

I liked her, this woman who could switch between Howard and Harvard, and whose cool, polished exterior only reinforced her interior strength. If we'd met in New York, I'd want to cultivate her friendship. "What happens next?" I asked.

Kenya said, "This isn't a case. It shouldn't go to court. What are the Powells going to recover? Damages from the Woodsons, who have nothing of value besides the chair? It's a power grab, not a legal maneuver."

"You want to stay out of court. Like my brother, the estate attorney. I think he feels he's failed if anyone goes to court."

"I'm a litigator. I don't mind going to court. But the suit has to have some merit."

"So," I said. "How do you plan to stay out of court?"

"There's something I've been thinking about since I learned about you. Finding proof of ownership would put this thing to rest. And that's apparently what you do."

"You want me to research the provenance." I sighed. "I'll need the Powells' permission to go through their papers again. And I'm on their shit list, to put it bluntly."

"I'd like to propose to their lawyer that we hire you jointly to look into the provenance."

"Work for adversarial parties?"

"Work to find the truth."

I was so surprised that I laughed. "You think that Mr. Sexton would agree? You think the Powells would agree?"

"We can ask, can't we? It saves time. It saves money. It saves face."

"That's some chutzpah," I said, echoing what she'd said to me.

"I'd like to float it with Brad Sexton. And I'd like you to accompany me when I meet with him." She gave me a sharp, appraising eye.

"You want me to be the Sotheby's expert with a Southern accent."

Now she laughed. "Half of litigation is theater," she said.

I OPENED my closet door and hesitated as I thought about what to wear to meet with the Powells' lawyer. Kenya would be in her most forbidding black suit, broadcasting I AM AN ATTORNEY. I thought briefly about wearing

Manhattan black in solidarity. Instead, I put on black silk trousers with a cream linen blazer, and as a nod to Southern taste, a floral scarf. Sotheby's, with a Southern accent.

The address Kenya had given me was an old building in downtown Memphis, a lawyer's office. The lobby was very much old South, deep homage to an English men's club, wood paneling, red leather upholstery, mediocre oil paintings on the walls. When I met Kenya there, I whispered, "They have lousy taste in art."

In the law office, the receptionist was slender and blonde, with a honeyed accent. That was old South too. She gave Kenya the side-eye and talked sweetly to me.

I said politely, "Ms. Davis has the appointment."

With reluctance, the receptionist spoke to Kenya. "What is this regarding?"

Kenya was armored by poise. "Mr. Sexton is expecting us."

We sat. We waited. The lawyers, the paralegals, the admins, and the clients who streamed by were all white. The only Black face was a man delivering office supplies. He gave the receptionist a big smile. At the sight of Kenya, his genial mask slipped.

I let it bother me.

Kenya asked, "You doing all right?"

"Getting upset on your behalf."

"Don't waste your energy."

We were ushered to Sexton's office by a white woman, fiftyish and dark-haired, in a floral print dress that seemed better suited to a garden party than a law office. Her manner toward me was friendly. She ignored Kenya.

"This way, dear," she said to me, and I was reminded of my grandmother Beardsley's friends. I thought, *We're not here for a garden party.*

We walked past offices, and through the open doors I glimpsed that everyone was white. Josh's firm had started to hire Black associates a decade ago. I'd met a few of them. They were painfully polite, and they looked as though the effort of leading the way made their blood pressure go up. I wondered if this firm had any Black employees.

Bradley Sexton's office had more paneling, dark red leather upholstery, an old-fashioned Persian carpet, and another bad oil painting. He gave Kenya a cool greeting and threw a "little lady" glance at me.

"Are you related to Josh Raskin?" he asked.

"He's my brother. Did you know my mother's people are Beardsleys? Eleanor Beardsley Reynolds, who lives in Cordova."

He was momentarily puzzled that I could be a Beardsley as well as a Raskin. "Isn't Bill Reynolds her son?"

"Yes, he's my uncle."

"We're acquainted. We've golfed together at the Memphis Club."

I rested my hand on the floral scarf and laid it on thick. "Oh, how is Uncle Bill's handicap?"

"Do you play?" Sexton asked me.

I smiled. "No. Don't even ask about my handicap." I looked down at the mahogany of the meeting table. It was brand-new. Nice wood. Not cheap, even for a new piece.

Sexton had trouble making eye contact with Kenya. When he spoke, his tone was veiled antagonism, as though they were already adversaries in court. "So, Ms. Davis, are your clients interested in negotiating?"

"Not yet, Counselor."

"Then why are you here? And why is Ms. Raskin here?"

I was a Raskin again, not a Beardsley.

Kenya said, "Ms. Raskin is an expert in American decorative art with fifteen years of experience at Sotheby's Auction House in New York."

"How is that relevant?"

"Ms. Raskin has researched the history of many nineteenth-century items, including furniture as well as paintings." Kenya glanced at the indifferent picture on the wall.

Sexton looked at me. Happy to educate him, I explained provenance.

"Proof of ownership," he said, as though we were too ignorant to make the connection.

Kenya said, "Ms. Raskin has the expertise to dig for that."

"Can she find it?" Sexton asked.

As my grandmother on the Raskin side would say, *What is this she business?* "I can try," I said. "I know the Powell family has papers that go back to the 1820s. I've looked at them once to establish the provenance of the chairs the Powell family owns. I'd like to go back for another look to see if we can do the same thing for the Woodson family's chair."

Sexton crossed his arms over his chest. "I'm not sure they'd agree to that."

Kenya said, "Prolonging this matter means time and

expense. It means diminishing the estate their mother left them."

"Of course, I realize that," he said. "I also know they're eager to pursue the matter. To press it, if necessary."

I rushed in. "Look, if I can establish the provenance, we can resolve this, without question."

He gave me a withering look: *You aren't the lawyer here.* "I'd be careful about asserting that."

I gave him the Sotheby's treatment. "I don't assert anything unless I have iron-clad documentation," I said. "Proof that can stand up in court."

"Did you go to court often at Sotheby's?"

"We didn't have to."

"I can broach the subject with them," he said.

"Will you let me know if they say yes?" I felt stubborn enough to insist.

"Why?"

"I'd like to meet with them when you do."

He said, "That's up to them, not you." His look said, *Pushy, aren't you?*

I touched the floral silk again, reminding myself I was a Southerner, too. "I might be able to help you. Since I know Owen. And I know Joyce."

"I hear they fired you," he said.

And you acted like you didn't know me when I walked in. I let him have it. "I lived in New York a long time. We ask for what we want." I glanced at Kenya, and she smothered a smile. *Chutzpah,* I thought.

Sexton looked sour, but he said, "I'll have my girl call you once we've scheduled."

After we left, we both waited until we were off the

elevator and in the main-floor lobby. I said, "You hate his guts, don't you?"

Kenya said, "I won't dignify that with an answer."

"And the feeling is mutual, I can tell."

Kenya said, "I wonder how old his secretary is."

"If she's over eighteen, she's not a girl," I said.

As I waited to hear from Bradley Sexton's admin, my personal business was in limbo, too. I had some news I had to deliver to Adam, and I'd never been so reluctant to talk to anyone.

Both Jude and Gideon noticed that I was preoccupied. Since he'd quoted me the Bible, Gideon had kept his observations to himself. He left right at closing time, and Jude helped me shut down the shop. She said, "Let me tally the daily sales."

"I've got it. I'm distracted, not addled."

"You have time for a drink after we close? E&H?"

"Sure."

She put her hand on the pile of receipts. "Let me total those. You go turn off the lights."

I shook my head.

In E&H, Jude said, "I'm buying."

"Just one beer. I want to get home in one piece."

When the drinks and the onion rings came, she said, "I shudder to watch you eat those."

"I'm a little old for that mama tone," I said, but I didn't really mind it.

"What's going on? I bet it's something you don't want to talk to your own mama about."

I asked, "Did you talk to Gideon?"

She said, "I couldn't stand it anymore. I did."

"Thanks a lot. He got mad as hell at me. Told me what a fool I've been."

"He isn't mad at you."

"Could have fooled me."

She said, "Can't you see it? He's mad at Adam. And at himself for not being able to do anything about it."

"Well, he should be happy to know what I'm intending to do."

Now she daintily picked the smallest ring from the basket and ate it in tiny bites. She wiped her fingers. "Spill it."

I said, "I'm going to break up with Adam."

I was braced to hear "I told you so," but she asked, "What happened?"

"He's in love with me, or he thinks he is."

"He said so?"

I nodded. "He wants to get serious. He wants to try again."

"And you don't."

I said, "I'm not in love with him. I can't possibly make a commitment to him." I felt misery wash over me. "I can't keep seeing him and letting him think there's a future, because there isn't." I thought of the verse Gideon had directed me to. "He wants to try again and do it right. There's no doing it right. I have to walk away."

She drank from the bottle, her eyes meeting mine.

I said, "Don't say it."

"What?"

"I told you so. I know you did. And you were right, too."

She shook her head.

I looked away. "I don't know how to break up with him so I don't hurt him."

Her expression hardened. "No," she said, leaning forward. "You need to break up with him so he doesn't hurt you."

"He's the one who's in too deep. I'm not."

She said, "I don't mean hurt your feelings."

"What do you mean?"

She'd been drinking from the bottle, and she set it down hard on the table, startling me. "I mean really hurt you."

Startled, I said, "You mean physically? He wouldn't do that."

She said, "When you tell him, do it in public."

"Why would you tell me that?"

"Trust me, I have a good reason."

I knew she'd had a rough divorce, but I didn't like understanding what she meant. "I know Adam," I said slowly. "He isn't like that."

She met my eyes, and I didn't like what I saw in her face. "That's what my family said about my husband. 'He isn't like that. He wouldn't do that.'"

And they'd been wrong. I'd never asked directly before. "What happened to you?"

She wasn't bitter. She was matter-of-fact, and that was worse. "Twist your arm hard enough to sprain your wrist? He wouldn't do that. Hit you hard enough to black your eye and split your lip? He wouldn't do that. Threaten to kill you if you left him? He wouldn't do that."

Evidently he'd done all of that.

"When I told my husband I wanted a divorce, he beat the crap out of me. He broke my nose and three of my ribs. He told me if I left him, he'd kill me. He meant it."

"I am so sorry," I said.

She said, "Don't be. Take care of yourself. Trust me on this. Break up with Adam in a public place."

I RETURNED to Bradley Sexton's office, where the receptionist didn't recognize me without Kenya in tow, and everyone was polite to me. In Sexton's office, Joyce and Owen waited. I was back in the principal's office, as I had been in Josh's office. Owen frowned as I sat. He said to Sexton, "I still don't understand why she's here."

I had nothing to lose here. "Nice to see you again, Owen."

Joyce said, "Hi, Nat. How have you been?"

"Just fine, Joyce," I said. *This is theater, and I'm doing my best to act in it.*

Sexton said, "I've shared Ms. Davis's proposal with the Powells, and they've agreed to discuss the possibility of hiring you to research the provenance of the disputed chair."

That was for Owen, still scowling, not for me. I thought, *That's Sexton's problem to manage, not mine.* I nodded.

Owen said, "I don't see why you need to come back to

look at our papers again. Didn't you already go through everything?"

"Yes, I did, but I was looking for the provenance on your chairs, not on the Woodson family's chair. If I go back with a fresh perspective, I may see something I didn't see before."

"How long will that take? And how much will it cost?"

"I'm going to give you an estimate on the fly. A week. Forty billable hours, including the research and the report. That's probably on the high side. If it's less, I'll charge less."

Sexton said, "The legal team will be hiring Ms. Raskin, just as we'd hire an investigator or any other consultant."

"You'll add it to our bill," Owen said.

Joyce shifted in her chair, her mouth pressed into a thin, angry line.

I was still in what-the-hell mode. "Seventy-five hundred dollars is a lot less than whatever it would cost to go to court."

Owen said, "How do we know we can trust you?"

Before I could remind him about my ethical and legal constraints, Joyce interjected. "What are you worried about? Do you think she's going to steal our dusty old papers?"

"After everything that's gone missing—"

Joyce said, "You're welcome to sit in the house with her while she goes through the papers. To make sure she doesn't walk off with anything."

Sexton said, "I'm sure that won't be necessary."

Owen raised his voice. "After everything that's gone wrong with this appraisal—"

So did Joyce. "What's the matter with you? Do you want to go to court and eat up everything Mother left us? Just schedule the estate sale and put the house on the market. And be done with it."

Owen leaned forward and curled his hands into fists on the tabletop. "That chair is ours."

Spots of color appeared on Joyce's pale cheeks. "Let Nat look. Let her find out whatever she finds out. If it's ours, we take it and we're done. If it's theirs, we know and we're done. Don't be a horse's hind end, Owen."

"And what if there's nothing to find?" Owen said.

Joyce shouted, "I don't care! And if you try to take it to court, I'll sue you myself!"

I heard two voices in my head, Josh's and Kenya's: *There's no grounds for a suit.*

Sexton said, "Please, both of you. It's only sensible to let Ms. Raskin do her research. And once we know what she's found, we'll be able to proceed."

Owen continued to glower.

Sexton said, "Will you allow her access to your family papers?"

Joyce crossed her arms and jutted out her jaw. "I will, and don't you try to stop me, Owen Powell."

"Is that a yes?" I asked, glancing from Owen to Joyce.

In the silence, no one said no.

Sexton said, "I believe it is, Ms. Raskin."

WHEN ADAM CAME OVER, the air was oppressively hot outside; inside, the new a/c system whispered. I hadn't put on music. I didn't want to associate a song or a voice I loved with this moment.

As Adam stood on my porch, I thought, *Oh, sir, you do me such an honor…*

He saw right away that I was upset. As soon as he walked in, he said, "Nat, is there something wrong?"

"Yes," I said.

He reached for me to pull me close. "Bad day?" he asked, fully attentive.

Pulling her gloved hand away… I didn't move, but I said, "No, it's bigger than that."

He released me and met my eyes. "Now you've got me worried."

"Let's sit down." I led him away from the loveseat. I sat him at the table.

"No music?" he asked. "No wine?"

I thought of Nana Raskin, mediating a confrontation between me and my father, telling me ruefully she didn't know what to serve for a family fight. "Not right now," I said.

"What's going on, Nat? What is this about?"

I took a deep breath. "It's about us," I said.

"So you've had time to think about what I said."

"Yes, I have."

He waited.

"We've been kidding about being on the rebound ever since we reconnected," I said. "And I think it's finally caught up with us."

"How so?" His voice cooled.

"You feel like you're ready to start a relationship. A

serious one. And since it's with me, you're hoping we can pick up where we left off in high school."

"I don't deny any of that."

But I must refuse… I laid my hands flat on the table. "Adam, my rebound is different. I'm not ready for any of that. A relationship. A commitment. A future."

He reached for my hand. "You know I'm willing to slow down. To let you catch up."

I felt sick. "That's not going to work out," I said. "Because I know I won't."

"You might change your mind."

With pain, I thought, *Do you remember?* "We had this conversation fifteen years ago. You asked me if I'd change my mind about breaking up. I knew I wouldn't. And I didn't."

He drew his brows together. "What are you telling me, Nat?"

"I can't keep doing this, Adam. I can't keep seeing you. I have to stop."

When he spoke, his voice was bitter. "This is just like last time," he said. "Do you remember?"

I closed my eyes, because I did, and the memory hurt.

He closed his hand over my wrist. "Look at me, Nat."

Alarmed, I opened my eyes and looked at him.

He said, "This is just like the last time. I got too close. You got scared. And now you're going to run away."

"No," I said. That was his interpretation, not mine.

"I know you too well," he said, but it wasn't kind or intimate. *I know you well enough to hurt you.*

"I think you should go."

"Just like that? Is this it?"

"Please."

He rose. "Just like last time," he said.

I rose and walked toward the door.

He followed me, and when I opened the door, he stood there, letting the heat of the summer evening rush into the house. Under the hurt on his face, anger began to smolder. "There's one thing that's different from last time," he said. "One way you've grown up a little. This time you didn't feel the need to pick a fight."

I watched him leave, and I thought, *It is just like last time. We got it wrong again, exactly the same way.*

16

WE LOST THE CIVIL WAR

T HE NEXT DAY, IN THE SHOP, J UDE PULLED ME ONTO THE sidewalk. "You look like hell," she said.

"I did it. It's over."

She shook her head.

I said, "Don't say anything to Gideon."

"I won't."

Later that morning, I asked both Jude and Gideon, "Would you guys be willing to work on the Powell estate again?"

Jude kept my confidence. She asked, "Have they scheduled the estate sale?"

"Unfortunately not." I told them about the suit and explained that both law firms had contributed to hiring me as a consultant to research the history of ownership.

"What are we looking for?" Jude asked.

"We're making sure we didn't miss something we weren't looking for the last time. Proof that somebody sold the chair. Or proof that they didn't."

"And what if we don't find it?"

"Let me worry about that when we get there."

"Those Civil War papers ever turn up?" Gideon asked.

"Not that I know of. We'll ask."

"Nat, you feeling okay?" he asked.

"I'll feel better once we go out to Cordova and get this done."

THE THREE OF US, Jude, Gideon, and myself, stood on the steps of the Powell house in Cordova, uncomfortable in the morning humidity that promised heat, waiting for Joyce. As Joyce opened the door, her eyes rested on Jude, then on Gideon. She said, "Well, it's the Three Musketeers, back again."

Jude said, "How do you know we're not the Three Stooges?"

Despite herself, Joyce laughed as she let us in.

The house was still and cool, as undisturbed as we'd left it. No one had been here since. "Joyce, where are the banker's boxes?" I asked.

She looked even more tired than before, her cheeks drawn, blue shadows under her blue eyes. "Right where you left them last time. In the study."

I said, "Thanks for going to bat to hire me."

"I just want to get this over and done with." She lifted the hair from her neck, even though it was much too cold to sweat in here. "I want to get the house on the market." She gestured to take in the room. "And get the estate sale on the calendar."

Jude said, "There's a local company I can recommend. Both Gideon and I have worked for them. They're good."

"Give me the contact info and I'll sit on Owen." She sighed. "For all the good it will do."

The bell rang. Joyce opened the door and Owen walked in. She followed him into the living room, where we all stood, waiting. She said, "Why did you come by? It's out of your way."

Owen took us in. "I wanted to keep an eye on things."

Joyce sighed again, this time in exasperation. "Do you really think Nat is going to steal the silver?"

"You know I don't trust her. And we've had too many things go missing already."

I pretended that was funny. "Don't worry, these two will keep an eye on me." I reminded him, "Jude Phelps and Gideon Fairchild. You've met them. They helped me with the stuff in the storage locker."

Owen said to Joyce, "You keep them in line."

Joyce said sharply, "You're one to talk. You get hold of yourself."

After Owen left, Jude said, "What's going on with your brother?"

Joyce said, "He's been acting like a horse's ass. I don't have time for it. I trust you to get the job done. Just go ahead and do it."

When Joyce was gone, we walked into the study, where the boxes were neatly stacked, five deep, covering the floor. I stared at them, and I sighed, too.

Gideon said, "Exactly what are we looking for, Nat?"

Today, we'd be friends who did business together. I could manage that. "We're going back through the post-

Civil War stuff to make sure we didn't miss anything related to the twelfth chair. We know the Powells owned it in 1861 when Lucullus Powell made his will. We know it was gone by 1893, when they only had eleven chairs to reupholster. But I'm worried that there's something in the papers for the intervening years that we didn't see, either because we didn't touch every piece of paper, or we touched it and we didn't realize what it told us."

"You sound tired," Jude said.

"I'm as tired as Joyce is."

Jude said, "I'm really surprised they let you come back to do this."

"They didn't hire me this time. The legal team did. Both lawyers pooled resources to bring me in as a consultant. The Powells had veto power, but their lawyer convinced them I was the best person for the job." I sighed again, glad to blame my mood on the job at hand. "It's not exactly a vote of confidence. I guess I was the fastest person. I really want to get this over with, too. Let's move as fast as we can."

We brought the boxes into the dining room. I gave everyone archival gloves, and we went to work. Gideon suggested that he look at the business records, since he knew them, but I said, "Fresh eyes."

"I'll look at them," Jude offered.

I looked at Gideon, and I felt a flicker of humor. "We'll look at the social butterfly records," I said. "You'll love them. Dance cards, scrapbooks, invitations, and holiday cards. Girl stuff."

Gideon said, "When you do an estate sale you put your hands on everything. And look at everything. I've dealt with worse than some teenaged girl's scrapbook with pink ribbons on it."

Jude began to laugh, and I said, "Are you thinking of something gross?"

"Yes," she said, and Gideon began to laugh, too.

"Spare me," I said.

Jude went to work, carefully scrutinizing every page. "This is boring," she said. "A zillion letters to their customers and their lawyer about selling cotton."

I said, "Don't grouse about the haystack. You want to find the needle."

By mid-morning I was tired and bored, too. I felt dusty and sweaty, as though I'd been working in a storage unit instead of the air-conditioned comfort of a living room in Cordova. I stood up and pressed my hands to my lower back.

Gideon said, "Here's something interesting."

"What?" I asked.

"Photograph. From the 1940s, I'd guess."

It was a young Black woman, well turned out in a dark tailored dress and a stylish hat with a little veil over her eyes.

Gideon asked, "Any idea who it is?"

I said, "That's Ruth Anne Thompson as a young woman."

"The housekeeper?" Jude asked. "Why would Evelyn keep a picture of her?"

"They knew each other from childhood. Maybe it was a closer relationship than we realize." Ruth Anne was smiling, and she looked pretty. "Jude, remember that picture of Evelyn Powell as a debutante?"

"I remember that. Gid, keep an eye out. You can't miss it. She's wearing a big poufy dress, and she has a bouquet in her hands. Why?"

I said, "I want to see them side by side."

"Young miss and her servant?" Jude asked.

"Gideon, let me know when you find it."

By lunchtime, we hadn't found anything about the chair, nor had we found Evelyn Powell's photograph. I'd seen this happen before in collections of papers. Sometimes you missed something in plain sight, and sometimes you couldn't find a document or photo you swore you put your hand on a week ago. Now I was unhappy that something else had gone missing.

Jude offered to make the lunch run, and while she was gone, my phone rang. I checked the number, and I put the phone back in my pocket.

Gideon said, "I've never seen you not answer your phone."

"Some callers are people I don't want to talk to."

"You pick up every call, and you talk to telemarketers because you think it might be business for the shop." I flushed, and Gideon said, "I get it. It's none of my business."

"There's no business to care about," I said. "It's over. I broke up with him. He keeps calling me anyway."

"Even though you told him to quit."

I flushed harder. "Of course I told him to quit. He hasn't."

He shook his head.

"I didn't want to mention it. I thought you'd say, 'I told you so.'"

"Well, I won't."

"It's over. Is there still something bothering you?"

He hesitated. "I was out of line with you."

"For quoting Scripture at me?"

"For losing my temper."

"Don't even think about it. We have work to do. I'm glad you're here to help."

"All right, I'll say it, and you can tell me to go to hell if you want."

"You have another Bible verse for me?"

He sighed. "I just wish you'd meet a guy who cares about you and treats you right."

I turned away because there were tears in my eyes.

He touched my shoulder. "Nat? You okay?"

I couldn't turn to face him. "I will be," I said.

He tapped my shoulder again. His voice was very soft. "Yes, you will."

On the second day, we finished going through the boxes. "Nothing," Jude said.

Gideon said, "And we haven't found those papers from the Civil War, either."

"They're still missing, evidently," I said. "I'll ask Joyce. It's beginning to make me a little crazy, how things disappear from this estate."

I called Joyce to ask if she could stop by a little early to close up. "Sure," she said. "I'm already on the road. I'll be there in half an hour."

I told Jude and Gideon to take off, and I waited in the

cool, hushed air of the living room. Where were the Civil War papers? I couldn't imagine the Powells, who had saved their grocery lists from 1823, throwing the ledgers and the diaries away.

The twelfth chair hadn't been hiding in plain sight. It wasn't there. And Evelyn Powell's debutante photograph was gone, too. Perhaps Joyce had found it and taken it as a memento of a happy moment in her mother's life. Perhaps she'd been struck by the strong resemblance between the young Evelyn and herself. It wasn't that important, but I should ask her. I wanted to see it again.

In archival research, as in medical diagnosis, a lot of effort went into ruling something out. Now it was clear that the proof I sought wasn't in the post–Civil War papers.

When Joyce arrived, I told her what we'd found—and what we hadn't. "Do you have any idea what happened to the papers from the Civil War years?"

"Not a clue. I thought we'd looked everywhere in the house. And in that storage unit. I can't imagine where they'd be."

I said, "They have to be somewhere." I sighed. "Don't tell Owen we haven't found them. Not yet."

We looked at each other. She said, "I can just hear him, mad that something else is missing."

"If I weren't so tired, I'd laugh," I said.

Joyce pushed her hair off her forehead. "Me too," she said. She was a little loopy. "Hey, why don't you call Ruth Anne and ask her if she knows where they are?"

"Don't even start."

The gap in the papers bothered me anew. It was

possible that the disruption of the war had prevented these methodical people from continuing to write in their ledgers and their diaries. Or that their papers had been destroyed somehow. I knew all about Sherman's march through Georgia; every Southerner did. I had relatives who still remembered and kept their grievance alive over it. Memphis had fallen to the Union army in July of 1862, a year before the siege of Vicksburg, but I'd never heard about Union army depredation in rural Shelby County. That didn't mean it hadn't happened. Maybe the Yankees had stomped through the Powell property, stolen their silver, and burned their cotton crop to the ground.

I'd been remiss about talking to my mother's side of the family since I returned to Memphis, and it was time to call on my mother's mother. She lived in Cordova, not far from the Powells, as a matter of fact, and I sometimes had a twinge of guilt when I drove out there. Now guilt was buttressed by a desire to unlock my grandmother's memory of the War of Northern Aggression.

Eleanor Beardsley Reynolds was an old-fashioned Southern lady, whose spine had never touched the back of a chair, and whose white hair had never known dye. Her affection for Josh and me had always been thorny. She had never gotten used to being related to people named "Raskin." It wasn't as much anti-Semitism as the old planter family's disdain for someone who had made a fortune by owning a clothing store. When I read Victorian literature and discovered that aristos hated rich tradesmen because they "smelled of the shop," I had to laugh, because I heard my grandmother's voice. Now I smelled of the shop, too. She'd been pleased by my job at

Sotheby's, and now she'd probably tell me how disappointed she was in me for running my own small business.

When she opened the door, she offered her cheek to be kissed. Her skin was powdery, wrinkled despite her lifelong effort to shield it from the sun. At home, at leisure, she wore a Tory Burch tunic over white trousers. She had Ferragamo pumps on her feet and her heirloom pearls at her throat. She didn't smell of commerce, but of Joy perfume, floral and old-fashioned now.

"Natalie," she said. She never used my nickname. She held me at arm's length, scrutinizing me. She'd known just how to make me miserable as an adolescent, telling me that I needed to watch my weight and learn how to walk with grace. My refusal to come out as a debutante at the cotillion had been my revenge on her. But today all she said was, "Come in and sit down."

Her housekeeper, a self-effacing Black woman I'd never met, brought in sesame cookies, a Southern delicacy I'd never eaten anywhere but in her house, and iced tea.

She sipped her tea and said, "Your mother has been keeping me up to date on you. Since you haven't."

"I've been bad, I know. I've been busy. Has Mom told you about the shop?"

"I see you borrowed my mother's name for it."

"It's my name too, Grandmother."

"I suppose so." She sighed. "Divorced," she said.

"He fell in love with someone else. Neither of us wanted to stay married."

She sighed again.

"Did Mom tell you that I was doing an estate appraisal for your neighbors, the Powells?"

"No, she didn't mention it. I wasn't close to Evelyn Powell. And in the last few years of her life, she was very ill. She didn't go out or receive visitors."

"She left quite an estate. As an appraiser, I enjoyed working on it. Lots of lovely things."

"They certainly had the means for lovely things."

"Grandmother, I'm finishing up the appraisal, and we're trying to figure out what happened to the family during the Civil War. I wondered if the Beardsleys had any family stories from that time. If there's anything you remember your own mother or grandmother talking about."

"We fought for the Confederacy. You already know that."

"I'm wondering if there are any stories about what happened in Shelby County after Memphis fell to the Union army."

"I remember my grandmother telling me how all the people on the place ran away. Picked up and ran off to Memphis."

"Did the Union army ever come through?"

"Natalie, have you called on me to ask for a history lesson?"

"Papa's family has stories about Russia in the 1880s. They still remember that stuff. I thought your family might remember the war the same way."

"I've told you what I know. Why don't you talk to the Shelby County Historical Commission? I know the director there."

"I might. But sometimes people remember surprising things that don't get into the archives."

She looked me up and down, an appraising gaze. "So this is how you're spending your time since you've come home. Looking at dusty old papers."

"Yes, when I'm not in the shop."

"Are you seeing anyone? If you want to get married again—"

She was the last person I'd tell about Adam. She hadn't approved of him the first time, either. "Not just yet. It's too soon after my divorce."

"In my day, when a girl got married, she stayed married," Grandmother said.

I couldn't let this anachronistic foolishness go. "Some people were happy doing that," I said. "Some people weren't. A divorce isn't always a bad thing, and being married isn't always good."

"Don't you want children?" she said.

She hadn't forgotten how to punch me in the gut. She just had a different method these days. I put my hand on the spot that ached in the middle of the night, protecting it. "Grandmother, please. Someday, when there's a baby to celebrate, I'll let you know."

I took a few more sips of my tea and I made my excuses and I left.

God, I was starting to hate being in Cordova.

On the way home, I cursed my own stupidity. How often had I watched my mother beg for her mother's love and attention? And fail to get it? My mother, scarred by her own upbringing, had struggled to be kinder and warmer to her children than her mother had been to hers.

My mother had succeeded, and Josh and I, well-adjusted with a few minor neuroses, were to her credit as much as to my warm-hearted and expressive father's. But she had never stopped hoping that her mother would love her more and show it, and she always returned from a visit to Grandmother Eleanor with a look of defeat and pain. She always looked as though she'd been sucker-punched in the gut. As I felt now.

THAT EVENING, I cranked up Otis Redding, the best companion I knew for a low moment, and listened to his voice as I drank a glass of wine, then another. My grandmother's judgment had stayed with me. I let it tell me the worst things about myself. I was divorced. I was childless. I had pushed away a man who said he loved me.

I let it get worse. I'd quit a job I was suited for, and I ran from the city where I belonged. Why had I come back to Memphis, this hot and humid Southern backwater? What kind of a life was I making for myself? None of the successes of the past few months—the shop and the community that had grown up around it, or the house, surrounded by like-minded neighbors I felt connected to —seemed to matter.

I felt it everywhere. Not just in my belly. Not just in my heart. But everywhere, mind and body and soul, as I listened to Otis Redding sing, the blues beneath the soul, the loss beneath the joy. Like Martin Luther King, another great spirit who had come to Memphis, Otis Redding had died too soon.

I poured myself another glass of wine, and when I finished it, I curled up on the uncomfortable little sofa, and I let myself feel every loss and every failure in my own life. I felt too low to cry, full of pain that would not go away.

I ALREADY FELT lousy when Calvin stopped by the shop, looking worse than I'd ever seen him.

I offered to show him the blue cat, and he followed me to the case in its quiet corner. Once we reached the case, he shook his head. "Don't even open it," he said. "Ain't never going to be able to buy that."

I knew how wrong it sounded, but I said, "You can always hope."

He said, "No, I can't."

I couldn't stand to see him so upset. "What's wrong?"

"I might be going right back to prison."

"Oh, Calvin," I said.

He shook his head at my tone, caught between fear and shame.

I said, "Not if Kenya has anything to say about it."

He didn't reply.

Gideon stepped into view. "Nat, will you mind the store for a bit?" To Calvin, he said, "You want to sit down for a moment? It's quiet in back, and there's bottled water, too."

Calvin raised his head. "You been listening to me? You eavesdropping on me?"

"Didn't hear a word," Gideon said, obviously lying. "It's

just that you look a bit peaked, like my grandmama used to say."

"And it ain't really your business, is it?"

Gideon said, "No, it ain't, but I'm used to people telling me that." He winked at me.

"Just to sit?" Calvin asked.

"And drink some water, if you want it. It's as hot as Hades outside."

Calvin rubbed the back of his neck, even though he wasn't sweating in our AC. "All right."

They disappeared into the back, where whatever they said was muffled. They stayed there long enough for a couple of looky-loos to come in, make a quick circuit, say, "You have so many lovely things here!" and not buy any of them.

When they emerged, I looked at Gideon, raising my eyebrows. He said, "Now this really ain't your business."

Calvin looked better, not so ashy. He said, "Takes one to know one."

"What?" I asked Gideon.

Gideon shook his head.

Calvin said, "I've got to go."

Puzzled, I said, "Take care, Calvin."

After he left, I asked Gideon, "What the heck did you say to him?"

Gideon leaned against the counter. "I told him that the job of a good lawyer is to keep you out of court and out of prison. And this time he has a good lawyer."

I asked, "And why would he believe you?"

Gideon said, "Because I had a good lawyer back in Nashville."

17

WHERE'S THE BOX?

As we closed, Gideon asked if Jude and I had time for a beer at E&H.

"You got something on your mind?" I asked him.

"Not much. Just that a beer would taste good right now."

Once we were settled at a table at E&H, Jude asked me if I'd made any progress on finding the papers that were missing from the Powells' house.

I shook my head. "I'm stumped. I need those Civil War papers, and I don't know where to look. I have a sickening feeling they didn't make it through the war."

Jude said, "We know these people. They've been pack-rats for all their stuff since they got to Shelby County. I don't think they burned their papers in the fireplace in 1865."

"Where are they? We know they aren't in the house. We cleaned out the storage unit. If they exist, where are they?"

Gideon took a swig from the bottle. "Think like an investigator for a moment."

"What do you mean?"

"Don't ask yourself, where are the papers? Ask yourself, where's the box?"

I groaned. "Yeah, I'll just call Ruth Anne Thompson, and she'll tell me. Do you think I want Curtis Thompson back in the shop, beating me up for bothering his auntie?"

Gideon said, "Was there anyone else in the house? Besides Evelyn Powell and Ruth Anne?"

I stared at him. "A nurse's aide," I said. "I'd bet my bottom dollar Ruth Anne hired home care at some point."

"There you go. Find the nurse's aide and ask her. Maybe she saw that box."

I groaned again. "How? Ruth Anne's the one who knows, and I can't ask her."

Jude asked, "How many home health care companies are there in Memphis? Ten? A dozen?"

"I don't know."

"Few enough so you can call each one, I bet," Gideon said.

"To ask if Evelyn Powell hired them, and who they sent? Do you think they'd tell me?"

He grinned like a naughty kid. "You don't ask them that. You fib."

"Like how?"

"You put on your best sugar-pie Southern accent, and you tell them that your poor dear grandmama needs care, and that your friend Joyce Enright said she had the best home health care aide for her mother. But Joyce is too upset to give you the name, because her mother just passed, but your grandmama is depending on you, and can they help you out?" He put a little sugar pie into his voice.

"Isn't that information confidential? Why would they tell me?"

"You'd be surprised what people will tell you."

I glanced at Jude, and I started to laugh. "Why is he so good at this?"

Gideon said, "Because I've been a miserable sinner for a long time. What do you have to lose? An hour of your time."

I said, "Someday I'm going to get your life story out of you. Every last miserable sin's worth."

"Maybe someday," he said, winking at me.

I PRINTED out the list of home health care companies and rehearsed a little before I picked up the phone. I was used to the kind of playacting necessary to sell Sotheby's services and placate nervous clients. Straight-out lying didn't come to me naturally.

At the first agency, I talked to the owner herself, whose sugar-pie accent softened her assertion that she couldn't give out a client's name. She would be happy to take my information and connect me with their nursing administrator. "I'm sure we can find just the right care for your grandmother!"

I thought I'd try the truth instead, and at the next agency I ended up talking to their head of HR. *Appraisal, item of value, family is fighting over it, looking for information, the nurse's aide who worked for them might be able to help.* It sounded like a mess to my own ears. I hoped she could make sense of it.

She was polite as could be, but she said, "Well, if you had the aide's name, I could tell you if she worked for us. But going into client records—we can't do that. That's confidential."

"I understand," I said. "If my grandmother was your client, I'd appreciate your discretion."

I didn't think it was worth going through the rest of the list. It didn't matter how I put it, no one could give out a client's name. As frustrated as I felt, I understood that these agencies were bound by confidentiality in their own way.

I called Gideon. There was an ungodly roaring sound in the background. "Where the hell are you?"

"County fair."

"What is that noise?"

"Drag race."

"You're a fan of drag racing?"

"I was, once. Today I'm here to play with a bluegrass band. What's up?"

"I fibbed my face off this morning."

"Get anything?"

"No. They can't give out information about clients, and they won't."

The roaring was overlaid by cheering. "Somebody won," he said, when the cheering subsided.

"That's great for somebody. What am I going to do next? Where's the box? Where's the nurse's aide?"

"Where are Miss Varina's letters?" he said, our joke from the early days of the appraisal.

"Ha-ha."

"I just thought of something. Isn't Letitia Woodson a nurse's aide?"

"She is, but she works for a nursing home."

"She might have an idea about finding someone who works as a health care aide. Or a suggestion about how to approach the home health companies. Would she talk to you?"

"I'm sure she's worried and upset, like Calvin is. I don't want to bother her."

"How did you get into the storage unit? Who leaned on Curtis Thompson?"

"His wife, Georgina."

"Can you call her?"

"Everyone in that family is touchy as can be."

"Ye of little faith."

"Yeah, that would be us Reform Jews. It's worth a try. I'll call Georgina."

The roaring began again. "Let me know what you find out."

EVEN THOUGH GEORGINA helped me before—she'd been the one to give Curtis a kick in the rear—I was nervous about calling her.

When she picked up, she was brusque. "Who is this?"

"It's Nat Raskin. The appraiser who was working with the Powells."

From her tone, I wasn't sure she remembered who I was. "I can't talk now," she said. "We're at the hospital."

"Are you all right? Is Curtis all right?"

"It's Ruth Anne," she said, upset as well as abrupt. "Chest pain. She's in for tests. I really can't talk."

Of course I worried. Ruth Anne was in her eighties, and I didn't know what her health was like, but I wondered if someone had been bothering her. Threatening her. I'd told the Powells to leave her alone. I was suddenly so angry that I had to stop myself from calling Joyce and giving her an earful. Not a good idea. I didn't know what had happened to send Ruth Anne to the hospital. Perhaps she'd had heart disease for years.

I didn't think so.

As I hesitated about calling Curtis to ask how Ruth Anne was doing, he called me. "Five Star Storage," my phone read, since I'd stored his number when I was negotiating with him about getting into the storage unit.

Without any preliminary, he shouted at me, "What the hell did you do?"

I forced myself to feel calm and sound calm. "Curtis, what is this about?"

"Ruth Anne was in the hospital with chest pain. She was there for three days while they ran tests on her. And it happened right after that detective bothered her."

"How is she now?"

"Did you hire that detective?"

Detective? "No, Curtis, I didn't."

"Did you tell the Powells to sic him on her?"

"No. What was this about? Do you know?"

"That damn ring. They think she stole it. They sent that detective to break into her house to look for it."

"I didn't have a clue. And I'm as upset as you are."

"Are you? Since it was your idea?"

"Curtis, listen to me. The Powells wanted to hire a detective to go in with guns blazing. I told them it was crazy. When they insisted, I got them to hire someone who did a discreet online search. Looked up her credit report. That kind of thing. He never even called her. And he told them there was nothing to find and they should leave her alone."

"This guy pounded on her door and forced his way into her house and wanted to toss the place. She was going to call the cops, but she had chest pain so bad her neighbors called an ambulance instead. And you tell me you don't know a thing about it?"

I was now as furious as he was, but not at him. "I don't. If you want to know who did this, call Owen Powell. I'm sure this was his idea."

Curtis was now yelling at top volume. "This is all your fault. You put us into this mess. It's all because of you. And this ain't the end of it." He hung up.

***

SHAKEN, I thought about what to do. I didn't want to call Joyce. I didn't have grounds to accuse Owen, and Joyce was now in my corner. I wanted to keep her there.

I called Kenya instead. She was hard to reach, since she was busy meeting with clients and making court appearances. When she called me back, she sounded a little tired.

"Is this a good time, Kenya?" I asked her.

Like Josh, she said, "As good as any. What's going on?"

"There's something that happened recently you should be aware of."

I could see her reaching for her legal pad. "What is it?"

"It's not about the suit or the research. But it's related."

Kenya said, "We're both part Yankee. Just spill it."

I told her about Curtis's call, Ruth Anne's stint in the hospital, and the enmity involved in the search for the missing ring.

Kenya said, "You're right, it isn't directly related, but there's a history of antagonism and threat. I'm not sure Joyce is blameless, even though she's being polite to you right now. Owen is obviously angry, and he's behaved in ways that could be a problem going forward, if he acts on his anger again."

"Is there anything I should do?"

"Absolutely not. I'll call Sexton and ask him to talk to Owen. See if he can rein Owen in, at least for the time being. Remind him not to hurt anybody. We want this to stay a civil suit."

"Great," I said.

"How are you coming along with your research?"

I figured my problem was small enough to admit to. "I've hit a snag. We're still looking for the Civil War papers. I'm leery of talking to Ruth Anne Thompson, who's the obvious person to ask where they went. I think Evelyn Powell hired a health aide who was in the house and who might know something about the papers."

"That's not a bad idea. What's the snag?"

"I've tried to find the health aide myself, and I can't."

She laughed in relief. "Is that all? That's what investigators are for. We have someone on retainer. She's excellent. I could ask her to look into it."

"Actually, there's someone local who's good. I've worked with him before."

"By all means, call him. Nat, why didn't you just go to him first?"

"I thought I'd try to do the obvious stuff myself. But it seems that nothing is obvious with this appraisal."

"Just have him bill us. My admin will send you the info for his invoice."

"Kenya, have you talked to Calvin recently?"

"A few days ago. Why?"

"He's talked to me. He's really upset. I wonder how Letitia is doing, too."

She said, "It's a stressful situation for all of them, I know."

"Did you know he'd been arrested?"

She was quiet, and then she sighed. "Yes, on drug charges."

"I think they're all reliving Calvin's arrest and trial."

Businesslike again, she said, "I realize that. I keep reminding them it's a civil trial, and our best way forward is to stay out of court." I could hear paper rustling. "That's where you come in."

I felt so much better I laughed. "No pressure," I said.

She laughed too. "No, not a bit."

THE INVESTIGATOR CALLED me a few days later with a name and an address.

"How do you do that?" I asked him.

He laughed. "When you find the proof of ownership on that chair, I'll be in awe, too," he said. "I've talked to her, and she's eager to talk to you. Says working for Evelyn Powell and Ruth Anne Thompson took ten years off her life. She's happy to give them as much trouble as possible. Her name is Vanessa Evans, and she lives in Bethel Grove."

Bethel Grove was just next door to Orange Mound, and like it, full of small houses in varying states of repair. Vanessa's house was in good shape, but the front yard was full of big plastic toys, like the ones my brother Josh's kids liked. I saw a well-used trike and a green dinosaur with a goofy grin.

Vanessa Evans came to the door. Laughing through the screen, she said, "Careful, the front is an obstacle course. The kids leave their stuff all over." She opened the door.

She was older than Letitia, and full-bodied, dressed in shorts and a T-shirt for comfort. She turned to call into the living room, "Darius, turn the TV down. I have a visitor I need to talk to." She turned to me. "You don't mind sitting in the kitchen? It's quieter."

I felt no twinge of uterine pain for this stranger's houseful. "Not at all," I said.

The kitchen had a little nook for a table and chairs. The appliances were newer than in Letitia's place, and the counters were cluttered with a toaster, a coffeemaker, and cookie jars. "Do you collect cookie jars?" I asked.

"I never meant to, but I inherited one from my

grandma, and then my husband gave me another one to match."

They were Red Wing pottery jars from the 1950s, the Dutch girl and the fat chef, in Red Wing's characteristic yellow glaze. "They're cute. Do you use them?"

She laughed. "With three kids? I sure do." She settled me at the table. "Do you want iced tea? It's not sweet. My doctor's after me to lose some weight. I can give you sugar for yours."

"No, that's fine."

She said, "I don't know how I can help you, but I'll do my best."

"How long did you work for Mrs. Powell?"

"I was there for three months, when she was failing and it was too much for Ruth Anne. I was there all day long, and I never sat down. Between the two of them, they wore me out. Not just the work. Their attitude, both of them."

"I've met Ruth Anne Thompson. I know what you mean. I hear you told the investigator that working for her took a few years off your life."

"More than that. After that job I changed careers. I got a certificate in medical records management. Now I work at Baptist Memorial, I have just one boss, and she's decent, even though she's a white lady. Now, what can I do for you?"

I explained about the papers we'd found and the ones that were missing.

"I never saw papers like that."

"They kept everything in boxes. Banker's boxes. I'm

actually looking for the box. We've looked everywhere in the house, and there's one box we can't find."

Her eyes widened. "Cardboard box? Box with a lid?"

"That's right."

"I'd forgotten all about that box. It was my last day there. That box!"

I waited.

"Mrs. Powell hadn't been doing well. She'd get agitated, and it was hard to calm her down. Ruth Anne told me she'd always been sharp as a tack, but by then, her mind was wandering. That day, that last day, she wouldn't get dressed and she wouldn't eat. She got out of bed in the middle of the morning, and she wandered into the hallway in her night-gown. She was carrying a box. Cardboard box with a lid. She didn't look all right. She said to me, 'The Yankees are coming. They'll be here any minute. You need to take this box into the backyard and bury it to keep it safe.' I thought, *She really isn't all right*, and I said, 'Here, give me the box, and I'll make sure it's safe.' I took it from her and set it down in the hallway. She got even more agitated. 'No, no. Take it into the backyard and bury it.' I said, 'You need to go back to your room and lie down. I promise you I'll put it somewhere safe.' I ran down the hallway, and as soon as I was out of her sight, I stashed it in an empty bedroom and shut the door. I figured I'd take it into the attic later and leave it with the rest of the boxes.

"That afternoon, she had a stroke, and in the commotion I forgot all about it. She went to the hospital, and she never came home. So that was my last day. I never went back to the house. That box. I'd forgotten all about it." She looked at me. "Does that help you?"

We'd been through every bedroom in the house, looking in every closet and under every bed. Jude knew to look under the beds. We hadn't found it. But it was good to know that the box, like Evelyn Powell herself, had been in the house until the day she left, never to return. "Yes, it does," I said.

As I left, I thought, *In the house. On the grounds. Hiding in plain sight.* Where?

18

AMELIA'S WAR

As I left, I felt light-headed. *It may be in the house somewhere.* When I got home, I called Gideon and told him what Vanessa had told me. "I can't imagine where. We looked everywhere in that house. And in all the outbuildings. You didn't miss anything?"

"I didn't dig up the rosebushes."

"Where could it be?"

He said, "Did you look in the mechanical room?"

"The utility room? Where the washer and dryer are? Jude and I looked there. It wasn't there."

"No, the room where the furnace is. The water heater. The fan for the a/c. I didn't look there. Did you?"

"I didn't realize they had a room for it. I thought the water heater was supposed to be in the garage."

"Not in a house like that."

"I don't know why it would be in there, but it's worth a shot. I'll call Joyce. We'll take a look."

I called Joyce to ask if she could let me in to see the

mechanical room. "I don't even know where that is," she said.

"You never had to service the water heater?"

"Ruth Anne would have taken care of that." She snorted. "I could ask her."

"Good luck with that."

She snorted again. "Well, why not? I can meet you there tomorrow morning."

I was the first to arrive at the Powell house in Cordova. Joyce pulled up. When she hopped from her SUV, the vehicle she'd called her kidmobile, she looked worse than I had before I slathered on the concealer.

I asked her, "Are you all right?"

She gave me an odd look, as though she was surprised I could be sympathetic. "Just the usual," she said. "Three messy kids, a husband who's worse than the kids, a dog who ate a sock yesterday, and Owen. I'm great."

"Is your dog okay?"

"He threw up the whole thing. He's fine."

"I never had a dog."

"It's like having another kid. Only he'll never get any smarter than he is now."

"Hide the socks."

She laughed a little as she unlocked the door.

I was glad I hadn't called her about Owen. If Sexton had talked to him, she hadn't heard about that, either. I followed her into the house, and we both looked into the expanse of the pristine, unlived-in living room. She said, "I talked to the estate sale company. We're trying to decide if we should hold the sale before we sell the house, or wait until after." She sighed. "Hard to believe that this place will be empty. And that it will change hands."

"It should be a weight off your shoulders."

"I still have to deal with Owen."

I asked, "Worse than usual?"

She said, "His usual is bad enough."

I held my breath, in case there was more, but she walked into the kitchen and dropped her purse on the counter without further comment. She said, "Let's go looking for this mechanical room. I don't have a clue where it is."

"In back, I'd think."

Next to the laundry room was a door. "I wonder if this is it," Joyce said.

"Open it."

It was bigger than I expected, the size of a walk-in closet. It was windowless and completely dark. Joyce fumbled for a light switch, and we saw that it was divided into two spaces. Against the back wall were the furnace and the water heater. Next to us was the toilet, the lid down, and a small sink.

Joyce and I looked at each other. I was surprised to see these fixtures in a house built at the end of the twentieth century, but every suburban house in Memphis built in the 1940s and 1950s had them. They were for the maid, hired to clean the upstairs bathrooms, but not allowed to use them.

I was upset enough to say, "Did Ruth Anne—"

"Goodness, no. When she stayed here, Ruth Anne had her own bedroom on the second floor, with its own bath. She used that."

On the commode sat a box. A cardboard box with a lid. A banker's box.

We looked at each other. I said, "Do you mind if I see what's inside?"

Joyce said, "Go ahead."

I pried off the lid and set it on the cement floor. Unlike every other box in this house, this box was a jumble of paper. I took the topmost sheet between my fingers.

It seemed to be a receipt for groceries. Flour, sugar, coffee, candles. It was handwritten. I read the date. "Joyce, look at this," I said, my voice hoarse with surprise.

"July 7, 1863."

I looked into the box. The piece of paper beneath the one I'd touched—*I shouldn't be touching this paper without archival gloves on*—was another receipt, dated October 1864. I didn't dare rummage in this box. The paper was old and fragile, and it hadn't had an easy war.

"What is it?" Joyce asked.

"They're from the Civil War." I stared at the sheet between my fingers. "It's the papers from the Civil War."

I put the paper back in the box and thought of all the anguish it had taken to find it. "It was here all the time," I whispered. "Hiding in plain sight."

"Is it what you were looking for?" Joyce asked.

"I don't know yet."

"I've got to see this," she said. "I don't have to be anywhere for a while. Can I look?"

"Let's take it upstairs."

I was about to put the box on the dining room table, but Joyce said, "Eww. It's been sitting on the commode. Let me find a tablecloth." She protected the tabletop, and I set up my laptop in the dining room, as I always had when working on the appraisal.

"Can I help?" Joyce asked.

"Let's sort through everything first. Then we'll figure out what it is. Then we can do the inventory."

She took the lid off the box. I said, "Wait, don't touch the paper with your bare hands."

"Why not? Is it dirty?"

"Probably. I'm more worried about the oils in your skin. They'll hurt the paper. And this paper has already had the hurt put to it." I pulled the gloves from my purse. "Put these on."

She said, "Like the gloves I wore to Easter services when I was little. But uglier."

I pulled on a pair, and she followed suit.

"Nat, what's this?" she asked, holding the sheet gingerly between her gloved fingers.

"It's a bill of sale. It's the same thing as a receipt, but it usually referred to a commercial transaction." I scanned it. "It's for the sale of cotton. Ten bales of cotton. 1863. Tell you what. Let's put the receipts for groceries in one pile and the bills of sale in another. Then we'll put them in chronological order."

The sheaf of paper wasn't very thick, and beneath it were notebooks. Not the leather of the ledgers or the cloth covers of the diaries. These were like a child's schoolbooks, with blue cardboard covers, much faded and battered, and cloth bindings, badly worn.

"What's that?"

I opened one, and I immediately recognized the handwriting. "A diary." I checked the date. "1862."

"Who was keeping a diary?"

"Amelia Powell. Your direct ancestor. She came to Shelby County from Virginia in the 1820s with her husband, Ezekiel."

"She was still alive then?"

"She was born in 1800. She was in her sixties when the war broke out."

"What does it say?"

"Let's pull them all out and put them in order. Then we'll take a look."

"You're so bossy," Joyce grumbled, but it was good-natured.

"In this, believe me, I know what I'm doing."

My phone rang, and I grabbed it from my purse. It was Adam. Why was he calling me again? I wished I could turn the ringer off.

"Do you need to get that?"

"No. It's the guy I just broke up with. He keeps calling, even though he knows it's hopeless."

Joyce laughed. "You should get a dog. You know what kind of idiot he'll be."

"Don't laugh on the fragile old beat-up Civil War–era paper."

When we got the notebooks out, there was something else in the box. Something wrapped in soft, faded cloth, fastened with a ragged scrap of fabric. Joyce reached for it. "I know, be careful," she said.

"Do the honors."

She fumbled with the tie. "It's harder with the gloves."

"You can take them off. The fabric's already ruined."

She got the knot undone. "Is the cloth old?"

"Probably. Go ahead. I'm dying to see what's in there."

It was oval, in a gilt frame that still shone brightly after so many decades, protected by a glass cover. The face, painted so daintily on the ivory background, was uniformly pale in the fashion of the day. The blonde hair spilled in artful curls around the face. The blue eyes met ours, almost two hundred years since the artist put his brush to the ivory surface.

I knew who she was, and Joyce didn't even have to ask. "It's Amelia Powell," I said. I was still wearing my gloves, and I touched the glass case with one finger, very gently, my fingertip to her cheek.

The expert in decorative art was droning inside my head. *Miniature portrait, watercolor on ivory, circa 1820, artist unknown, Virginia.* But I ignored it. *I know you,* I thought.

"Nat?"

"She was so young when this was painted. It was probably before she got married. Her whole life was ahead of her, and she had no idea how it would turn out."

Joyce was a little surprised at my emotion. "Well, none of us know that, do we?"

I held my breath because I was afraid that a sob would come out. "No, we don't."

"You love that portrait," Joyce said.

"I feel like I know Amelia. I like her a lot."

"You should have it."

"No, I can't take anything from the estate. Ethics. Besides, it's yours. She's a flesh-and-blood ancestor. She belongs with you."

"I wish you could have it."

"Don't sell it. Tell you what. Take a good picture of it, a

really nice one, and send that to me. That way I can have her forever. No moral problems attached."

"That's all you want?"

"Oh, I want a lot of things. But I'll settle for that."

In a soft voice, Joyce said, "What should we do now?"

I righted myself. "Let's put everything in order."

As soon as the bills of sale and the receipts were arranged, we saw a pattern. "Look, Joyce. She goes into Memphis and sells ten bales of cotton to the broker at $100 a bale, and then she walks down the street and buys enough in staples to eat up every dime of her thousand dollars." I checked the dates. "Every three months."

The receipt and the bills of sale were the bare bones of Amelia's life during the war. I knew how she fleshed them out. I said, "Let me show you something. Let's find a diary entry for one of those visits to Memphis."

MAY 5, 1861

Lucullus has mustered into the Confederate army and awaits instructions to go to Virginia. How odd that our old home is now the seat of war. His wife is already behaving like a widow, drooping over the furniture and sobbing into her handkerchief. I don't know why such a hot young man married a girl with a spine like a washrag. Well, I will carry on, with Harriet and Tobias to help me, as they always have. We have nearly forty hands in the cotton fields, and they know what they're doing, under the watchful eyes of their overseer and their driver. Thank goodness for that.

. . .

November 1861

God is jesting with us. We had a bumper cotton crop this year, and because of the blockade, we have no means to sell it. I had the hands gin and bale it and store it into a tin shed, to guard against fire. The war cannot go on forever. The blockade will end sometime.

I hear of cotton planters, especially in Mississippi, who have braved the blockade. It sits badly with me. We may be in rebellion, but running the blockade seems like a fool's risk. Lucullus has written to me to consider it, but at night, when I can't sleep for worry, I argue with Ezekiel's ghost about it. The ghost is the more reasonable of the two.

MAY *1862*

Lucullus wrote to us on the eve of the battle at Shiloh, and once the reports began to come to us, I was full of dismay. Now that the news is certain, I am stricken. There's no time to grieve. My daughter-in-law put on the black clothes Harriet and I dyed for her and sobbed more than ever. I have no rest. I have a plantation to run.

May God forgive me, but I grieved a long time ago for the man I hoped Lucullus would become. I think he began to spoil for war when he was a tiny boy. He followed the star of Mars, the god of war, and I believe he may have found his proper place on the field of battle. Am I a monster to think so? I remember the way he tried to despoil Rosetta, and I think not. I have never forgiven him for that.

JULY *1862*

Memphis has fallen to the Union Army. The town is full of blue-bellies, as my neighbors call them, and even though I hear they behave themselves fairly well, the people of Memphis do not like being conquered. We feel the war differently in Shelby County. We have not been visited by the Yankee soldiers, but our slaves are very restless. On the neighboring places, half a dozen have run away to the Union lines.

I asked Harriet if she wanted to run away. She said that she did not. I asked Tobey if he had thought about running away, and he dropped his eyes to the ground and didn't answer me.

August 1862

Since Memphis fell last month, the slaves have become ever bolder about running away. The Yankees call them "contraband of war," but taking them in is nothing short of theft, in my opinion.

Tobey and his family are gone. They ran away in the dark of night. After so many years, they left me without a word.

If more of our people leave—if the field hands go—I don't know how we'll harvest the cotton crop this year. Not that we can sell it. But it makes me sick to my stomach to think of bales and bales of cotton rotting on the stem instead of sitting in the tin shed, awaiting the end of the blockade.

August 1862

There's trade in cotton again in Memphis. The Yankees are buying it. Southern brokers can get licenses to sell it to the army, and they'll buy it from anyone who has bales of cotton to sell.

Because we have no cash, we haven't had flour since the blockade began. Or sugar, or coffee. We eat corn bread and honey, and we go without coffee rather than drink that dreadful brew made from powdered acorns. There are some things we can't make ourselves or do without. Our shoes are worn through. We've patched and patched them until there's nothing left to patch.

To think that we bought silk and brandy before the war without a thought for what it cost or whether there would be more.

We have a hundred bales of the 1861 crop in our shed. Cotton is going for nearly two dollars a pound in England, but the local men are buying it for 25 cents a pound. That's a hundred dollars a bale. If I sold some of our cotton—ten bales, say—I'd have cash. I shudder to think of what flour and sugar and shoes will cost me in Memphis, where the speculators have run riot.

I hate to sell the cotton. It is the only thing between us and ruin. The war can't last forever. The blockade can't last forever. I don't know how we'll grow cotton again, if the slaves stay with the Union army and refuse to return.

One struggle at a time—dear Lord, help me—

August 1862

I decided to take ten bales of cotton to Memphis to see what I could get for it. It was quite an effort to load the wagon, since all our prime hands, and their stout wives, are gone. The only servants who remain are Pompey and his wife, Dinah, who are too old and too infirm to run away. But we managed it, and we set off to find a cotton broker in Memphis.

I couldn't ask Pompey to drive, but he accompanied me. As though this poor feeble old man could help me if the blue-bellies wanted to despoil us. The horse, unused to the road, was loath to go briskly. Pompey suggested I whup him, but I had no more desire to beat the animal than I would to beat a slave.

Memphis was overrun with men in blue coats. I was afraid they would stop us or try to take our cotton as contraband, but no one gave us a second glance. It's odd that the city has barely been disturbed by the war. We drove down the main street and stopped before a building to which a sign was affixed: William Epley, Cotton Broker. Mr. Epley had brokered cotton for us before the war. He was still here and still in business.

I left Pompey in the wagon and went inside. It was surprisingly crowded. The cotton business was brisk again. I had never done business with Mr. Epley in person, but he would know my name. When I introduced myself, he apologized that there was no place to sit and no refreshment. I told him that I could hardly blame him for it.

After some pleasantries, I told him that I had ten bales of cotton to sell. He glanced out the window to see Pompey asleep on the wagon seat. Mr. Epley told me to drive the wagon around in the back, and his men would unload it and weigh it for me. I stayed inside while they did so, and shortly, Mr. Epley began to write up the bill of sale. I had hoped for better, but it was as I expected—ten bales, five hundred pounds apiece, twenty-five cents a pound, twelve hundred and fifty dollars in total. He gave me cash in greenbacks, telling me that the Yankees paid him the same way. Once the money was stuffed into my reticule, I breathed a sigh of relief.

I walked down the street to the general store. The prices shocked me. The blockade had been lifted in Memphis, but spec-

ulation had taken its place. Once I had bought flour, sugar, candles, needles and thread, a few lengths of cotton cloth, and shoes, I was nearly broke. I hesitated at the price of coffee, but why was I saving my money? We couldn't eat greenbacks. We could drink coffee.

The storekeeper's porter loaded my wagon with our staples—they took up so much less room than the cotton—and I nearly wept to think of how little my money had bought me.

January 1863

Now that the slaves have been declared "emancipated," they are more brazen than ever. They roam the countryside and refuse to work for anyone. They end up in Memphis, dwelling in squalor next to the army, and they count themselves pleased to live in "freedom" in conditions that the chickens would have disdained at home. Those who have left don't send word back. I have never had news of Tobey and his family, even though they must be close by in Memphis. Tobey's departure hurt me as the others did not. We had always treated him with kindness and consideration, and we thought of him as a member of the family. Evidently he saw things differently.

We had gone through every bit of the provisions I bought last summer, and it was time to load the wagon and make the slow journey back to Memphis and to Mr. Epley, the cotton broker. This time, everything cost even more at the general store —the price of flour astonished me!—and I had to forgo the coffee. I bought the cheapest cotton cloth to patch our clothes, which are nearly too ragged to wear. What was it like to buy new dresses every six months? I can no longer remember. Shoes were out of the question this time.

The fighting goes on, and even though we still have eighty bales of cotton in our shed, I worry that it will not outlast the war. I cannot think of what we will do—

AFTER JOYCE READ the diary entries, she said, "It's like *Gone with the Wind.*"

"*Gone with the Wind* wasn't real," I said. "This is."

Joyce said, "Oh, look at the time. I have to run." She rose. "Once you read the rest of it, you'll have to tell me how it comes out."

I said, "The war? I think you know."

She laughed as she left.

After I ate lunch, I stopped reading. I went into the office to figure out how to scan the pages. I wanted a copy. I worried about losing this box again.

I was sitting at the dining room table, the papers and diaries spread before me, when I heard the key turn in the lock. That was odd. Joyce usually called me to warn me she was nearby. The tread was heavier than Joyce's.

It was Owen.

He walked into the dining room, stopping beside me, standing to look down at the table. He smelled of whiskey. He stared at the pages, the paper yellowed, the ink faded against the opulent surface of the mahogany table. "What are you doing?"

I put my hand over the nearest pages, the way my mother would put her arm over me when we made a hasty stop in the car. "I've been scanning. Making copies."

"Why? Don't you trust us?"

I ignored the scorn in his voice. "The legal team asked for them."

He sat in the chair nearest me and spread his hand on the table. "Did you sic my lawyer on me?" he asked.

"Sic? Of course not."

"Sexton called me on the carpet. Told me to shape up. Embarrassed me. You're sure you didn't put him up to it?"

I said, "Your lawyer wouldn't listen to the time of day from me. You know that."

He leaned forward, and the smell of whiskey was even stronger. "You go crying to that lawyer in Atlanta?"

"Ms. Davis and I are in touch about the progress of the research," I said.

He pulled the box toward him. "What's in here?" Without waiting for an answer, he began to rummage in it.

I said, "You're welcome to look, but please put on some archival gloves and handle everything carefully."

He didn't remove his hand, and he said, "These papers are mine, and I can do anything I want with them. Touch them. Take them with me. Or throw them out."

I thought, *Why didn't I tell Kenya I found the box? Why didn't I insist we keep it somewhere safe?* "You surely can," I said, "but while you're here, and I'm here to watch you, please be careful with them."

"And if I'm not? What are you going to do? Tattle to Ms. Davis about me?" He managed to put a lot of contempt into it.

"I think the legal team would prefer to have them in one piece," I said.

He didn't move his hand. "I want you out of here."

"Just let me finish up. It will only be a few minutes."

"If you touch that box, I'll call the police and have you arrested for theft."

"What?"

"I mean it." He pulled out his phone.

"Owen, please don't do this."

"You think I'm bluffing?"

"What are they going to arrest me for? Fulfilling the contract I signed with your legal team?"

"Get the hell out."

I rose. "Okay. I'll go. But I want you to walk me out."

"Why?"

I was shaking. I didn't know whether I was more afraid for the papers or for myself. "I want to see you lock the door and drive away. Without that box."

He stood, too, and came close. Much too close. "Aren't you full of yourself," he said.

I said, "Don't come any closer. You touch me, that's assault. I'll call the cops."

He didn't back off. He flexed his fingers as though he wanted to make a fist. "Get the hell out," he said.

"I'm not leaving unless you leave too."

"Jesus," he said.

"If you hit me, that is assault," I said.

In disgust, he said, "You aren't worth the trouble," and he dropped his hand to his side. "All right, come on."

Even though I was shaking, I followed him. I waited until we both walked through the door and he'd locked it behind us.

"Now what are you waiting for?" he asked, his voice dripping contempt.

"I'm going to stand here to watch. I want to see you drive away."

"And if I don't?"

"I'll call your sister. Then I'll call your lawyer."

He turned his back on me and walked into the drive. "See?" he said. "I'm walking to my car." He wrenched open the door. "I'm getting in." He slammed the door shut and gunned the engine.

I waited until he'd driven away. I was still shaking. I pulled my phone from my bag. I called Joyce and, to my surprise, got voicemail. I left her a message. "Owen came to lock up today, so you don't have to. Call me back as soon as you can. It's important."

19

THE BRICK

THE SOUND OF SHATTERING GLASS WOKE ME FIRST, AND AT the thud of something heavy on the living room floor, I was completely awake. I sat up, and something slid from my torso to tinkle on the floor. Glass. Shards of glass. I was covered in bits of glass.

The window next to the sofa had been shattered.

My heart pounded. My head ached. I froze, afraid to move, and listened for the sound of an intruder in the house.

I saw the brick on the floor, sitting in the middle of a puddle of glass. Just like the break-in at the shop.

Why didn't I have a dog? Why didn't I have a gun? Why didn't I have an alarm system?

911. Call 911. Where had I left my phone? I stared at my bare feet. I couldn't walk across glass in bare feet. I'd kicked off my shoes to lie on the sofa. Where were my shoes?

Turn on the light to find them.

What if someone was in the house? I listened. Nothing. No footsteps. No rustling. No breathing. No sound of a voice.

I turned on the lamp. Damn these old houses, no overhead lights in the living room. You were supposed to make do with floor lamps and table lamps, like I did. The lamp cast its light, which had been romantic when Adam visited me. Now it was too dim, and who knew what lurked in the shadows in the far corners of the room.

Shoes. They were on the floor next to the sofa. I nearly stuck my foot in the nearest shoe when I realized that they were probably full of glass. I bent down and shook out first one, then the other. The glass tinkled as it fell to the floor.

I hoped I'd gotten enough glass out not to cut myself. I put on my shoes. No pain. I took off the shoe to check for bleeding. Nothing. Good.

Where was the phone? I hadn't set it on the lamp table. I tried to remember where I'd left it. God, my head ached. How much wine had I drunk before I fell asleep?

I stood. My head cleared a little.

I heard a sound, and I froze again.

It was outside. A scrabbling sound in the shrubs. I didn't dare draw close to the broken window to look. I waited.

And heard the distinctive chirp that belonged to a squirrel.

I walked gingerly across the floor, wincing at the sound of glass crunching under my feet. I was shod and I wasn't hurt. I thought of the glass scratching the pine boards of the floor, the ninety-year-old flooring that had been refinished just before I moved in.

This was a hell of a time to be a preservationist.

911. Call 911.

When I picked up the phone, my hand was shaking so badly I could barely punch in the numbers. The woman who answered sounded like Mavis, a capable voice with an undertone of compassion, and for a moment I was so confused that all I could do was stammer.

She asked me questions I could answer. My address. My phone number. My name. By then I knew she wasn't Mavis, but a stranger, and I was able to talk again. Not normally. But the words came out.

"What is your emergency?" she asked, and I told her.

She said, "Help is on the way."

When I got off the phone, I was shaking again. I picked my way across the glass again and turned on the porch light, as though the cops were guests who needed the light to guide them in.

The sound of the siren brought my neighbors to their front windows, and the flashing light of the police car drew them onto their front lawns. The last emergency vehicle on this street was probably the ambulance that took the previous resident of my house, elderly, ailing Miss Augusta, to the hospital. A quiet, nervous crowd gathered on the sidewalk as the cops parked and emerged from the black-and-white. The police didn't have to restrain this crowd. My neighbors, teachers and social workers and civil servants and artists, stood back because they trusted the police to do their job.

Like the cops who had been called to the break-in at the shop, this was a male-female duo. The man was broad-shouldered and burly; the woman was shorter, but she looked fit and muscular. Their guns and night-sticks gave them a bulk that looked all wrong on my porch. At the door, I said—and immediately realized how idiotic I sounded—"Careful, there's glass all over the floor."

They wanted to know if I'd seen an intruder, and like the cops at the shop, they went looking through the house first. When they were satisfied that the house was empty, we talked in the dining room. They wanted to know if I'd seen anyone. I said, "I was asleep when it happened." I pointed to the sofa and saw how lucky I'd been. I could have been badly hurt by the shattering glass. I started to shake again.

They asked me if I had any idea who might have done this.

Yes. I thought of Curtis Thompson, who hadn't forgiven me for hurting his aunt. I thought of Owen Powell, who was furious with me and who didn't mind threatening people he hated.

It wouldn't help me to tell the police. It might only make things worse.

The female cop asked me, "Is there an ex-husband in the picture?"

I was so addled I answered it literally. "I'm divorced, but it was amicable, and he lives in New York."

"A boyfriend?"

That hit me. Like a brick. Oh, God.

Adam.

It couldn't be.

Now my voice was shaking too. "No."

She looked at me as though she listened to people lie

to her all the time. She said, "Here's my card. If you think of anything else, you can call me."

"Do you want to file a report?" the man asked.

"Yes, for the insurance." What was wrong with me? Someone could have cut me to ribbons with flying glass and I was worried about the finish on my floor and my homeowner's insurance policy.

The cops talked briefly to the neighbors, still waiting anxiously on the sidewalk, and then they got in their patrol car and drove away.

Emmy and Val detached themselves from the worried cluster on the sidewalk. I let them in. Emmy asked, "How are you?"

"Not hurt. Just shook up." I started to shake again.

Val said, "Would you like us to stay with you?"

"I have to call the emergency glass company," I said, sounding stupid to myself.

"We can stay with you until they get here."

"There's glass all over."

Emmy and Val exchanged a look. "We'll help you clean it up."

In the balmy night air, I was cold and shaking. Emmy made me a cup of tea, and Val found a sweater for me. They didn't pry. They stayed until my window was boarded up.

"I can't thank you enough," I said. "And on a week-night, too."

Emmy laughed. "I'll live. Val's the one to suffer. She's on the day shift tomorrow."

I DIDN'T GET BACK to sleep that night. Whenever I dropped off, I heard the glass and the brick.

At four in the morning, I realized that Joyce hadn't called me back.

After I showered and drank a cup of coffee, I called the insurance company. I emailed the head of the neighborhood preservation group to find out whether there were rules about restoring a broken window in a house in a historic district. I vacuumed the living room, including the sofa cushions, and thought darkly about selling the sofa.

I thought darkly about selling the house, too.

I didn't call my parents or Josh. They would worry, and there was nothing they could do.

There was nothing the police could do if I didn't tell them who I suspected.

As I was about to leave for the shop, Joyce called me. "I'm sorry I didn't call you back sooner," she said. She sounded exhausted.

"Are you okay?"

"My youngest boy was up all night with stomach flu. I was up all night, too."

"Oh no. How's he doing?"

"Better. Not throwing up, thank goodness. I did three loads of laundry last night." She sighed. "You said Owen locked up yesterday?"

"Yes, he did." *She must be really frazzled,* I thought. *She didn't ask me why he came by.*

"And that you wanted to talk about something important."

"I know this is a bad day for you. Can you get to the house in Cordova?"

"Why? It's locked up now, isn't it?"

"I need to know that the box is still there."

She seemed to wake up. "What happened when Owen came over?"

"He was in a state," I said, an expression I'd learned from my Beardsley grandmother.

Her voice rose. "Did he mess with the papers? Did he mess with the box?"

"Not before we both left." I debated with myself —*Should I tell her about the brick?* I was still afraid of disturbing her goodwill. "But he may have gone back later. That's what I'm afraid of."

"To take it? Why?"

I said, "You know better than I do." *His usual is bad enough.*

She groaned. "Today of all days," she said.

"I wouldn't ask unless it was an emergency."

She made a strangled sound that was half a laugh and half a sob. "An emergency over a box of old papers," she said.

"If he's taken them—if he's destroyed them, like he threatened to yesterday—you'll be in court for months."

She made another strangled sound. "I may kill him," she said. "Then we'll really go to court."

"Don't do that. If you can drive over there and make sure the box is okay—"

She said, "As long as he's not throwing up, my kid can ride stretched out in back. I'll do it. You want me to take the box home with me?"

"Yes," I said. *If it's there.* "Call me as soon as you get there."

"I'll kill him," she repeated.

"Don't. No one wants to go to court."

I got to the shop fifteen minutes early and opened. As soon as Jude walked in, she knew something was wrong. "What happened?" she asked.

I didn't want to talk about the box. I was afraid that if I admitted to my worry, it would be gone. Instead, I told her about the brick.

She grabbed my arm. "Why didn't you call me?" she said. When I flinched, she was contrite. "Did I hurt you?"

"Only my ears. I didn't call you because I knew you would be asleep."

Gideon came in, and Jude said indignantly, "Nat got broken into at home and she didn't call us! She said she wanted to let me sleep!"

Gideon was immediately and visibly upset. "I'm never asleep in the middle of the night. Why didn't you call me?"

I was so tired I felt dizzy. "Because I called the police. They're handling it."

Gideon said, "Yeah, they'll file a report, and they'll never find out who did it."

I shook my head.

Jude said, "You should put in an alarm system."

"Maybe. I'm not worried about my stuff. Whoever did this left my collection alone. My midcentury pottery is fine."

Gideon said, "Whoever did this could have hurt you. You should buy a gun and learn how to use it. I could teach you."

"No, thanks. I don't think the world will be a better place if I know how to handle a firearm."

Gideon said, "I can think of a few people the police don't know about. Curtis Thompson, that sorehead. And Owen Powell, who's an even bigger sorehead."

I lost my temper. "And what good would it do me to finger either of them? To have them come back and try something worse?"

"Why are you here?" Gideon said. "Why didn't you stay home and take it easy today?"

"It's worse if I'm home. I think about it, over and over. It's better to be here."

I spent the morning staring at my phone, willing it to ring. I left it on the counter when I was there and put it in my pocket if I needed to be on the shop floor.

Neither Gideon nor Jude teased me about it.

It was nearly noon when Joyce called me. "It's gone," she said.

My heart pounded so hard that I had to cough. "What the hell, Joyce?"

"I looked all over. In the dining room, the den where the computer is, up in the attic. I even went back into the utility room. It's gone."

"I can't believe it," I said.

"If Owen has it—"

"If he doesn't have it—"

She said, "Meet me at his office. He's in Germantown. Let me give you the address."

When I got off the phone, I said, "I need to cut out for an hour or so."

Gideon said, "You look like you're going to faint."

"I've got to deal with the appraisal."

"There's something else going on? Besides the brick?" Jude asked.

"The damn box went missing again," I said, and I ran out the door to my car.

WE MET in the parking lot next to the two-story brick building that housed Owen's office. Joyce held the hand of her son, a seven-year-old who had managed to get dressed but who looked pale and woozy. "This is Zeke," she said.

I bent down. "How are you feeling, buddy?" I asked.

He pressed against Joyce, and she wrapped her arm protectively around him. She said, "It's all right, sweetie, none of us is having a good day."

We left Joyce's son with the receptionist, a smiling woman who must have kids of her own, because she settled him with a cup of cola and let him stretch out on the sofa. She ruffled his hair and said, "If you feel sick, honey, you tell me right away." He nodded, curled up, and put his fist to his mouth, the way kids did when they'd outgrown a thumb but they wanted comfort.

The receptionist called Owen to let him know we were out front, and he came out. He didn't look happy to see either of us.

Joyce said, "We have something to talk to you about. In private. In your office."

"You need investment advice now?" He threw a glance at his nephew. "Why is he here?"

"In private, Owney," Joyce said.

Joyce was in no mood to sit down. As soon as he shut his office door, she put her hands on her hips. "The box. It isn't in the house in Cordova. Did you take it?"

He said, "What the hell, Joyce?"

"Nat told me what you did yesterday. Stomped in. Threatened to take the box. Threatened to destroy the papers. Threatened her. Did you go back there and take the box?"

"Why would I do that?"

"Then where is it?"

"Did you look around?"

"Don't give me that. Of course I did. It was you, I know it was. Where is it?"

He threw me a poisonous glance. I was reminded of Curtis's outburst. *This is all your fault.* "Calm down, Joyce. We'll find it."

"We don't need to look very hard if you took it. Where is it? Did you take it home? Or did you toss it in a dumpster somewhere?"

He couldn't look to me for sympathy. I wasn't his ally. "Joyce, please."

I said, "Maybe I can help your memory. Last night someone threw a brick through my front window. Middle of the night. I seem to remember you said some pretty threatening things to me yesterday as we were leaving the place in Cordova."

"Are you accusing me of something?"

"Did I say that? I have to tell you, when the cops asked me if I had any idea who did it, I said no. But I can change my mind. I can tell them they should talk to you."

He shouted at me, "How dare you?"

Joyce grabbed him by both arms. "Do you know anything about this? Did you do this?"

Furious, he said, "What do you think, Joyce? Do you think I'm that kind of idiot?"

There was a tap on the door. "What is it?" Owen said, his voice brusque.

"It's Angie. I have to talk to Joyce. It's about Zeke."

"Zeke? Why?"

"Let her come in, Owen," Joyce said.

Owen opened the door, and Angie put her head in. "Joyce, he's not feeling well."

"Like he's going to throw up again?"

"No, but he says he doesn't feel good and he wants to go home."

Owen said, "You brought Zeke here sick?"

"What was I going to do?" Joyce flared. "Leave him home by himself?"

"He's sitting in the waiting room by himself? Sick?" He reached into his pocket and pulled out his car key. "I'm going home right now."

Joyce said, "We'll meet you there."

He glared at his sister. "How sick is he?"

"Better than last night. Get going, Owen."

In the reception area, Zeke was lying flat on the sofa, looking pale and tired. Owen bent down and smoothed his nephew's forehead. "Hey, buddy," he said. "I hear you don't feel too good."

Zeke struggled to sit up. "I want to go home," he said.

Joyce rushed to her son. "We need to stop for a minute

at Uncle Owen's house," she said. "Then we'll go home and you can take it easy."

Owen stood and threw an unhappy look at me. I shook my head. For once, none of this was my fault.

In the parking lot, Joyce said, "Nat, ride with us." It wasn't an invitation. It was a command, and it sounded strange coming from Joyce. I heard the voice of generations of steel-spined Southern women in it. I obeyed her.

"Zeke, honey? You doing all right?" his mother asked.

"I don't feel good," he said, his voice plaintive.

My heart went out to him. "Do you mind if I sit with him, Joyce?"

Surprised, she said, "No, I don't."

Zeke was too listless to sit up. He stretched out, oblivious to the way his back met my leg. I felt the bones of his shoulder and his spine against me.

When we pulled up, Owen's car was already in the driveway. Joyce parked, got out, and helped Zeke onto the sidewalk. "Just a few minutes here," she said. She smoothed his forehead. "I am so sorry about this."

Between my fear for the box and my concern for Zeke, I was too wrought up to notice Owen Powell's décor. Inside, Joyce settled Zeke on the sofa, where he sat back against the cushions and watched us.

"Owen, the box," Joyce said.

Owen glanced at his nephew and didn't reply. He disappeared down the hall and returned with the box in his arms.

Joyce stared at him. *I don't trust you either.* "Did you take anything out of this?"

"No."

She lifted the lid and pulled out the topmost piece of paper. I recognized it as a bill of sale. She glanced at it and said to me, "1864."

Owen reddened. "I didn't touch it, Joyce. Just to take it home with me."

I thought, *We know what you intended for it.*

"Give it to me."

He handed it to her. She set it down. "Now give me the house key."

"The key? Why?"

"Because I don't want you bothering Nat while she's working there."

I knew, as Joyce did, that he wanted to argue with her. He wanted to lose his temper. But his eyes slid to the little figure propped up on the sofa pillows. He met the watchful blue eyes in the wan little face. His cheeks reddened further with the effort of containing himself. He reached into his pocket again. Joyce held out her hand, palm up, and he dropped the key into it.

She didn't thank him. She picked up the box and handed it to me. Then she scooped up her son from the sofa and buried her face in his hair. "Just one more stop, sweetie, and we'll be on the way home," she said.

She settled Zeke in the back seat of the van, then took the box from me to stash it in the storage area. I got in back again with Zeke. Before Joyce started the car, she called softly, "Zeke, sugar? You all right back there?"

I looked down. His eyes were shut. I resisted the impulse to touch his forehead. "He's asleep," I said. Very softly, I asked Joyce, "How are you doing?"

"Now I feel like I'm going to throw up," she said, letting the strain of the last hour show in her face.

"I know what you mean."

I HAD a bad delayed reaction to the stress. I went home and shook and cried for a long time. When I was tired of crying, I still wasn't all right. I wished I could call the police, but I wouldn't.

I called Kenya.

"You sound awful," she said. "Are you sick?"

"Just exhausted."

"Is there a problem?"

"You have your legal pad ready?"

"I always do. What's the situation?"

Like the woman who answered the 911 calls. *What is your emergency?* I told her about the brick and the broken window.

"That's an old Klan trick."

"I know." My grandfather, Morris Raskin, had gotten a brick through the window—at the shop and at home—when he insisted on selling to Black customers in the 1960s. "But I doubt the Klan is involved here."

"You have your suspicions."

I told her who I suspected. And I told her I hadn't shared my suspicions with the police.

She said, "I'm thinking this through. It doesn't make sense to me that Curtis Thompson would risk his business and his reputation to do something like this. And even though I haven't met Owen Powell, he strikes me as the kind of person who hires a lawyer if he wants to harass someone."

"There's more."

"Go ahead."

I told her about the box—the threat, the theft, and the retrieval.

Kenya said, "So his sister read him the riot act."

"That's right."

"Is there anything else?"

I'd kept Adam's name out of it, but suddenly I was so tired of keeping everything close that I told her about him, too. The breakup and the calls since.

She was quiet for a while.

"Kenya?"

"You won't like to hear this."

"Yankee to Yankee. Just tell me."

"This is a personal hunch, not a lawyer's opinion, but my money is on your ex-boyfriend for the brick."

"But he's a nice Jewish boy from Germantown!"

She sighed. "If a comfortable suburban upbringing, a good education, and weekly synagogue attendance inoculated people from acting violent and cruel, this would be a very different world," she said.

"He's a lawyer! If he's charged with a crime, he'll be disbarred!"

"Throwing a brick through a window is a misdemeanor, not a felony, and the worst that would happen to him is a reprimand and a temporary suspension while he works on his problems with anger management. Which wouldn't be such a bad thing."

"I can't do that to him. I just can't."

"Nat, I do pro bono work for a battered women's shelter. What I'm hearing bothers me. You need to protect yourself."

"I'm having an alarm system installed."

"That's a start."

AS THOUGH HE KNEW

I met Joyce at the house in Cordova. Once she'd placed the precious box on the dining room table, and after she'd left and I'd closed the door behind her, I wasn't ready to get to work. The house was quiet, but my nerves were not. A distant roar from somewhere outside rattled me, until I realized it was the sound of the neighbors' landscaper, starting a lawnmower. I sat at the table, listening for the slightest sound. Was that a car coming down the street? I knew that Owen couldn't get into the house unless he rang the bell and I opened the door for him. It didn't help. I was more than skittish. I felt afraid.

I thought of Calvin, mired in his own fear about going back to prison. I owed him the effort to keep this matter out of court. I owed myself something, too—to find out how Amelia's war turned out. I sighed and reached for the lid of the box.

Since the brick through my window, I kept my phone at hand all the time, even if I checked caller ID before I answered.

I had to finish looking at the papers. If the Civil War held any clues for me, I wanted to find them.

Owen had rummaged through the box and jarred its contents when he carried it away, but it wasn't in much disarray. The diary from 1864, which I'd been prevented from reading, was still on top of the pile. Just beneath it were the bills of sale and receipts for that year. I pulled on my gloves and opened the diary.

On the first page was an entry for January of 1864, when Amelia planned to make her next trip into Memphis to sell her cotton.

JANUARY 1864

We have sold sixty bales of our precious store of cotton, and the remaining forty will have to last us until the war ends. Perhaps beyond that, because nothing will recover overnight. I have lain awake at night, unable to sleep for worry. My daughter-in-law is oblivious. If it were piety, I could bear it better. But it's pure selfishness. She is still the pampered planter's daughter she was before the war, and none of our privations have moved her or changed her. Except for her widowhood, which excuses her from tending the garden, doing the weekly wash, or cooking our meals.

Little Robert, who is six years old, understands our plight better than his mother does. When I told him last month that we would do our best to have Christmas for him, he asked, "Does it cost a lot to have Christmas?" He is a dear boy, and too young to worry as I do.

We need the cotton, but there are other things we can sacrifice to raise money. We don't need the silver. I took it out and asked Harriet to help me polish it. She looked puzzled. "Are you planning to use it, ma'am?"

"No, to sell it. It will fetch more if it looks bright."

It hurt me to wrap it in rags and pack it up—the coffee set, the serving dishes, the goblets, the hollowware. Some of it came from Virginia, and the rest, Ezekiel bought for me as our fortunes increased before the war. But we can't eat or drink silver. We need cash. And even if the Yankees don't care for the old-fashioned look of these things, silver itself is worth money. I hefted our box, and the weight assured me that the metal alone has value.

I thought of selling my jewelry, too, but I have little of value. The most expensive piece of jewelry in this house is the sapphire and diamond ring my son gave his wife when they became engaged, and she swears that she will wear that ring to the grave. I will let her have it.

How hard I've become. My daughter-in-law cries about everything. I cannot weep at all.

I THOUGHT of the woman who had wept into her diary after her last miscarriage and I missed her, too.

My phone rang. My heart pounded as I checked the caller ID. It was Gideon. "Where are you?" he asked.

"I'm at the Powell place in Cordova."

"You all right?"

I'd told Gideon and Jude the story of the box. "It's quiet as can be here. I'm fine."

"You sure? You sounded rattled when you picked up."

"I'm just jumpy. Considering."

"You want company?"

"No, it's all right."

"You have any trouble, Nat, you call."

"I promise I'll call the cops first."

"That ain't funny."

I put down the phone and picked up the next receipt.

It wasn't like the others. It was an ordinary piece of paper torn from one of the diaries. And it was in Amelia Powell's handwriting. I read the date, and I reached for the diaries, looking for August of 1865.

AUGUST 5, 1865

The war is over, but our circumstances are no better than before. I've kept back ten bales of cotton, but we're no closer to being able to plant a crop next year. The former slaves are now free, and they roam the countryside, going between places in Shelby County and Memphis as they please. They refuse to work in the cotton fields unless they are paid. How would I pay anyone? We have no cash for anything, not even for ourselves.

Robert now goes barefoot, even in the worst of weather, as the former slave children do, because I cannot afford to buy him shoes.

If we struggle, we can manage to plant a corn crop and a kitchen garden. The pigs keep themselves, thank goodness, and the cow finds what she can. The chickens can eat corn. If we work as hard as slaves used to, we won't starve.

But next year looms before me, a greater worry. How will we manage? I don't know.

· · ·

I COULDN'T REMEMBER if Joyce had taken the portrait of Amelia Powell or not. With care, gloves on, I emptied the box until I found the portrait, re-wrapped in its deteriorated fabric. Joyce had even replaced the ribbon, re-tying the frayed scrap into a little bow.

I thought of Joyce in Owen's office, full of fury, so intent on the papers that she'd momentarily entrusted her son to a stranger. I'd have to ask her if Zeke Enright was named after the progenitor of the Powell family, Amelia's husband, Ezekiel.

I unwrapped the portrait and set it on the table. The blue eyes, intelligent and observant in the pretty, doll-like face, seemed to meet mine.

What did she have to tell me?

August 8, 1865

Today we had a visitor—someone I never expected to see again. Two men, driving a wagon, pulled up by the front door. Their horse was sturdy and well-fed, unlike the horses that are left in rural Shelby County. They were both decently dressed in white shirts, nankeen trousers, and new hats.

Both were Black, and both were familiar.

It was Tobey and his oldest son.

They got off the wagon and walked to the front porch, where my daughter-in-law and I sat. I shelled peas for dinner, and she watched me with a sour humor.

"Ma'am," Tobey said, touching the brim of his hat but not doffing it. His son also murmured, "Ma'am."

I rose. "Tobey," I said.

"Ma'am, no disrespect, but these days I call myself Mr. Tobias Woodson."

I couldn't call him that. "How have you been?" I asked him.

"We're in Memphis. We all work for the Union army. My boys and I do carpentry work, and my wife and my girls work as seamstresses."

I said, "Why didn't you tell me you were leaving? Why did you run away?"

"I reckoned you'd try to stop me."

He was right. I asked, "Why have you come back?"

"I left my tools behind," he said. "Some of the Union men asked me about making furniture. I'd like to oblige them."

"You aren't thinking of stealing them." That was unkind of me. But I was still bitter about the way he'd gone, stealing himself and his family away in the middle of the night without a word.

"No, ma'am, I'm not." He pushed his hat back and lifted his face to look at me. "I came here to buy them."

"Buy them? With what?"

He said, "The Army pays me in greenbacks, ma'am."

I had forgotten about the woodworking tools. I had never realized they might be something to sell. And he had good Union money, not Confederate paper or scrip.

"We aren't selling anything to him!" my daughter-in-law hissed.

I gave my daughter-in-law a gimlet eye. "And what are we going to live on this winter?" I asked.

"I'd rather starve!"

"I'd rather not." I said to Tobey, "I want a hundred fifty dollars for the tools and the chest."

He said, "That's a little high, ma'am. I'd offer you fifty dollars." He patted his pocket.

"And that's much too low. Could you see a hundred twenty-five?"

I met his eyes. He wasn't desperate. He had a gleam in his eye. "Seventy-five?"

My daughter-in-law was watching us with distaste. I didn't care. "How about a hundred?"

"Yes, I could see a hundred," he said, and I wished we'd been able to agree on more.

I waited for him to pull out his greenbacks, but he said, "There's one more thing, ma'am."

"Yes, Tobey? What is it?"

"I'd like to buy the chair. The one that matches the others."

He meant the replacement for the chair that Lucullus had destroyed. "Why?"

"The chair I made with my own hands. The one I marked with my name. I want to buy it from you."

That poor, cursed chair. Let it go, I thought. And make him pay for it. "$200."

He smiled. "You know that's too high," he said.

"What would you give me? For the chair you want so much?"

"$100."

I sighed. "We could dicker and dither about it, but $150 is in the middle. Would that satisfy you?"

He deliberated for a moment. Was he thinking about the asking price or the history of the chair? I didn't know. He said, "I'll meet you in the middle." He held out his hand to me to shake it.

I couldn't do it. I said, "All right. $150 for the chair, and $100 for the toolchest."

Now he put his hand into his pocket and pulled out a wad of greenbacks. I stared at the money in surprise. He said, "Ma'am, will you write us both a bill of sale? So everyone will know I bought these things fair and square, and no one will think I stole them."

I PICKED up the bill of sale.

AUGUST 8, 1865

Sold by Mrs. Amelia Powell, of Shelby County, Tennessee

Sold to Tobey, also known as Tobias Woodson, the following items:

A toolchest and its contents, a set of woodworking tools, for the sum of $100

A chair in the Chippendale style, made by his own hand, for the sum of $150

In total, a sum of $250

Received in full this day, August 8, 1865

Signed,

Tobias Woodson

THE SIGNATURE on the page matched the mark on the chair.

I thought, *As though he'd known.*

I looked away from the page. I felt their presence, both of them, Tobias and Amelia, imagining the weight of his hand on my right shoulder, and the light touch of her hand on my left arm.

I picked up the pages and took them into the study to scan them. Then I uploaded the images and messaged them to Kenya. "I found this. Is it enough?"

Wherever she was, Kenya replied right away.

"Yes."

THIS BELONGS TO YOU

OWEN REALIZED HE HAD TO DROP THE SUIT, BUT HE WAS still angry. He insisted on authenticating the sales receipt. I didn't want to get involved. I called Sexton and told him to contact the Tennessee Historical Society for the name of a neutral expert. I never met the expert, but I read his report, which attested that the ink and paper were nineteenth century, and the handwriting on the receipt matched Amelia's handwriting in the diaries.

Joyce called me. "Owen doesn't like it, but he knows he can't argue any more. We're done," she said. "I called the realty agency this morning."

"They must be happy."

"They're ecstatic. They're going to put it on the market for one point six million dollars. The agent thinks we have a good chance of getting that much or more."

"That's great."

"I'm just so relieved," she said. "I'm so glad it's resolved."

"Me too."

"Now you know we'll pay you."

I laughed. "I never doubted that," I said. "Joyce, I have a question for you."

"What?"

"Did you ever see that old photograph of your mother? A picture of her as a debutante?"

"I did. I saw that you found it, and I took it home. It's such a nice picture of her. A nice memory."

"I thought so. Would you mind meeting me at the house and bringing it along?"

"No, I don't, but why?"

"There's another photograph I want to show you."

I'd found it and set it aside the last time I was there. I didn't want anything else in this estate to go astray.

Joyce met me outside the house, and we went inside together. She pulled the photograph from her handbag. "I just wrapped it in some plastic. Is that all right? It isn't hundreds of years old."

"Since it's under glass, it's fine."

"I'm really curious why we're here."

I led her to the dining room table. "Set your photo down," I said. "Next to the other one."

She did. Puzzled, she asked, "Who is that?" She answered her own question. "It's Ruth Anne, isn't it?"

"It is. It looks like it was taken about the same time as your mother's coming-out photo."

"This was in her things?"

"The things she saved."

Joyce looked surprised.

I asked her, "What do you see?" It was the first question I'd learned to ask at Sotheby's. It was the first question I asked myself whenever I looked carefully at an object. Now I asked it of Joyce.

She looked, from one image to the other, from the slight, fine-boned white girl in her debutante's dress, to the slight, fine-boned Black woman in her Sunday best. She bent close, as though scrutiny would help her. Then she stood back and put her hand over her mouth.

When she took it away, she said, "Oh, my stars."

"What do you see?" I repeated, as gently as I could.

She shook her head. "I can't believe I never saw it before."

"What do you see?"

She met my eyes. "You don't need one of those DNA tests to know," she said.

I said, "Do you remember you told me you always thought the ring should go to a family member?"

She looked at the photographs again. She nodded.

I said, "Do you still want it back?"

She gazed at the image of her mother. She picked up the image of Ruth Anne and stared at it, seeing the connection, unable to unsee it, ever again.

She put Ruth Anne's picture back on the table, next to her mother's. Side by side. She looked at me. "No," she said.

A FEW DAYS LATER, Curtis walked into the shop. At the counter, he said to me, "I'm here to see you."

I said, "Is there something you're looking for? Something you want to sell?"

"No, it's not that." He held a brown paper bag, a lunch sack, in his hand. He reached inside it and put the contents on the counter. "Ruth Anne gave this to me, and I thought it was a dandy birthday present. I just found out that it wasn't hers to give."

It was the baseball. Owen's baseball.

"When did she tell you?"

"A few days ago."

"Did she say why she wanted you to know?"

"Just that I should know. So I could decide what to do with it."

I wondered if Joyce had talked to her. I'd probably never find out.

He looked rueful. "I never knew a thing about Bob Gibson before she gave this to me. I did some research on him. He was a great ballplayer, and he was a trailblazer, too." He rested his hand on the ball. "I'm going to miss this."

I turned my head and asked Gideon, "You know anything about sports memorabilia?"

"A little."

"Do you think we could find Mr. Thompson a nice 1959 season ball with an authenticated Bob Gibson signature? For a reasonable price?"

"If Mr. Thompson wants one," Gideon said.

Curtis said, "I don't think so."

"If you change your mind, you tell us," Gideon said.

He rested his hand on the ball again and said to me, "I know I've given you a rough time."

"I won't argue with you."

"I don't feel good about it. Especially since Georgina told me I should do what a churchgoing man should do."

"I appreciate it. I'm sure it wasn't easy."

"It wasn't."

"Curtis, may I ask you a question?"

"Depends on what it is.

"The answer would help me out. Would you mind doing that?"

"Got myself right into that. Since I'm a good church-going man. What is it?"

I said, "Someone put a brick through my front window. At home. You wouldn't happen to know anything about that?"

"No, but I'm mighty sorry to hear about it."

He was in an atoning mood, but I shouldn't press my luck.

He said, "You'll make sure that goes back where it belongs?"

"I will."

He nodded. He said to Gideon, "If I do change my mind, I'll call you." And he was gone.

I CALLED OWEN. "Something came into the shop that I'm sure you'd like to see," I said.

He sounded better than he ever had. More relaxed. "I won't try to guess what it is."

"You don't have to. Can you stop by? We're open until five, but I can stay later if it's convenient for you."

"Now you've got me curious. I can be there around three."

He walked into the shop looking a little suspicious. Still Owen, even if he'd calmed down a little. He came up to the counter. "Who sells the guitars?"

"They're Gideon's."

Gideon grinned at him. "You in the market for one?"

"Ha-ha. Like I need a guitar. You've got quite the display, that's all."

"If you ever feel the need for a vintage electric guitar, you know we're here."

He said to me, "Okay, I came all the way from Germantown. What have you got?"

I put it on the counter.

His eyes went wide. "Is that what I think it is?"

"You tell me."

He picked it up and cradled it in his hands. He turned it around, and as he examined the signatures, as he checked the wear, the years fell from his face. He was a boy again. Still holding the baseball, he said, "How the hell did you find this?"

I said, "It turned up. Like I told you. Like I always thought it would."

"How did it turn up?"

"Curtis found it," I said.

"Where did he get it?"

"It just turned up," I said.

"Ruth Anne's in this somehow, isn't she?"

"Let's not go there," I said.

"Joyce told me about Ruth Anne. About the photograph you showed her."

"So you know."

"Yes, I know." He looked down at the baseball and set his hand on it. He smiled a little. "So it turned up."

He was suddenly far away. He was his nephew Zeke's age, and he was in the study with his father, who loved the baseball and the memories that went along with it. He stared at it and shook his head. Then he looked at me. "I was pretty hard on you," he said.

"I noticed that."

"I'm not proud of myself for it. I've been having a rough time."

"Joyce said something about it."

"She tell you the specifics?"

"No, she said it was just some trouble in business. She didn't know the specifics, either."

His mouth twitched. "You wouldn't know to look at her. Little slip of a thing, my baby sister, and she's quite the fighter when it comes to taking care of anyone she cares about."

I thought of Amelia, who had passed that spirit to her female descendants.

"I know I caused you a lot of trouble."

At that I said, "Was that trouble? I thought it was just that you were a client."

He laughed.

I said, "I'm curious about something."

"What?"

"I had some trouble myself a while back. A brick came through my front window. Would you know anything about that?"

"Jesus, no," he said. "You know me. When I get mad, I

sue." He picked up the baseball and cradled it in his palms. "I'm sorry," he said, and it wasn't clear whether he was sorry about my trouble or the trouble he'd caused me.

I didn't press him.

He stared at the baseball again and chuckled. "Turned up," he said.

"Like I said it would."

<hr>

NOW I KNEW who'd thrown the brick.

I still had it. It sat on my front porch, a malevolent little presence, which bothered me when I noticed it and remembered it was there. I called Adam, and he let my call go to voicemail. I left him a message, telling him I needed to talk to him, and I'd prefer to see him in person.

He waited a day before he called back, and his voice was cool. "I thought you never wanted to see me again."

"I don't want to go out with you again. But there's something important I need to discuss with you."

He grudgingly agreed to meet me at a coffee shop in Midtown. I was there early, a cup of coffee I didn't want at my elbow. I sat in a quiet corner. I didn't like the idea of strangers eavesdropping on this conversation.

He came in from work, dressed in a suit. He looked remarkably good for a man who'd just had a rotten breakup. I wondered if he'd found someone else, someone more pliable. He didn't order anything. He sat at the table and said, "What is this about?"

I reached into my bag and pulled it out. I couldn't

prevent the clunk as I set it on the table. "I believe this is yours," I said. "I thought you might want it back."

At the sight of the brick his face crumpled. He looked as though he would cry. His voice husky, he said, "That's the worst thing I've ever done."

"I don't know everything you did in Nashville, but I'd say it's definitely on the list. It's in the top three."

"Nat, I am so sorry—"

"Don't apologize."

"Did you call the police?"

"Yes, for the insurance. I didn't give them your name."

"You could have," he said.

"It didn't seem fair to ruin your life and your career for something mean and stupid."

"Thank you," he said.

I shook my head.

"I'm leaving Memphis," he said.

"Going back to Nashville?"

"Going back to Warner, but not to Nashville. I just got a job in New York. Counsel to the division of streaming services." When I didn't reply, he said, "It's a great opportunity."

Stiffly, I said, "Good for you." I thought, *Geh gesunterhayt*, which was Yiddish for "bless your heart." I said, "After this I never want to see you again. Or talk to you again."

He bent his head. "I understand."

"Do you?"

"Yes," he said. He rose. "Goodbye, Nat."

After he left, I realized he hadn't taken the brick with

him. It was still in the middle of the table. It was still mine to get rid of.

Fuming, I put it back in my bag and drove back to the shop, where Jude said, "How did it go?"

I said, "He's gone. This damn thing isn't." I pulled the brick from my bag and set it on the counter. "What am I going to do with it? I should throw it into the Mississippi River."

Jude said, "Don't. There's too much junk in the river already. I'll take it."

"What are you going to do with it?"

"Use it in someone's décor. Put it in a stranger's garden. Give it good karma for a change."

I shook my head.

She picked it up. "I'll make it go away," she said.

2 2

THE AUCTION

SOTHEBY'S decided to make the WOODSON chair the centerpiece of their January auction. Its photograph graced the catalog cover and the front page of the website. Inside, the curator of early American decorative art had written a two-page essay about its history. The Woodson chair was more than special; it was significant. It was a superstar.

My old boss was so glad to see me that he risked a hug instead of a handshake. "We've missed you, Nat," he said.

When I extricated myself, I said, "There was a reason I went back to Memphis. To find you the Woodson chair."

He grinned. "We're very grateful."

"I saw the piece in the *Times*. PR's been busy."

"There's a lot of interest, believe me. The Met and the Smithsonian have gotten their big donors—well, worked up."

"Anyone I know? Or is it all on the down-low?"

He dropped his voice. "Come to the auction. You'll see how worked up."

I'd accompanied the Woodsons to New York, where Sotheby's had put them up in a luxury hotel, fed them gourmet dinners, and arranged to squire them around to tourist attractions. Letitia wanted to see the Statue of Liberty, and Ayesha asked for a history tour of Harlem.

Calvin wanted to go antiquing, and he didn't ask the Sotheby's tour guide to take him around. He asked me.

"Where do you want to go?" I asked him.

He said, "Not somewhere so fancy I'll feel like I don't belong there. A nice place, like yours."

I knew just the shop; I'd bought from there for myself when I lived in New York. The owner remembered me and said he'd missed seeing me.

"I moved away. I went back to my hometown. Memphis, Tennessee. I opened an antique shop there. We're doing well."

"And you brought a friend with you."

"A friend and a customer from Memphis."

He asked Calvin, "What brings you to New York?"

"I'm going to an auction at Sotheby's tomorrow."

The owner looked at Calvin with surprise.

Calvin said, "I'm selling, not buying."

I said, "Did you see anything about the Chippendale chair made by the enslaved artisan?"

The owner said, "I saw the article in the *Times*. The only known example of a signed chair by an enslaved cabinetmaker."

"That's right," Calvin said. "The man who made it was my ancestor."

"That's really something," the owner said.

"No shit!" Calvin said, laughing. "May I look around?"

Calvin was completely at ease in the shop. He poked around. He asked questions. He picked up the objects that interested him, holding them capably in his big, graceful hands. He nonchalantly looked for marks.

He finally said, "You have lots of good things here, but I have my eye on something back home. I'm going to see how well we do tomorrow."

I knew what he had his eye on. We hadn't sold it yet.

———

IT WAS strange to attend a Sotheby's auction as a member of the audience. It was a moneyed crowd, diverse but slender and beautifully dressed, where the Woodsons stood out, like the tourists from Memphis that they were. It didn't matter. They'd brought Sotheby's a special thing, a celebrity in its own right. They were welcome in the auction room.

They stood clustered together with their tour guide, their eyes wide, too keyed up to drink the champagne or eat the hors d'oeuvres.

At the auction, I recognized the curator from the Met's early American decorative art department talking to a woman I didn't know. They were both smiling. He waved me over. He introduced us; she was a curator from the Smithsonian's African American museum. He explained, "Nat's the one who found these chairs down in Memphis, Tennessee!"

The Smithsonian's curator laughed. "Now that's what I call a good eye."

I'd always felt a rush before an auction. Now I smiled too, drawn into their excitement. "And I trust the two of you have found some buyers who will want to fight over it."

She said, "We certainly hope so!"

As I looked for the Woodsons, a familiar voice said, "Nat Raskin, it's great to see you."

"Likewise, Pete." It was Pete Gurevich, who had made his money in New York real estate and whose wife Helen had refined his taste in early American decorative art. "Do you see something you like?"

Despite his money, Pete was unpretentious, a stocky man with unruly hair, who'd always reminded me of the Jewish businessmen I'd known in Memphis. "Yes, I do," he said. "I hear you found it."

Pete had a long-standing relationship with the Met. I kidded him, "I got lucky. I hope you do too."

He laughed. "Luck, and a few dollars to go with it," he said, sounding just like Ben Levy.

The young woman who was taking care of the Woodsons tapped me on the arm. "Showtime, Nat," she said, and I followed her to sit down. She sat on one side of the Woodsons, and I sat on the other. Between us, Ayesha and Letitia flanked Calvin.

I watched as lot after lot sold. Nice brown American furniture, the kind of thing I used to worry about when I worked here. I let it go by. Now I was spoiled for lesser things.

Ayesha nudged me. "The other chairs are coming up next."

The Powell chairs had received some attention too, because of their relationship with the Woodson chair. We all watched as the bidders raised their paddles. There were several bidders on the phone, too. Besides the Gureviches, I saw other familiar faces, all well-to-do collectors who liked early American furniture. There was lively interest in the Powell chairs, and that raised their price. They sold for a premium. When the hammer fell, the Powells, *bless their hearts*, were $375,000 richer. I turned to scan the audience. The Met's curator was smiling.

Several lots intervened before the Woodson chair came up. Ayesha drew in her breath as the auctioneer introduced the chair and talked up its history.

When he started the bidding at $275,000, all three Woodsons gasped in surprise. I felt a flutter of excitement. As the number climbed higher, the Woodsons began to stare in astonishment. When it topped $750,000, they grabbed each other's hands and held them tightly. I stole a look behind me, even though it was hard to be discreet from the front row. Did I see Pete Gurevich holding up his paddle? I didn't stare, but I believe I did.

The Woodsons were dumbstruck as the bidding went on. The number hit $1,000,000, and it didn't stop.

I stole another look, but I didn't recognize the competing bidders. There were several phone bidders, too.

Now the curator from the Smithsonian was smiling, too.

The number hit $1.2 million. Ayesha's eyes were bright with excitement. Calvin leaned forward. Letitia looked as though she might burst into tears.

My heart was pounding, just as it always had when we sold a great thing. I wished Kenya were here. She hadn't anticipated this kind of restitution, but she would be delighted by it.

$1.3 million. $1.5 million.

When the hammer fell, the chair sold for $1.6 million.

Afterwards, the arts reporter from the *Times* pulled the Woodsons aside, and the photographer took a lovely photo of them, looking stunned in the best possible way. Letitia gave them the quote they wanted. As tears streaked her face, she said, "All my life I've had dreams. Now I can realize them. That's the gift Tobias Woodson gave us."

WHEN I CAME BACK to Memphis, Jude and Gideon took me out for a celebratory dinner. "$1.6 million!" Jude said. Gideon lifted his glass. I'd ordered bourbon, a Southern girl tonight, and I clinked glasses with him. I said, "The Woodsons deserved every dime."

"You earned your salt," Jude said.

"And I heard something interesting from my friend who's a curator at the Met. They bought both the Powell chairs and the Woodson chair."

Gideon laughed. "Put the set back together."

"Now we all know where the twelfth chair is," Jude said.

I snorted. "But the Met is going to loan the Woodson chair to the African American museum at the Smithsonian for a special exhibition. That's just what the Woodsons hoped for. It's the best possible outcome."

The word went around, and the appraisal jobs came to me. They were easy insurance appraisals for well-behaved clients. Not a one of them said, "Owen Powell referred you."

Calvin didn't come by the shop, and I thought about calling him. I decided he'd let me know when he wanted to talk to me.

It was mid-February when he walked into the shop. He looked completely different from the man I'd first met. He looked years younger, all the weight of worry smoothed from his face. He was casually dressed, but he looked sharp as a Midtown hipster.

He looked like a man uplifted by money.

I emerged from behind the counter and held out my hand. He shook it as he smiled. "It's good to see you, Nat," he said. He waved at Gideon. "And to be back here, too."

"We've missed you."

"I've been busy. Big changes for all of us."

"How is Letitia?"

"She decided to move to Atlanta. She applied to nursing school at Georgia State, and she'll be starting there in the summer."

"I'm so glad to hear that. How is Ayesha?"

"She's crazy about Kenya Davis. She's going to do an internship at Kenya's law firm over the summer. All excited about it."

"What about you? Are you still living here?"

"I sure am. After I invested most of my money so the tax man didn't get it, I spent some of it. I bought a house."

"Where?"

"Vollentine. Right next door to you in Evergreen. Fixer-upper that I got cheap. I've been busy fixing it up. I'm learning how to carpenter. Turns out I'm good at it." He laughed. "I'm a wood man! I take after Tobias."

"That's wonderful."

"Is that blue kittycat still here? The Theodore Deck?"

I smiled. "It's still here."

"I want to see it."

I picked up the case key, and he followed me there, smiling as he watched me unlock the case and extricate the cat. He handled it with affection, reluctant to let it go. I knew what that meant. *I want to take this home with me.*

Cradling it against his chest, he said, "Would you see to take $2500 for it?"

Just like Tobias Woodson. I smiled. "It's on consignment. I don't think the seller would go for it. I could do fifteen percent."

He calculated. "Do you think your seller would go for $3,000?"

"Let me call her."

He followed me back to the counter, where he set the cat down but kept his hand on it, as though it was alive and liked the touch of his fingers on its fur.

I got the seller on the phone. I said, "I've got a motivated buyer here. All ready to take out his credit card. How do you feel about $3,000?"

As she spoke, I nodded at Calvin, who was smiling as he rested his hand on the ceramic flank.

I hung up the phone. "You've got a deal."

He continued to grin as I ran the card and Gideon

carefully wrapped the cat in tissue paper and bubble wrap. We gave him a bag with handles, more secure to carry, but he left with the package clasped to his chest, next to his heart.

We did all right that day, no matter what the daily sales form said.

Gideon walked me outside and through the yard to the parking lot. The sun had set, and it was as dark as it would ever get on neon-bright South Main. As we lingered, I heard a welcome sound. The high-pitched hoot of a great horned owl.

And to my surprise, a call in a lower key.

"What's that?" I asked Gideon.

"Boy owl."

The girl owl called back, and the boy owl responded.

Gideon said, "She's got a suitor. They're courting."

We stood in the dark, beneath the live oak that never lost its foliage, listening.

Gideon said, "Did you know they mate for life?"

I smiled at him as the two owls, male and female, called back and forth. "I wish them the best," I said.

THE END

WANT MORE OF NAT? Get the prequel to the Memphis series, *Debutante of Memphis,* for free when you sign up for my at https://www.sabrawaldfogel.com/sign-up.

Memphis, 1994. Nat Raskin is half Southern Jew and half Southern belle. She's in conflict with herself and her family. Which side will win?

And visit my website to learn more about my other books at https://www.sabrawaldfogel.com/.

HISTORICAL NOTE

In reality, I have never seen a reference to a Chippendale-style chair made (and signed) by an enslaved artisan. The "object of desire" in this story is purely my invention. But the idea is rooted in information from the historical record.

There were Black chairmakers in nineteenth-century Tennessee, both free and enslaved. Enslaved chairmakers fell into two categories. Many of them lived on plantations—in Tennessee, most plantations were small—and made everyday furniture for the plantation itself or for its immediate neighbors. Skilled enslaved artisans were indeed rented out for their services, and most of them never received any compensation. The other group of Black enslaved cabinetmakers worked in towns for white chairmakers and cabinetmakers. As with white apprentices, none of them signed the work. Most of the furniture made in antebellum Tennessee was practical, although a few urban furniture makers added the carving and flourishes typical of the Chippendale and Queen Anne styles.

In reality, none of the Tennessee makers achieved the finesse of the Philadelphia workshops like Thomas Tufft's.

There were a handful of free Black chair- and cabinet-makers in antebellum Tennessee; there were more in Charleston and New Orleans, both of which had a substantial free Black population before the Civil War.

The other inspiration for this story was the pottery of David Drake, who was born in about 1800 and died in Edgefield, South Carolina, in 1865, meaning that he spent most of his life enslaved. He made pieces that were both beautiful and practical. He was more than a talented potter. He was literate, and he was a poet. He inscribed about forty of his pieces with rhyming couplets full of sly observation and humor.

The idea of "adding a zero" came from the sales history of David Drake's pottery. In the first decade of the twenty-first century, when this story is set, Drake's pieces were fetching about ten times the value of pieces made by white potters of the same time period. Since then, Drake's work has become more prized—and more valuable. In 2021, one of his inscribed jars sold for $1.56 million at auction, destined for a museum collection.

The rest is fiction.

ABOUT THE AUTHOR

Sabra Waldfogel grew up far from the South in Minneapolis, Minnesota. She studied history at Harvard University and got a PhD in American history from the University of Minnesota. Since then, she has been fascinated by the drama of slavery and freedom in the decades before and after the Civil War.

Her first novel, *Sister of Mine*, published by Lake Union, was named the winner of the 2017 Audio Publishers Association Audie Award for fiction. The sequel, *Let Me Fly*, was published in 2018.